A Perfect Stone

A Perfect Stone

S.C. Karakaltsas

Karadie Publishing
Melbourne, Australia

Publisher: Karadie Publishing (Email:Karadiepublishing@gmail.com)

Catalogue-in-publication entry details are available from the National Library of Australia
www.trove.nla.gov.au
ISBN 978 0 994 5032 68

Cover Design by Jonny Lynch (https://jonnylynchgraphics.wixsite.com/ media)

For every child who was, and is, a refugee seeking the right to a better life.

1

The Scarecrow

August 1947

The scarecrow, like the ones propped on a stake in the fields to frighten the birds from the corn, sways oddly in the gentle breeze. Its head hangs limp and awkward to one side, and the trouser legs are filled with something more solid than straw.

From where Dimitri stands he knows something isn't right. Some of the older boys gathered beneath the scarecrow begin shouting and someone runs back to the village.

He's torn when his mother's urgent call stops him from catching up to the others to get a closer look. He should have been doing his chores and instead stands between her and the scarecrow he so desperately wants to see. His mother shades her eyes and begins walking toward him.

"Dimitri! Come home right now!"

Pulling himself away, he runs down the dry grassy slope toward her. "I'm coming."

A quick glance over his shoulder at the growing crowd in front of the scarecrow, Dimitri's heart thumps not from the threat of punishment but what his mother will do when she finds out. He runs as hard as he can to reach her before she notices.

"Why don't you come when I call you?" Her ragged brown dress covered in a tattered apron swings around her legs. In her hand is a long thin piece of reed.

When he reaches her he touches her arm gently and swallows. His tongue finds the tooth hanging loose and he wriggles it back and forth as he thinks of what to tell her.

When the blood-curdling scream comes, her eyes widen in fright and her hand flutters to her chest as she turns toward the scarecrow. Dropping the reed, she reaches for him, fingers tight around his thin arm and, despite her limp, they run. Several women from the village bolt out of their houses and hurry past them toward the crowd.

When mother and son burst through the thick wooden door of their tiny stone house, she leans heavily against it, flings back the latch, then slumps to the floor with her head in her hands and sobs.

From outside, the wailing begins.

2

The Stone and the Diary

March 2016. Was he abducted or did his mother willingly give him up? Thoughts tumble like a poker machine until Jim settles on one. She was definitely distraught. Punching the keyboard hard, he forces the words across the screen.

Tapping the enter button, he swears under his breath. He's not ready for the new line, yet there it is. Running his hand through his thin grey hair, he stares at her smiling face in the photo frame on his desk and clicks his dentures. She'd hated it when he did that. They're uncomfortable, he'd retorted in his defence.

He stares at the keyboard. "Which one was it?" he says aloud to her. But she's no help. There are days when he remembers and there are days when he doesn't. This is one of those days. His mind blank, he leans back in his chair and fixes on the cobweb swinging from the ceiling. Following it with his eyes to the bare lightbulb that hangs listlessly in the dim room, he takes a deep breath.

"Helen! Helen, I need help!" he bellows.

A woman hastily makes her way down the hallway, high heels clattering on the timber floor. Standing in the doorway, she wipes her hands on a tea towel bearing the faded picture of a Melbourne Tram.

"What now?" says Helen, a petite middle-aged woman dressed in blue jeans and a white shirt.

"How do I get back to the last line?"

Helen purses her lips, rolls her blue eyes and snaps. "For goodness' sake! How many times do I have to tell you? Have you checked your notes?"

"It's quicker if I ask you, love," he says, breaking into a grin.

"Humph. Is that right?" There's a hint of a smile in her eyes and she folds her arms.

"So what do I do?"

"Try backspace."

He makes no move to press the key and instead swivels around to face her as she steps into the room. "I keep forgetting."

"You know what to do. It's slow at first, but you'll get better with practice," she says gently, before pulling the floral curtains open. Sunlight floods the room and he blinks, surprised by the day.

Glancing at the piles of boxes littered along the wall, he watches Helen frown as she runs her finger across the window ledge. "What are you doing anyway?" Wiping her finger on the tea towel slung across her arm, she peers over his shoulder but the screen is blank. His nose twitches from the smell of her faint perfume.

"I've been thinking about writing my memoir, if you must know."

"What a great idea! I suppose sorting out all this stuff has brought back a lot of memories?" She scrutinises him, her eyes narrowing before nodding. "You definitely should write your story. You're quite the self-made man. Leaving school at fifteen, working in the textile factory where you met Mum. Then working your way through night school."

Jim grins. "I don't know about that. But there are things I'd like to get down. Before it's too late."

"Too late? Don't be ridiculous. You're as strong as an ox. Maybe I can help?"

"I think I'll be right."

"Don't forget the best bits like the birth of your one and only amazing daughter; CEO of a highly successful multinational company."

"It's not about you." He rolls his eyes but allows a smile.

"When can I read it?"

"When I'm ready for you to read it."

"Ooh. Have you got a sinister past that I don't know about? Have you killed a man and stuffed him in a drum and sent him down a river?" Her eyes crease as she laughs, showing off white front teeth.

His heart thumps and he searches her face to see what she

knows. But she's examining the pile of bills sitting on a box. "I know," she says, looking up, "you got a girl pregnant and I've got a big sister somewhere. How funny would that be?"

"Don't be stupid, girl."

"Yes, that's it. A big sister or brother." Warming to the idea, she giggles. "Or, or what about this? You were a spy and Jim is your alias." She laughs hard. "Imagine the headlines: 'hard-nosed accountant for one of the biggest retailers in the country was really a spy.' Hilarious."

"For goodness' sake…" He spins his wedding ring, trying to stay calm. "I'm glad you find me so amusing."

She frowns. "By the way, you really should file these bills."

"When I get a chance. Now, can you let me concentrate?"

"All right, all right. I'll finish cleaning the kitchen then fix us some lunch." She giggles as she clatters back to the kitchen, her noisy heels jarring him.

"Little does she know," he mumbles as he stares at the screen.

But he can't concentrate. Maybe she does know. He'd read in the newspaper that the internet knows what you feel, where you've been and what you like. Maybe she's searched one of those infernal ancestor sites. He reassures himself with the belief his history can't be there. He's distracted by the commotion in the kitchen. His shoulders slump as Helen comes back down the hall and into his study, the clatter of her high heels resounding off the walls.

She frowns as she puts her hands on her hips. "Dad, the

place is a mess. I found rat droppings on the bench behind the toaster."

"Stop fussing. I wiped the bench," he says, still intent on the blank screen.

"When? Last week?" Helen leaves the room muttering.

Why doesn't she speak up? he thinks. She knows he can't hear properly but he can't be bothered calling out to find out what she's said. Instead he examines the keyboard.

"Backspace," he mutters. "I've got to remember that." He scrolls back, reads the first few lines and deletes the last. Images roll around his head like a thrown dice, each side showing something different. What did he know and what could he remember?

Uniforms. A cigarette hanging limply on the side of his father's mouth and the smell of tobacco when he was near. He was always away. In the war, his mother had said.

The games with his grandmother; her stories; stooped on a walking stick. Running his hands over her whiskered, leathery face. When she laughed, hairs on a large mole on her neck danced. Crying. Her breathless voice dying with her.

Be proud of who you are. Never forget it. But he did.

Now he remembers too clearly.

Punching in a new sentence he misses a word. "How do I fix that?" he murmurs to himself. He thinks twice about asking Helen for help. She'll yell at him again about reading the notes. Where are the notes?

Helen is just like Anna. It's almost as if she's followed in her mother's footsteps. His beautiful Anna; the love of his life for more than sixty-two years.

Helen wanted to clear out the cupboard but he'd stopped her. It was in a box that he'd found the only two photos of his parents that Aunt Vera had thrust into his hands before he left. His wrinkled hand trembled as it touched the framed photo of his father in an army uniform. His mother's photo curled and yellowing at the edges showed a young woman, hair tied back laughing at something. He remembered her laugh but not much else and it saddened him.

Sighing, he began closing the box when he noticed an old, yellowing notebook and a small round stone. The stone fitted snugly in the palm of his other hand. It felt smaller than he remembered but it still held a power over him. In the beginning they'd agreed never to tell anyone. But as Helen got older, Anna said she had a right to know. They'd argued and he'd won – or so he thought. Then her dying words to him, "She has a right to know. We should have told her but now it's up to you."

He opened the front page. Her cursive handwriting said: *For my darling Jim and Helen – the two most important people in the world.* He couldn't read more than a page before the memories came back, the ones he'd pushed away and not thought about for more than sixty years. They weren't as difficult to remember as he'd thought, and painful as it was he'd found the nerve to start his story several days ago, just as Anna would have wanted.

He opens the desk drawer and the round stone lies there.

Stones skipping across the water.

Was there ever a time when the bombs didn't fall?

Hunger. Winter cold. The noise of planes overhead. Blackbirds. Hiding in the forest. Mud oozing between his toes. His bare feet cut to shreds climbing over rocks buried beneath the snow. So much pain. The soldier. Running.

Running hard.

"You told me that you'd thrown this out a long time ago," he whispers to the photo on the desk.

3

Humiliation

June 1945. A hot dry wind arrives early and whirls dust up the street of the small village of Baeti which was nestled close to the mountains of Northern Greece. Dimitri's grandmother fusses around him, slipping a white tunic over his head, then a red vest emblazoned with yellow embroidery. His blonde hair pasted flat, his ears and face sting from her scrubbing.

"Do I look like a grownup school boy now, Baba?"

He stands proudly in the costume. Night after night his grandmother had bent over it with a needle and thread. He'd stood straight and proud, spinning while she measured and fitted it to him. He was sure he must have looked just like his father.

After the Germans left, his father and other men of the village returned. Some families rejoiced while others grieved. Then the celebrations began. Dressed in traditional white costumes with red and yellow embroidered vests, the men danced in a large circle in the village square. Following the lead dancer, who waved a brightly coloured handkerchief above his head, they twirled in time to the shrill of the clarinet and the beat of the drums, kicking their feet into the air. The heady smell of roasting meat filled the village. Dimitri and the other children clapped their hands as they proudly watched the odd spectacle of their parents and grandparents laughing and dancing. It was a happy time.

The tiny village returned to normal. The church re-opened and everyone headed to the fields to sow crops or look after their goats and cows. A teacher was found, the school re-opened and it was time for Dimitri's first day.

"Of course you do. You look perfect." Clutching his head with both hands, Baba plants a kiss on his cheek, leaving a whiff of stale garlic, then squeezes him tightly as if she's scared of losing him.

"When you learn to read and write you can read the newspaper to me." Baba spits on her handkerchief before scrubbing an imagined mark off his cheek. Almost smothering him, she hugs him again, pinning his head somewhere between her sweating underarm and her ample bosom. Finally, she lets him go and he escapes through the front door to the dusty road outside.

"When you come home I'll have your favourite chicken soup ready," she calls out, waving her wobbling arms.

Glancing back, he sets off, feeling nervous and so excited that he's forgotten his mother's instructions from the night before.

He opens the gate to the school and eyes a boy he's seen around. Lazo is a similar height with a shock of thick, curly black hair. They're shy at first, until Dimitri kicks a stone toward him. Lazo kicks it back. They play with the stone until it's time to go into the one-room schoolhouse.

Dimitri fails to notice the sniggers of the other children until he shuffles into the classroom. Their stares unsettle him. Perhaps they're wondering why a boy of my age is so good at kicking a stone, he thinks. He'd shown Lazo a thing or two when he aimed for a piece of wood and kicked the stone exactly where he wanted it. To find a perfect stone was a joy, especially one for skipping. The day after the dancing celebrations, his father had taken him to the nearby river where they found round, flat stones. Throwing one with the flick of his wrist, he'd shown him how it skipped across the water before it sank. Dimitri made it skip once at first and practised for days afterward.

He finds a desk next to his new friend who whispers, "Have you ever hit a bird with a stone?"

Dimitri nods. "Easy. Can you skip stones across the river?"

"Why aren't you speaking Greek?" Spittle flies from the mouth of the thickly bearded teacher as he roars. The entire class of mixed-age children jump in unison and fall into sudden silence.

"You!" the teacher snarls.

Dimitri swings his head around the room. The other children sag in their seats, their eyes to the floor. Striding toward him, the teacher looms above Dimitri. "You! What's your name?"

Pulling himself to his feet he shakes, biting his lip trying desperately not to cry. "My name is Dimitri Filipidis."

"Who gave you permission to speak in that tongue?"

"This is what we speak at home."

"You are all Greek!" The teacher glares around the room until his eyes return to rest on Dimitri. "And you are to speak Greek. At all times. Don't ever forget it."

Before he knows what's happening, the teacher drags Dimitri by his ear and pushes him to the dusty floor. "Why are you wearing that?"

Wiping away a tear, he splutters, "My baba made it for school. I thought…"

"I don't care. You shouldn't wear those disgusting colours or speak that awful language. Didn't your parents tell you that? I could have you and your family sent to jail." The teacher snaps his fingers. "Just like that. Get out and don't come back until you're dressed properly. You're Greek and should be proud of it."

Biting down on his trembling bottom lip, Dimitri hangs his head, feeling the stares of the other children like bugs crawling across his back. Someone behind him bitingly whispers, "Barbarian."

Another older Greek boy sniggers and mutters the worst insult, "Bulgari."

Walking past his desk, he glances at Lazo, whose eyes search the floor. He must not cry, Dimitri tells himself over and over until he reaches the gate. Then he runs as fast as he can – crying until he bursts through the front door of his house.

"What are you doing home so early? What's the matter, my Dimitri?" Baba puts down her knitting and pulls him to her. She rocks him, waiting for him to settle, but he's too distraught to tell her. She offers a spoonful of precious sugar, and it's enough to calm him and for the words to tumble out.

"Those bastards," she yells to the sky. "They take everything. Our land, our names … I'm an old woman. I can't be expected to learn Greek. I curse the teacher, the government and their families. May they go to the devil and burn in hell. May their offspring be struck down with disease." She spits out the word 'Greek' as if it's venom in her mouth.

While she rants and raves, Dimitri slips into the bedroom. His once beautiful clothes feel like worms slithering over him. Ripping them off, he flings them onto the floor and changes into his old clothes. Gathering them up he goes outside where he digs a hole and buries the bundle vowing never to wear them or step foot in the school again.

His mother returns from the fields to collect the lunches. Hugging him, she smells like freshly turned soil. When she pulls away she looks at him carefully and can tell from his face that something is wrong. The story pours out of him.

His mother rolls her eyes skywards, turning her rage to his grandmother. "You're a stupid old woman. What did you think you were doing putting your only grandson at risk? Everything is different now. You put us all in danger."

"I didn't know. They're the finest clothes. He should be able to wear them. I thought it would be all right," Baba says softly.

His mother shakes her head. "You know perfectly well that we can't draw attention to being Macedonian now. I told you he couldn't wear that outside of the house. Don't try to tell me you've forgotten. You remember when you want to, you old crone."

"I don't know what you're talking about."

"You can't be trusted with my child. You've just made our lives even more difficult. We'll probably be a target now. The Greek police picked up Mitra for speaking Macedonian to her grandson in her garden. They pierced her tongue with a needle. Last week, they executed the great Mirka Ginova who stood up for our freedom. What hope do we have when the leader of the Macedonian Front can't save us? Don't you understand?" his mother says in Macedonian.

The old woman retorts, "She should have been at home with her husband and children. Now she's brought dishonour on her family."

"You're the one who brings dishonour. Mirka fought against the Germans and she fought hard for us to have freedom, and now she's lost her life. They tortured then executed her and that proves they'll stop at nothing. I'll not have you say a bad word against her."

"Maybe you should go into the mountains with the

Partisans," the old woman grumbles. "So high and mighty. Your parents, the Grecomans."

"What did you say?"

"Nothing."

"My parents were not Grecoman. They were wrongly accused. Wait till your son hears about what you did." Then she mutters, "You're a stupid, selfish old witch."

Baba looks defeated as if her strength has given out. She slumps clasping her chest, into the rickety chair. Dimitri feels bad and wants to protect her but he daren't say anything to attract his mother's anger.

Baba and his mother had never got along and he hated it when they argued. Ever since Dimitri could remember, they'd called each other names. Baba called his mother a Grecoman; an insult used on Macedonians who thought of themselves as Greek.

His mother kneels in front of her son. "Dimitri, I told you last night you must never speak our language outside the house."

"But my new friend spoke to me in Macedonian and I answered. I was only whispering. I forgot." He bursts into tears again.

"You're going back to school and I will speak to the teacher."

"No! No! I can't go back," Dimitri cries out. His sobs and pleading do nothing to stop his mother. "Please don't make me go back."

"Look at the boy. Look at what they did to him. He can

stay here with me. I never went to school and he doesn't have to either," Baba says.

Dimitri looks at his mother in hope.

"Shut up! He's my son," his mother yells at the old woman. "You've already done enough damage."

"Listen," she says, wiping Dimitri's eyes. "We can never let them beat us. They can take our land and change our names but they can't take away what is in our hearts and in our heads. If you run away, you'll be weak and they'll see that. Now stop your crying. Blow your nose. Let's go."

And so the skinny small boy follows his thin limping mother to school where she meets with the teacher. Dimitri doesn't know what she says but the next day he learns to count to five in Greek.

4

The Trouble with Water

"Dad! It's time for lunch," Helen yells from the kitchen.

Jim sighs and feels with his foot for the tattered slipper lost under the desk. Hauling himself up on his walking stick, he shuffles into the kitchen, which is dated and aged like him. Helen had tried to convince him to update the stove and the oven, which worked just fine. Not that he used the oven. He had to admit that since he'd read about someone's gas oven exploding he was nervous. When Helen's new kitchen was being installed she came over and put a leg of lamb in his oven, then left. He had sat with the fire extinguisher in his lap and watched it closely, in case it exploded. He didn't tell her, but you can't be too careful, he thought.

He settles himself on the vinyl kitchen chair in front of a plate of sandwiches. "Aren't you having any?" Lifting a slice of brown bread, he peers at the lettuce, tomato and cardboard-tasting cheese within. "It's looks nice, love." He's always hated brown bread, but that's all she and the quack will let him have.

His daughter leans against the sink with her arms crossed.

"Is that a new hairdo? It looks good," he says, biting into the fresh bread.

"I went to the hairdresser yesterday to get rid of the greys. Thanks for noticing. Have you taken your tablets?"

"Ah … no. Can you get them?"

She places three packets on the table in front of him with a glass of water, then resumes her place leaning against the sink. He can tell she's got something on her mind and, for a moment, he fears the inevitable lecture.

His arthritic fingers fumble as he painstakingly takes one tablet at a time, as if in slow motion. "Sit down for goodness' sake. You make me nervous standing there." He blows crumbs across his tea.

Taking the seat opposite, Helen continues to stare as if he has two heads, and it makes him squirm.

"Did you save the crusts for the maggies?"

"Yes. They're on the plate over there. You really should stop feeding the magpies. Have you seen the mess they're making of the deck? If Mum were here, she'd have a fit."

"They depend on me. There's a whole family who visits." He loves those magpies. The young ones eat out of his hand now. Helen doesn't understand what it's like to be alone. The magpies keep him company. Whenever he's in the garden, they come from wherever they are and follow him as he checks the water levels in the buckets.

"How're Jazzy and Alex going at school?"

Her frown deepens and he wonders what he's said wrong.

She narrows her eyes. "Jasmine lives in Brisbane now. She finished uni two years ago and Alex lives in New York. Don't you remember?"

"Of course I remember. That's what I meant. I meant how are they going in their jobs."

He wonders if he's convinced her as he picks out a yellowing leaf of lettuce.

"They're both good and send you their love."

A silence settles between them as he tries to remember what his grandchildren look like. He's disturbed by Helen drumming her nails on the table. That's it, he thinks. She wants him to notice them. They're bright enough.

"Is that new nail polish, too?" he says, after swallowing the last tablet.

He's very proud of her, although he can't remember the last time he told her. It's a pity about that weedy bloke she's shacked up with, he thinks. What's wrong with people these days? When he was young, it was simple. You met the love of your life, married, bought a house and had children. The first bloke she was with was a good man. He'd liked him. Brian had come from a nice family with a good job as a doctor. He was the first fellow she'd gone out with who he approved of. Now she's with what's his name – Tony, the National Retail Sales Manager. It's a rubbish job, and he's too slick and smarmy – a no-hoper, he'd told his daughter. "Go back to Brian. He's a good man," he'd said. "He's a doctor."

"He's a dull bore, which is what a Doctor of Philosophy is, Dad," she'd shot back.

She's saying something – her lips are moving – but he's still thinking about the no-hoper.

"What love?"

"I said, I was looking through your new digital camera."

"Yes?" He picks up the second half of the sandwich. "Why aren't you eating?" He hopes she's not getting that disease, what is it? Anorexia! He'd seen something about it on TV. She's looks too skinny. Come to think of it, he never sees her eat.

"Dad, the photos on the camera. What are you doing?"

"What do you mean? I'm taking photos, like you showed me." He clicks his dentures to remove a bit of food that's caught.

"But Dad, they're photos of the water meter."

"It's good isn't it?" He grins. "I can see exactly how much water I'm using each day. Those bastards are cheating me. Did you see the last bill? They charged me $250 last month."

"Why, then, is there water in the bathtub?"

He places the remaining sandwich on his plate and looks her squarely in the eye.

"Helen, in case you haven't noticed, there's a drought. I'm simply conserving water."

"But Dad, you put in three water tanks, which is enough to irrigate your tiny garden and all the neighbours' gardens too. You also have buckets at the end of the storm water pipes running off the pergola."

Jim swallows the last remnant of the sandwich then washes it down with a gulp of tea.

"Plus, your toilet is disgusting. I take it you're not flushing to save water."

"That was nice, love."

"Well?"

"Well what?"

"The toilet? The bath?"

"I'm conserving water. What's wrong with that?"

Really! Young people today, he thinks. They run water to wash one dish, then leave it running to wash another. He isn't going to tell her that he boiled the water from the bath and washed himself with a bucket of water – just like he did growing up. She wouldn't understand or listen. He rang the water people and they gave him some mumbo jumbo. He didn't understand why the woman on the line was so terse. Told him he was rude, when all along she refused to give him answers about why his water use was so high.

Then Helen had given him a digital camera for his eightieth birthday. He didn't know what he was expected to do with it, and told her she'd wasted her money. He took some photos of flowers and the magpies in the garden. Then he got the brainwave to track his water usage. Taking a photo every day, he writes down the figures to measure how much water he's using. He's itching to catch them out. Thank goodness Helen hasn't seen the photos of the gas meter.

"Dad. There's mosquito larvae in the bath. The toilet stinks of urine and the kitchen has mice running everywhere.

You've got to use water to clean. I haven't got time to come here every day to do it for you. I'll organise a cleaner for you if it's too much."

He scrapes back his chair. "NO! I'll not have someone in here fussing about." He gets up and shuffles to his study. He's grateful to his daughter but surely he can run his house the way he wants to.

She follows him. "Dad. I'm not trying to nag but you have to take better care of yourself," she says softly. "I'm worried, that's all."

"Don't worry about me. Everything is neat and tidy, isn't it?" He always has a place for everything. He can't see the sense of replacing something just because it's broken or worn out. He takes pride in fixing everything. He never did understand why dust disturbed women so much. It's just part of life, that's all. It does no harm. Even after Helen dusts, it resettles again. He tried to tell Anna, but, like Helen, she ignored him too.

He stares at the dark screen instead of his daughter and wonders where his words have disappeared to.

"What happened to the screen? It's gone black."

Helen sighs and leans in toward the keyboard. "It's just gone to sleep that's all." She shakes the mouse. "See, there it is." She frowns. "*Dimitri was abducted when he was ten,*" she reads out loud. "What's going on? What are you writing?"

"It's nothing. I'm playing around with a story."

"I thought you were writing your memoir."

He swivels on his chair to face her. "You're right. I'll empty the bath and try to remember to flush the toilet. Look, love, you can head off if you like. I've got a few things to do."

He stands up and walks out into the kitchen with her. He hopes she'll bugger off. He loves her but she can be annoying. If she gets a sniff of what he's up to, he'll never hear the end of it. She'll ask questions that he's not yet ready to answer. He has to sort out his memories. Write them down before he forgets everything.

"I suppose I could go if you don't want anything else. I'm happy to help you with the boxes."

"No, I'll deal with it. If I need any help I'll call you."

"Okay. Oh, I put some pumpkin soup and a lasagne in the fridge. And I brought you our leftover cheese platter. We had it last night and I thought you might like it as a snack."

"Thanks, love. It sounds good. I'll save the soup for tomorrow night. I think I'll have eggs tonight."

"Have the soup tonight." She opens the fridge and brings out the carton of eggs. "You can't have these. They're two weeks past the use-by date."

"There's nothing wrong with them. Waste not, want not," he says.

Helen holds tightly onto the carton. "They're going into the bin! That's all I need; you getting salmonella poisoning to top it all off."

She opens the front door with the eggs under her arm.

"I'll drop by on Wednesday to take you to the specialist and then we'll go to the supermarket. Bye, Dad," she calls out from the bottom of the steps. "And please get rid of the water in the tub."

"It's all right. I'll drive to the eye specialist. You don't need to take me," he calls out.

She stops and turns around. The set line of her mouth and the squint of her blue eyes; just like her mother when she was about to explode. "You will not be driving. The doctor said you're not allowed," she yells and starts back up the driveway.

"There's no need to yell, Helen," he says calmly.

"You're trying my patience. The doctor said you can't drive for at least three weeks after the cataract surgery."

"Isn't it already three weeks?"

"Let's not take any risks. Anyway, I want to come to the specialist too," she says, standing at the bottom of the steps.

"All right then. See you Wednesday."

Thank goodness that's over, he thinks, as he limps back inside to his desk. He knows she's talked to the specialist and tried to stop him driving. He's not an idiot. She thought he didn't know what he was doing. But if he only takes left-hand turns on roads he's driven on for the last forty years he knows he'll be fine.

"Now, where was I? Damn, the screen's gone black again. What do I have to do?"

5

The Stick, the Stone and the Donkey

May 1946. The ground is hard and the air cold. The sun's dull heat coaxes the beginnings of buds on the trees. Across the flat fields, villagers plant their crops – Dimitri's father and grandfather amongst them. The snow-covered mountains surrounding the valley are silhouetted against a cloudless sky.

Fighting rages some distance from their village and all anyone talks about is the Fascists and the Partisans; terms Dimitri doesn't understand or can be bothered with. Except for the occasional military plane high above, all is peaceful and Dimitri's life is spent with chores and play.

With his only friend, Lazo, away visiting his grandparents, Dimitri has little to do. He kicks at the dirt until his feet are covered in a fine brown dust. Then, with a stick, he ferrets around for worms. He worries a yappy dog, straining on its leash, by offering a worm he's dug up.

Growing bored, he chases a starling as it flies between the olive trees. He stops when he comes upon a group of older boys. They're gathered under a large fig tree filled with loudly chirping birds. An older Greek boy he knows as Vassili, picks up a stick and flings it at the lower bough, hitting it and scattering several birds. He remembers that the boy called him names at school. The other boys cheer and dance around their beaming friend.

Edging closer, Dimitri searches the ground and finds a long stick lying alongside the dusty path. The older boys watch and wait. The birds, not easily scared off, repossess the tree. He picks out a bough for his target. It's high and he's uncertain, now that he has the boys' attention.

"Go on. Throw it," Vassili shouts. The others chant, *"Throw it! Throw it! Throw it!"*

Dimitri swings his arm back and flings the stick as high as he can, but it falls short and lands a few feet away. The boys laugh. "Maybe when you're bigger."

"I told you he couldn't do it," says another.

Losing interest, they turn away in search of more weapons. It isn't their snub that disturbs him, but the pain of the splinter in his palm that seeps with blood. He turns and runs for his mother.

He finds her in the house kneading bread, while deep in conversation with their neighbour, Eleni. She's a sour woman who lives across the street from them and is always dressed in black after losing her husband during the war. Her house is as unkempt as she is and she visits every day to complain about her swollen ankles, food shortages and her lot in life. Today, she's crying as usual, wiping her eyes on her apron, when he bursts through the door.

"What's wrong, my love?" his mother says, seeing his distress.

His mother, a slight woman with a hobble leans against the table. She smiles and laughs but never when Eleni is present. When he's with his mother, he always feels like he's the most important thing to her. She kisses and hugs him a lot. Sometimes too much. Nearly eight years old, he still loves it when his mother lifts him and cuddles him, although he knows he's too big. He'd asked her once why she hobbled but she'd only grunted. Dedo, his grandfather, told him she'd slipped down the steps.

Wiping her flour-covered hands on her apron, she scoops him into her arms, installing him on the bench near the window where the light is the brightest. He uncurls his small hand to show her. Wisps of grey-streaked hair peek out from under her brown head scarf. Her worn, weathered hands hold his hand to the light. Eleni looks on, annoyed at the interruption.

"My goodness, what have we here? It looks like a big splinter. Have you been throwing sticks again?"

His round wet eyes blink as he gazes into her lovely face. The crow's feet crinkle as she squints at his hand.

"Such a lot of fuss, Dimitri. Why didn't you just pull it out yourself?" Eleni says, barely glancing at him. "Really, you shouldn't be bothering your mother with a little thing like that." Emphasising her annoyance, she folds her arms across her ample chest and frowns.

"It's a very big splinter," his mother says, ignoring Eleni. "There."

The pain sharpens again and before he knows it, she's dabbing at the wound with the edge of a wet cloth. She swings him down from the bench and pats him on the head.

"Will I get a scar like yours?" he asks.

"I don't think so," she says, frowning. "Off you go now."

"You smother that boy," Dimitri hears Eleni say. "You treat him like a baby. He needs to learn toughness. Life is hard and you shouldn't protect him from it."

"If you can't love your only child, what else is there?" his mother replies.

Dimitri hesitates on the front step and wonders if what Eleni says is true.

"The bloody Fascists," Eleni says. "Without salt and flour how can I make bread or make anything taste decent? If they ban that, what'll be next? You'll see. It's going to get worse."

He jumps from the top step instead of taking the three steps one at a time. Babies can't do that he thinks, as he runs back to the fig tree, but the other boys have gone.

***

A few months later, returning from running an errand for his mother, Dimitri kicks a good-sized stone all the way down the centre of the dirt road. He loves how it rolls exactly where he wants it. He's careful to avoid the large holes pockmarked here and there, where the planes dropped bombs several nights before.

The village had panicked. Dimitri, shaking with fear, had hidden with his parents under the bed until the planes had gone. His mother muttered prayers under her breath. His father said the bombs were dropped as a warning. Dimitri never understood what they were being warned about.

Their village is luckier than those closest to the mountainous border, his mother says. Later, he overhears his father telling his grandfather that many people have died. Lying in bed at night he listens and the words Partisans, bombs and war worries him. He strains to listen to his mother's whispers. He knows she wants to leave. She's packed and unpacked the bags many times. But since Baba's death, Dedo is too frail to leave, his father tells her. Waking one morning, several months earlier, Dimitri was told Baba had gone. Died in her sleep, his mother said. There was a lot of crying and sorrow. Now his father won't leave Dedo. Maybe he doesn't want to leave Baba's graveside, Dimitri thinks.

All Dimitri knows is that his carefree life has ended. Now, he has many worries and some are overwhelming. Fire worries him. The scars on his mother's arms have something to do with his fear, and he worries that he, too, will be scarred like her. Baba told him a cigarette fell from Dedo's mouth when he fell asleep. Dimitri was playing on the floor. There was smoke and screams. Arms snatched him up and, although his mother never mentioned it, he knew from Baba that she'd fought the blaze and saved them all that day.

Apart from fire, bombs scare him more than anything. He hates the sound, the whistle, then the echoing boom. All he can do is put his fingers in his ears and hope one doesn't fall on him like it did to Vassili's brother. There was nothing left of him after the bomb fell out of the sky. Eleni said there were bits hanging off a nearby tree and he wonders which bits they were. There was a lot of wailing that day.

He worries about holes in the ground made by the bombs and that one day he could fall into a deep crater and never come out ... that the hole might take him down into a dark place. He can't help but worry that one day he will come home and no-one will be there. That they will have disappeared and never be found. These are the things he thinks about as he kicks the stone.

When he arrives home, it seems all of the neighbours are crowded into the small kitchen. In the centre is his mother. Everyone is crying and it alarms him, although it's a common enough occurrence in his village. Some wail and rock back and forth, and Eleni is wailing the loudest. He surveys them then walks into the bedroom he shares with his parents. Two suitcases stand next to the bed. Perhaps they are leaving after all.

He skulks about but no-one notices him so, after a while, he slips outside to kick the stone again. The donkey nearby turns his head and their eyes meet. Dimitri thinks about his mother. It's not like he hasn't seen her cry before, but something seems different. With his bare foot, he manoeuvres the stone onto a tuft of grass next to the fence and kicks. It veers in the wrong direction and settles in a shallow hole close to the donkey's hind legs. Maybe this time we're really leaving, he thinks.

Standing behind the donkey, he leans in to grab the stone. He decides leaving would be a good thing. The donkey's tail swishes across his face. As he stretches his arm, a hind leg lashes out, knocking him into the dust.

The next thing he sees is his mother's tear-stained face above him, along with all the other women. He feels his body lift with hands gripping him firmly until he's dropped into his mother's lap on a cart.

"Majka?"

"Hush. You're going to be all right."

His face is wet. Has he been crying? He feels foggy and the pain behind his eye is sharp. Lifting his hand, he sees the blood and attempts to sit bolt upright from his mother's lap. But she's too strong and holds him close.

"Don't move, my love. We'll be there soon."

The cart rocks and sways behind the old horse for what seems like ages. Finally, it stops and his mother carefully lifts him out and sets him down. While she speaks to the man in the cart, Dimitri looks around the village, which is bigger than his own. An old war jeep rumbles past, billowing dust, and he coughs.

"Can you walk?"

He nods and his mother cradles her arm around his

shoulder. Inside the stone house she speaks quickly to a woman dressed in white.

The room is so crowded that he sits on the floor in front of his mother's feet. Another small, bald-headed child in brown shorts with dirty feet crouches in the opposite corner. He holds a small stone, which he throws from one hand to the other while Dimitri watches.

Names are called and people disappear into a room and emerge later rubbing their arms. A name is called, Marika Ginova. The child who Dimitri thinks is a grubby little boy, stands up. The stone slides to the floor and Marika disappears into the room.

Dimitri scurries along the floor and snatches up the stone. "Come back here and sit still," his mother calls out. She pulls him onto her lap and looks carefully at his face. "Is it sore?"

"No, Majka. It's fine. Can we go?"

"No, son, we have to let them look at you and while we're here …" She says something else but he's not listening.

He's too intent on gazing at his prize; his head and pain forgotten. He angles it into the light to catch the speckles; it's almost perfectly round and smooth. He, too, rolls it from one hand to the other and visualises throwing it at the birds, and hitting one.

As Dimitri holds the stone to the light, Marika comes out rubbing her arm. She stares at him on his mother's lap, then at the stone and her lip curls into a sneer.

At that moment his mother stands up and Dimitri slides to his feet as his name is called. The two children face each other. Dimitri holds out his palm with the stone in the middle.

Marika snatches it. "You're a baby," she hisses, and disappears through the door.

He stares after the girl who looks like a boy as his mother pulls him into the room.

"Well, young man," the lady in white says, "what's happened to you?"

But Dimitri is still thinking about the girl and the perfect round stone.

6

The Phone

It's dark. After Helen has left, Jim sits at his desk for what seems like hours. He looks at his watch. Half past five. The computer screen is black again.

He wanders into the kitchen and opens the fridge door. The eggs are gone. Damn that girl. He'd had his heart set on scrambled eggs on toast. Pulling the pot of soup from the fridge, he lifts the lid; an aroma of garlic makes his stomach growl.

As he puts it on the stove to heat, the telephone rings.

"Hello, is that James Philips?" asks the heavily accented female voice.

"It's Jim Philips."

"How are you today? Have you had a nice day?"

"Ah … err, I suppose so."

"I'm Naomi Wilson from Solar Panels Australia. I won't

keep you but I'm just getting back to you about the government subsidy for solar panels."

"Didn't you ring me last week about this? I'm not interested."

"But lots of people in your area are getting them. Now, what's the best time for one of our contractors to come out to measure?"

"I don't want anyone to come out and I'm not interested."

"Now, Jim. Don't be like that. I'm only trying to save you money. Don't you want to do the right thing by the environment?"

"Get it through your thick head, I'm not interested. I don't want you to ring me anymore!" he roars.

The soup bubbles furiously in the pot and the bread pops in the toaster.

"But Jim, you asked me to ring you back with some information," the woman persists.

This stops him in his tracks. He thinks hard. Has he asked? "Nah. I'm pretty sure I didn't ask. Don't ring me again. Goodbye." He slams the telephone down hard on its cradle and moves quickly to turn the gas down.

"What's a man got to do to get some peace around here!" he grumbles.

After pouring his soup into a bowl, he sets up the tray table in front of the television. Then he brings out the cheese platter. There are olives and feta cheese, cheddar and blue vein. Doesn't she know that he doesn't like feta? Helen never puts enough salt in the soup so he sprays some liberally across the steaming bowl before settling to watch the news.

Someone is rabbiting on that cars should only be permitted in the CBD on even numbered days unless you own an electric car. How ridiculous? As if he's going to replace his old Holden Calais with one of those newfangled electric things. He's always had a Holden. Even if there's no longer a Holden manufacturer in the country. Ian, next door, kept telling him his Calais was going to be an antique and worth big bucks. He bought it brand new in 1996. He'd proudly told Ian it hadn't even clocked one hundred thousand kilometres.

He never trusted mechanics and serviced it himself, ever since the brakes failed one day after being replaced. He was sure the mechanic had stuffed it up. He told the bloke he'd run into that it wasn't his fault. The insurance company didn't believe him either. So he cancelled his insurance and learnt how to fix his car himself. At least he knew then it was a good job. Anna had protested but he'd won the argument that day.

He's surprised to see his bowl is empty and so nibbles on the cheese, avoiding the feta. After a while he heaves himself off the couch and clears the dishes. Scooping a bucket of water out of the bath, he lugs it into the kitchen and pours it into a large saucepan in the sink.

"She wants me to empty the bath," he mutters.

He tries to light the gas but finds it already on. Shrugging, he places the saucepan on the stove and wanders into the lounge to pick up the platter of leftover olives and cheese, popping an olive into his mouth as he wanders back to the kitchen. The feta lies on the plate taunting him. He breaks off a piece and throws it into his mouth. It tastes better than he'd remembered.

He peers into the saucepan of water – no sign of life. He could have run the hot water out of the tap but that would be wasteful when he has a whole bath of perfectly good water collected from the rain buckets. When they start rationing water, Helen will be around every day. He bets his shirt on it. Won't she feel stupid then for telling him off for storing it in the first place?

Flicking on the switch for the kettle, he rummages in the cupboard for the teapot. Anna had liked tea bags but he couldn't see the sense of them. They cost a fortune and you couldn't throw them in the garden, like you could tea leaves.

The phone rings again.

"What now?" he mutters. "Hello," he snaps.

There's silence at the other end.

"Hello," he repeats. Silence still. "Listen, you twerp, stop ringing if you're not going to speak." And he hangs up.

What's wrong with people these days that they ring and don't talk? The water bubbles on the stove and he pours it carefully into the sink full of dishes. The olives and bits of cheese bob up from their hiding places and float to the top of the water line.

"Damn! Must concentrate on what I'm doing. Except I can't if that infernal phone KEEPS RINGING," he yells.

He pulls the olives out of the water and tastes one. "Mmm

… it's fine." Then he scoops out bits of cheese and puts what he can onto a clean plate.

The phone rings again.

"What now?" he yells.

"Hello, Jim. Thanks so much for giving your donation to …"

He presses the off switch and places the phone on the cradle and glares at it, daring it to ring again. It stares back as if to say they were only asking for a donation.

"I don't care. I need a donation myself," he mutters. "Now for the dishes." But they sit like icebergs in a sea of tepid water. He swishes them around before placing them on the drainer, reasoning that the boiling water has done its job. Then he pours his tea, only to find that he's forgotten to put the tea leaves into the teapot. Why is everything so complicated?

The phone rings again and he looks at it accusingly.

"Whose side are you on anyway? You can ring all you like but I'm not picking up. You've had your chance. I'm going to have my cup of tea in peace."

While the phone rings every half hour for the next two hours, his mind wanders to the last time he'd eaten feta cheese.

7

Feta and Rakia

August 1947

There's no peace for anyone. The bombing gets worse.
The Partisans exchange fire with the Fascist government
forces during the day and planes drop their bombs at night.
The mountains behind the village glow with flames and a
smoky haze fills the valley.

Each night, Dimitri is dragged out of bed by his parents
as they run to hide in the forest. Sometimes it's an hour and
other times it's all night. Often they find their neighbours and
huddle next to them. Mothers and grandmothers cradle their
crying children, desperate to keep them quiet. Then, as the
new day dawns, they assess the damage. Luckily, the bombs
fall around them onto roads and fields. An old stone house
is damaged but the occupants are long gone. Villages nearby
and in the mountains are not so fortunate. Even the school

closes when the last teacher runs off to fight with the Partisans yelling, "Death to the Fascists."

Then, one sunny day, the fighting stops and Dimitri and Lazo are allowed to venture outside after what seems like weeks hiding in fear. The sticks they play with are make-believe guns, which they fire at each other. Rolling over and over, Dimitri pretends he's been shot.

"You have to die straight away. If you've been shot you can't keep rolling," Lazo says. "I asked my father and he said if you've been shot, you die."

"Arggh, arggh," Dimitri yells, before he settles under a thick bush. He points his stick and fires at Lazo. "Take that. Now I've shot you."

"That's not fair. I got you first. Now play fair and die."

Dimitri's eyes widen in his hiding spot under the bush. Behind Lazo stride two large bearded men in tattered, dirty clothes. Real rifles are slung over their shoulders as they stand behind his friend in mud-splattered boots.

"Who are you trying to kill, lad?" asks one of the men.

Lazo looks behind him and freezes in fear. Dimitri holds his breath, praying that Lazo will not give him away, and edges himself further back into the undergrowth.

"No, no, no-one sir," Lazo says.

The eyes of the taller man sweep across the bush where he's hidden and he holds his breath watching the man.

"Do you live in this village?" asks the other man.

Lazo nods.

"Come on. Let's go and visit your parents. We need food."

Dimitri watches the men follow Lazo away. When they're gone he runs home to tell his mother and father what happened. Already clustered around the rickety kitchen table is his father, grandfather and two men he doesn't know. Chewing on his bottom lip, a metallic taste floods his mouth as he takes in the dull brown of two rifles propped like sentries against the wall behind the men. His mother hunches over the stove, stirring something in a pot, her lips moving in soundless prayer. His grandfather lifts his hand to quickly wipe blood from his face, leaving a menacing red mark on his cheek.

"This is my son, Dimitri." He's reassured by his father's warm hand resting on his shoulder.

The strangers ignore him; their eyes bore instead into his grandfather.

"We're going to eat. Sit down next to your father," his mother whispers. Her top lip glistens with a film of sweat even though it's cool inside.

"We suffered some casualties but we've beaten them back," says the first man. Dimitri can't help but stare at the gap where two teeth should have been; the rest are brown and crooked. Having lost several of his own teeth in the last few years, Dimitri desperately wants to know what's happened to this man's mouth. But he knows to keep quiet.

"Surely you can see already that things have improved, now that we've taken control. You'll have your freedom if you help us. The Fascists are only interested in one thing and that's themselves. They don't care about the peasants, socialists, the Macedonians, or any minority. They want one Greece. Everyone must be Greek. With Tito behind us, we'll have our own state and respect for everyone's own culture and language. We need men like you. You fought against the Nazis?"

"Yes I did," his father says.

"Then you know. The American money is helping the government build the Greek Army. The King is nothing but a pawn they brought back from exile. And we need more people if we are to succeed and make life better for everyone."

"But I must look after my family. They'll starve if I don't go out into the fields. You can see an old man, a crippled woman, a young child who depend on me to be here."

The gap-toothed man's intense gaze flits to his mother first and then to Dimitri.

"We need women too. Can you knit?"

"Yes, she can knit," his grandfather says too quickly, lifting his head. The bloodied smear has dried on his face.

Dimitri has questions, but settles on quick glances at the two strangers. The other one taps his grubby finger on the table. He looks young, maybe sixteen, and his thick neck seems to disappear into the ragged collar of his filthy clothes.

"Then you can help. As for the child, we always need messengers."

"No!" his mother says. "He's too small. Look at him." Dimitri squirms under their gaze. It's true, he is small. The other children his age are much taller; he's still the size of a six or seven-year-old but he's not worried. He only has to look at his own father, who'd also been small as a child. Now he's almost as tall as the top of the door.

"How old are you, son?" the gap-toothed man asks.

"I think nine, sir," Dimitri answers proudly. He might be small but he's old enough. "I know a lot and can do all sorts of things like read and write." Only the look on his mother's face tells him he's said the wrong thing.

"Excellent," says the grinning gap-toothed man. "Then he's old enough to help. Might do you good, old man, to follow this youngster's attitude."

The soup is ladled into bowls, most to the men, then his father and grandfather, two spoonfuls for him and one for his mother. Dimitri looks at the soup, which is the same every night – murky water with a few beans. Concentrating on his meal, Dimitri hears the noisy slurps from around the table, which remind him of the sound of the job he hates the most – the slosh of the night bucket onto the garden.

"Now that we control the valley and mountains, everyone in the village will need to supply us with food for a while," the gap-toothed man says, his spittle spraying against the fading light from the window.

"Of course, we'll help. And I'll think about what you've said," his father says. "Cheese with your bread?"

He holds out a plate with feta cheese on it, and the gap-toothed man reaches out a dirty hand, breaks off a piece and throws it into his mouth.

Dimitri loves feta nearly as much as he loves olives. He likes to roll the cheese around his mouth, savouring the saltiness. When the plate is offered he takes a large piece and pops it in.

"It's time to celebrate our victory. Rakia?" The gap-toothed man smiles expectantly, his tongue searching for remnants of crumbs on his lips.

"No, we've run out," his mother says too sharply. Everyone stops eating. Dimitri is surprised. Hadn't they made some only a few weeks earlier? It's always a family affair each year. They make Rakia to sell mostly, but always keep some for themselves. Dimitri was encouraged to try it but he could never see why grownups liked it so much. It tasted like cough medicine he'd had once when he was smaller. Perhaps he was wrong.

"That's a shame. I've heard you people have the best in the valley." He leans back in his chair and reaches for his rifle. He runs his hand down the barrel. "Son, why don't you come over here. Would you like to see a rifle up close?" He holds his hand toward Dimitri, who peers at the bulging veins on the man's arms that wind their way up like worms.

He looks from his mother, whose eyes widen in fright, to his father. Should he go to the man? His father says nothing but gives a faint nod. The day outside has almost gone but no-one moves to light the lamp.

The man pulls Dimitri close enough for him to smell his stale sweat and an ugly breath of cheese and swampy water. The feta sticks to the dry walls of his throat and mouth. The gap-toothed man stands the rifle so that the muzzle is under Dimitri's chin. If he chews, his chin will touch the gun.

Holding his breath, the cheese oozes between his teeth, sliding down his throat. A trio of moths have found their way into the house and he watches their wings beat against the grubby window pane.

"You sure you haven't got any?"

His father meets the man's stare for what seems like hours. He eventually looks away. "I'll check again. Son, why don't you come and help me look?"

The man laughs and pushes him to his father.

"Go boy. Go look for some Rakia. It'll be better if you do."

8

Stinky Spiro

Spiro Tatelidos is a small, skinny man not much taller than five feet. Grey speckles his unshaven face, moustache and greasy hair. The villagers call him Stinky Spiro behind his back – some claim they can smell him coming down the street if the breeze is blowing in the right direction. It wasn't always so, but after his wife died five years ago he cares nothing for himself or the village. He's convinced they were responsible for his beloved wife's death as no-one bothered to help her when she fell ill.

Although not well liked, the café he's owned for the last ten years is the only place where men in the village can escape their nagging wives, crying children and every other woe they have. They play cards, drink ouzo or coffee and talk. When the Germans invaded they talked about the war. Then business died as the men went off to fight. Stinky Spiro was forced to close the café to join the army too. But, being a cowardly man, he ran into the mountains and hid for days when the Germans came near.

After the war ended the men came back to his café to talk about their crops, politics and how hard their lives were. But things steadily got worse. There were taxes for this and taxes for that. They worried how to feed their families. A new war was on everyone's lips and the Partisans won a lot of sympathy. Many a spirited argument followed with everyone throwing in their opinions, sometimes trading blows.

Although not a clever businessman, Spiro scratched his greasy hair and thought about the looming conflict drawing away his customers, as villagers one by one disappeared to join the Partisans. He looked for opportunities to make extra money. When the authorities slipped him money to gather information, he spent more time wiping down tables while discreetly listening to what was being said.

Three villagers were repairing the road, which had been peppered with craters by bombs dropped from planes. One boasted of being a war-time hero and thought too highly of himself. The other two owned too much land. Stinky overheard they'd been repairing the road for the carts to deliver produce to the next village. He told the authorities the men were digging trenches for the Partisans. The villagers were rounded up, tried and executed. Stinky's reward was a pocketful of drachma. He felt no remorse.

Now, while Stinky pours the coffee, he listens.

When the Partisans capture the village, Stinky stays low.

The café is closed and a sign says he's gone to visit relatives at another village.

In truth, he hides in his house next door to the Filipidis family. Sometimes the curtains move and his watchful eye peers through.

One morning, two burly, ragged men with rifles slung across their shoulders ruffle the boy's head as they stand with Dimitri's father and laugh at the front door. Two more Partisans leave Eleni's house.

Dimitri plays outside and throws a stick up into the tree in front of Stinky's house. More Partisans come out of another house further down the street. The stick lands in front of his window. Stinky sees the boy just in time and lets the curtain drop.

9

The Arrest

One morning, Dimitri wakes to hear birds singing. A sparrow on the olive tree outside his window looks in. By opening one eye then closing it and opening the other, he makes the bird move across the branch.

The bed next to his is empty. His mother hums in the kitchen. Outside, wood is split. Then laughter. Even the roosters crow echoes across the early morning.

No sounds of fighting; the Partisans have gone.

The village relaxes. Music plays again and name days are celebrated with much dancing, and what little food everyone has is shared.

Men sit in Stinky's café again and women gather in the street to gossip about the handful of younger women who have gone with the Partisans into the mountain to fight. Some say they're looking for husbands. Others argue they're helping the cause for freedom but secretly agree it's for husbands.

The school re-opens and, despite his protests, his mother marches Dimitri back to class. As always, he keeps his head down and mouth shut when the teacher is around, and he prays that, like the others, this teacher will run off and fight too.

He tells his friend what happened with the Partisans.

"I hate them too. They took my sister." Lazo looks sullen.

"But didn't she want to go?"

"My mother said we should tell everyone that she wanted to go, so that she can hold her head high. I don't know why she has to hold her head up." Tears fill his eyes. "Those men said if she didn't go they'd shoot each one of us." He sniffs. "It's all my fault. If we weren't playing that stupid game with the sticks, they wouldn't have found us."

Dimitri kicks at the dirt in the road and says nothing. He can't help but agree.

***

Two weeks later, Dimitri and his family huddle around their table ready to eat the evening meal when they hear a commotion. A loud scream comes from outside.

Peering through the window, his mother drops the spoon she's holding.

"Oh God! They've got Eleni."

They rush to the window to see soldiers dragging Eleni along the street by her long hair.

"Get back from the window," his mother hisses. "What should we do?" she says to his father.

Before he can answer, three loud thuds crash on their front door. They freeze. Another thud and the door bursts open; splinters fly.

Two soldiers in military uniforms storm into the room, guns raised. The tallest one, whose cap is askew, stares at each of them before his eyes rest on his father. "Are you Petro Filipidis?"

"Yes."

"Come with us."

His mother wails, "No." And his grandfather holds her back.

"You. Old man." The soldier moves closer and his gun almost touches his grandfather's stomach. "Who are you?"

Hearing the answer, they decide they aren't interested in him. They want only one person.

Dimitri's father takes a deep breath. "Why?"

"You're under arrest."

"But why? What for? I've done nothing wrong." Putting the cigarette to his lips, his fingers quiver as he rubs his head trying to understand.

Dimitri stands perfectly still, and yet he can't stop warm pee sliding down the inside of his leg. Reaching for his mother's hand, his eyes stay on the soldiers and the guns as they reach for his father.

His mother wrenches herself from his grandfather's grip and jumps on the soldiers, screaming and hitting them. They throw her off with a punch and she falls heavily against the wall. Dimitri's face is wet and he tries not to whimper but he can't stifle his sobs.

"Control her, old man, or we'll arrest her too."

"No!" she screams. "No!"

And before they know it, his father disappears out of the door and down the street with two rifles prodded into his back.

***

The soldier's large shiny boots crunch on the gravel as Dimitri, his distraught mother and grandfather follow at a short distance. When they arrive at the village square, Petro is nudged forward by a rifle and ordered to stand in line next to five others. A soldier moves behind them to bind their hands behind their backs.

More villagers gather.

Eleni, their next-door neighbour, is quietly sobbing. Her dress is torn and her hair dishevelled. The others are men they all know.

The sun is overhead and sweat pools in the clutches of his mother's firm hand. Dimitri cranes his neck to see what is happening. His father – last in the line – has his head bowed. An officer paces impatiently in front of the six, looking at a piece of paper.

"What's going on?" a woman whispers to Dimitri's mother, but she's too distraught to answer.

"Do you know anything?" his grandfather asks. "Why do they have my son?"

"I don't know. They have my son too," says another old man who lives close by.

The officer coughs. "Is everyone here?"

A voice from behind the crowd answers, "Yes. They're all here."

"These people are accused of conspiring to harbour the enemy." The officer's black eyes stare into the crowd.

"That's not true," one of the accused says, lifting his head suddenly.

But all he gets for his trouble is a rifle butt to his back so hard that he pitches forward face first into the dry, hard ground. The soldier smirks as he surveys the sprawled man, then stares at the faces of the villagers who murmur in fright.

"You will be tried for your crimes," the officer says to the man whose face contorts with pain as he struggles to stand up. "As for the rest of you…" he turns to the crowd. "We know what you eat, what you say and what you do. Anyone helping the enemy will be similarly dealt with."

The crowd gasps but no-one is brave enough to speak up.

The prisoners are ordered to turn around and, with the soldiers, they march single file out of the village, leaving behind fear and distrust.

On the way back to the house, his mother dabbing her eyes, she whispers to his grandfather, "It must have been when the Partisans came."

Another woman walking with them overhears.

"They came to our house and stole all of our food. But

no-one in my family was arrested," the woman says in a low voice.

"No house was untouched by the Partisans. Why not arrest the whole village?" his grandfather says. Families disperse into their own streets leaving the saddened families to walk up Dimitri's street together, pondering.

"Oh God! They only arrested people in our street. Don't you see. Someone has spied. Someone here is a traitor," his mother exclaims loud enough for all to hear.

"Shush," his grandfather says, pulling on his mother's arm.

The small group stop in front of their house and gather around his mother.

"Think about it," she whispers, anger replacing her grief. "Every one of those taken away live here. Not in the next street but here."

"Yeah, you're right," murmurs another.

Dimitri, thinking about his father, unwinds his mother's fingers from his sweating hand. He kicks a stone aimlessly and watches it roll into a small depression in the road. His father would have clapped and beamed his approval before kicking it back. Fear has been replaced with anger as everyone talks over the top of each other.

Dimitri blinks back tears when he thinks about his father and looks down the road, hoping he might reappear. But all he sees is the lonely figure of Stinky Spiro with his head bowed, walking quickly toward his house with a small package under his arm. He hesitates, glancing at the group, and quickens his pace.

"Where was he?" a voice calls out. "Hiding out as usual."

"He was giving the Fascists coffee and information. That's where he was," says another.

"You," says someone else.

"It was you. You're the traitor."

Stinky stops, just feet from his front door. Dimitri's mother breaks from the group and marches up to him.

"Did you tell the authorities?" she hisses, pointing a finger at the trembling man who shakes his head.

"I, I didn't. I swear to you."

Two older men stand on either side of Stinky.

"We think you did. Where have you been?"

"What's in that package?"

"I... I've been at the café," Stinky says.

"We think you told them about the Partisans in our houses."

"No! I wasn't even here," Stinky pleads. "How could I know? I was away visiting my sister in the next village. Remember? I had to shut the café."

There was silence.

"Then who could it be?" says a tearful woman. "What will I do now? I have no husband." She begins to wail and the women turn to comfort her before slipping back into their homes, taking their fear with them.

Once inside, Dimitri stands next to the window and watches the birds gather in the tree outside. Dimitri sees Stinky Spiro look around before going inside. He slams his door shut and closes the curtains.

"Come away from the window. Wash your hands," his mother says, wiping her eyes with the apron, which is always permanently tied around her waist. His grandfather slumps in his chair.

Dimitri washes his hands. "Majka, why did Stinky say he was in another village when the Partisans came?"

"He probably ran away. I don't trust him." His mother stirs the pot before turning to his grandfather. "How do we find out where Petro is?"

His grandfather shrugs. "I'll go into Ptolemaida tomorrow and see what I can find out."

"That's going to take you all day to walk there. You're too frail and weak."

"I'm all right. It's a big village. Someone will know something. I have to go."

"He must have come back because I saw him," Dimitri says, rolling a small stone around and around on the table.

"Yes. You're right," his mother says, deep in thought.

"He was looking out of the window when those men left," Dimitri says.

His mother frowns and turns to Dimitri. "What are you talking about?"

"Son. Listen to me. Did you see Stinky on the day the Partisans left?" his grandfather asks.

"Uh-huh." Dimitri aims for the saucer and rolls the stone. "He was looking out of the window when I was throwing a stick into his tree. I was trying to hit one of the birds but it was too high up."

His grandfather stands up so suddenly that his chair falls over – his fists clenched. "Why, that no good snivelling weasel. I'm going to tear him limb from limb!"

Dimitri stops his game and watches his grandfather and mother.

"Stop! It'll do no good if you take matters into your own hands. Do you want the authorities to get you too? Think about it."

His grandfather scowls, picks up the overturned chair and sits back down.

Dimitri looks from one to the other. "Did I do something wrong?"

His mother hugs him. "No. Now go out and play. But keep your mouth shut. Tell no-one about Stinky. Do you understand? No-one."

"But isn't it dinner time?"

"Not yet. I'll call you. You're a very good little boy," she says. But the wild look in his mother's eyes terrifies him and Dimitri knows then that he has done something wrong, but he's not sure what.

10

The Knocking

Jim is roused from his thoughts by an urgent knocking at the door. His face wet with tears he quickly wipes them away with a large handkerchief. The television is blaring and he peers at the screen. More knocking rouses him and he hurriedly shoves the photo frame under the cushion and gets up to see who it is.

"What the hell are you doing?" Helen says, bursting into the house.

"And to what do I owe the pleasure of your company at this ungodly hour?"

"It's seven thirty so it's not exactly ungodly."

"Well, come in then. It's so nice you dropped in, again. Do you want a cup of tea?"

"No, I don't. I've been worried sick. Why haven't you picked up the phone? I've been ringing you for the last two hours." She looks him up and down and moves closer to inspect him. "Humph. Surprisingly, you look all right."

"Of course I'm all right."

Helen follows Jim into the lounge room. *MasterChef* is blaring on the TV.

"Can you turn down the volume? I can hardly hear myself. Why haven't you got your hearing aid in?" Not waiting for an answer, Helen grabs the remote control and adjusts the sound.

"Sit down, love. You need to relax. Is everything all right?"

"You didn't answer my question."

Jim's attention is on the latest news flash. *Police hunt a hit and run driver in Melton.*

"What sort of bastard does that? Sorry. What did you ask?"

"Why didn't you pick up the phone?"

"Don't get me started. Those bloody telemarketers have been harassing me all evening. So I've decided to teach them all a lesson and not answer the phone."

"But I was trying to ring you. What if there was an emergency?"

He closes his eyes trying to remember if the phone had rung.

"Is there one?"

"No. But what if there were?"

"Well there isn't, so no need to worry."

Jim stares at the television to avoid the anger in her eyes. Her mother's eyes.

"All I'm saying is that you should answer the phone. That

way I won't worry. When you didn't pick up I thought something had happened to you. You might have slipped in the shower. Or fallen over in the garden. Or something."

Jim frowns. "But none of those things happened."

"But they could have. And I notice you're not wearing your necklace monitor."

"I'm not going to wear a blasted necklace. For goodness' sake, I'm perfectly fine." If only I could keel over and die, then I could have peace, he wants to say.

"Why were you calling anyway? Didn't you just come over here this afternoon? Really, Helen, you need to get a life."

Pushing her glasses up her nose, she tries to hide a look of hurt. "I was wondering if you liked the cheese platter, that's all."

"It was nice." He feels guilty now. "Why don't you go home? As you can see, I'm perfectly fine. In fact, I want to go to bed."

He gets up and so does she. He walks her to the front of the house.

"I'm glad you're all right, Dad. See you on Wednesday," she says, kissing him on the cheek.

"Yep, you will," he says, closing the door.

"What's happening on Wednesday?" he wonders out loud.

11

Kitty

Dimitri tosses and turns.

He's playing with Lazo in a large field of corn. It's tall enough to hide in and they weave in and out, chasing each other. He pants in his hiding spot. Then he sees the tip of a rifle, or is it a stick looking like a rifle? He squeezes his eyes shut the image is sealed in. The corn sways in the breeze. Licking his dry lips, he tries to call Lazo's name but nothing comes out. He tries again but can't get his mouth to work. He sees a man's hand and freezes. Although the sun burns his face and legs, he feels chilled.

He wakes with a start. His sheet is wet under him and he's frightened. You're too old for this, his mother will say. He sits up and leans on his elbow and peers across at his parents' bed. It's empty. Good, he thinks. Then he remembers: his father, arrested. Is his mother still up? All is dark and quiet. He gets up and gropes for a towel to lay across the wetness. The wooden floor creaks. He slips off his shorts and gets another from the cupboard after kicking the wet pair under his bed.

When he's satisfied that he's covered up the mishap, he listens again. Where are Majka and Dedo? He tiptoes to the darkened room they use as the kitchen and sitting room. His grandfather's room is empty too. There are only three rooms in the house yet he can't find his mother. He steps out the back door to the outhouse. She's not there. Peering into the darkness he makes his way up the side of the house to the street.

In front of Stinky's house, the tall tree sways in the breeze. He thinks he hears muffled voices. Are the soldiers back? Has Majka been caught? Through Stinky's window he sees a roaming light. Is it a candle? He peers down the street. No lights. No sound, except for a dog barking somewhere far off. Even the light in Stinky's house has gone now. Nearby a dark shape looms. He sucks in the cold night air, hoping to calm the thumping in his chest. Is it someone? Majka? He releases his breath when he sees it's a bush.

He shivers and turns to go back inside while willing himself not to cry. She'll be somewhere safe, he tells himself. Something warm touches his bare leg and he jumps. Then he bends down and allows a relieved smile. It meows. He picks up the animal and holds it close to his face, feeling its softness before going inside with it. His mother will disapprove. Climbing into his bed, he's comforted by the kitten's purr as it nestles on his chest under the covers, and he lies awake to wait for his mother, but his eyelids are too heavy. The warmth of the kitten calms him and he strokes its soft fur. He whispers its new name – Kitty. In the morning, he'll ask if he can keep it.

***

"Dimitri. Get up. You're late. What's gotten into you?"

His mother stands in the doorway, wiping her hands on her apron, staring at him. She's back and he's relieved.

"Get up!"

Sitting up, he rubs his eyes as his mother goes back into the kitchen. He stretches and yawns. Then glances at his parents' bed – his heart sinks.

He changes and wanders out to his mother. She pecks him on the cheek and hands him a slice of bread.

"Can I have an olive?"

"There aren't any. Eat that and get yourself off to school."

"Where's Dedo?"

"He's already gone to Ptolemaida to find your father. He left very early. I know what you're trying to do, but it'll do no good. You still have to go to school before it closes down again."

Just then, Dimitri hears a noise and unfortunately so does his mother. A small meow.

"What's that?"

Kitty wanders out and wraps itself around Dimitri's legs.

"Dimitri! What is that thing doing in my house … in my bedroom?"

"Ah … I don't know."

"Get it out. Now!"

Dimitri is not brave enough in the daylight to ask if he can keep it. Instead, he scoops up the kitten and drops it outside before going to school.

***

Kitty is still there when he comes home, lying in the sun in front of his house, licking her paw. Ignoring him until Dimitri puts his foot on the front step, she sits up and meows. Her scrawny body brushes against his leg before meowing again.

"Shh, Majka will hear you." He picks Kitty up and examines her. Black with a white face and paws, the kitten stares back as if daring him to put her down. Instead, he carries her to the tree in front of Spiro's house. He places her down gently and, with a pat, walks quickly back to his house. But Kitty follows him. He picks her up again and takes her further down the street, then runs back in time to see his mother open the front door.

"There you are," she says, wiping her mouth with her apron. "I managed to get watermelon. Come and have some," she says before going in.

Dimitri glances over his shoulder, relieved Kitty has gone.

It's dark before his grandfather comes home. His clothes are dusty and the lines on his face etch deep into his skin as he slumps in the chair.

"What did you find out?"

His eyes closed, he shakes his head.

"Don't just shake your head. What?" His mother slams a bowl and a glass down in front of his grandfather.

65

"Dedo, did you find Tato?"

His grandfather gulps the water before thumping the glass on the table. "They were taken to Ptolemaida where they picked up more prisoners. No-one knows for sure but some people told me they went in the direction of Solun. Tomorrow I'll go to Solun. I'll need some food and water and I won't come back until I find him."

His mother looks crestfallen and tears fall silently down her cheek. "It's too far. It'll take you weeks to get there."

"What choice have we got?"

Shrugging, she quickly wipes away her tears with the back of her hand.

"Is it done?" his grandfather asks.

A dark look passes between his mother and grandfather before his mother nods.

"Now eat," she commands as she goes to the cupboard to gather supplies for his grandfather's journey.

Dimitri wanders outside with some cheese hidden in his pocket in case he sees Kitty. But the street is deserted.

12

The Stench

The late blast of the summer heat in October stifles the village.

It's been just the two of them for a month with no word about his father or Dedo. Dimitri is on edge, sidestepping his mother's bad temper and constant crying.

"Can I go to Lazo's house for soup?"

"What soup? How did his mother make soup?" his mother snaps. "Who does she think she is? Trying to take my child with offers of better food. She throws the fact that she still has a husband in my face."

"Please, Majka."

His mother looks wildly at him.

"No. You're eating here. Bread and the last of the beans." She sniffs and retrieves two plates from under the bench. Dimitri involuntarily groans. He's always hungry but he knows she puts more on his plate than on hers yet doesn't question her growing stomach.

"If it's good enough for me, it's good enough for you."

They've had bread and beans for weeks. The bread is hard and tasteless and there's no salt to be had. The government forces have seized all the crops and no other supplies can get through. The last of their flour has now gone and all they have is some of the meagre crops left in their vegetable patch out the back. Lazo's mother is only trying to help. But since his father's arrest, Dimitri's mother keeps to herself. Shunning all offers, she avoids everyone, spending hours lying on her bed staring upwards. Dimitri knows she's not well and he tiptoes about and keeps out of her way.

"Go out to the garden and see if there's a tomato. They might have missed one."

"It stinks out there."

She glares. "Go!"

Thankfully, the garden has yielded a few watermelons, some beans and new tomatoes, which will soon be ripe and hold off starvation unless the soldiers or Partisans get to them first. But theirs is a small garden and his mother can barely manage it. Her back is sore and her legs are swollen. Dimitri has had to do more and more to help. After bringing water from the well he digs the weeds or picks that night's meal. On the days when the air is hot, it stinks so badly that he shelters inside. The neighbours complain of the stench but no-one knows where it comes from.

In the cool of the evening he plays with Kitty under a tree.

Sometimes he sneaks the kitten into bed to help him sleep. The purrs block out his mother's sobs.

That evening, sharing one unripened tomato, they eat their evening meal lost in their own thoughts. Dimitri plots to get Kitty into the house. A knock at the door makes them jump and they look at each other in fear, so rare is it for a night-time visitor. His mother gets up and opens the door. Mika from across the street stands there in the dusk light.

"Have you heard?" Mika asks breathlessly.

Dimitri hopes it's news about his father or grandfather.

"What?" Dimitri's mother asks. "Come in. Sit down, dear Mika." Dimitri knows her contempt for this woman and he wonders at the fake, eager smile on his mother's face.

"You'll never guess. It's Stinky."

"Oh him. I don't care to hear anything about him."

"You will now that he's been found dead. Just a little water dear."

Dimitri watches Mika take in the room and surveys the table while his mother fills a glass of water from a jug. His mother looks tired and shrunken as she sets it on the table in front of Mika, who has helped herself to his mother's chair.

"That was the stink." Mika sips. "His throat was cut. In his bed, he was. Effie on the other side of him complained about the smell and they found him. Funny how everyone thought he'd gone to his sister's."

His mother absorbs the news while scraping dirt from under her fingernails. Mika finishes the water and moves to leave.

"Thanks for telling me, Mika."

"Thought you'd want to know."

"Do they know how long he's been dead?"

"At least a month. Between you and me…" Mika lowers her voice, "I'm glad that traitor is gone. He got what he deserved. Any word on Petro or your father-in-law? He's been gone for a long time now, hasn't he?"

"No word. No word at all. I just wait and pray. That's all I can do."

"Yes, that's all anyone can do. See you tomorrow."

Dimitri watches his mother close the door. When she turns, he's puzzled to see for the first time in a long time a hint of a smile.

***

The authorities doorknock every house in the village looking for Stinky's killer. The neighbours in the street live in fear as rumours circulate. Tensions are even higher in Dimitri's house. His mother jumps at every sound. She paces the floor every night in despair, while Dimitri worries about his father, Dedo and now Stinky. Stinky's dark eyes at the window haunt him. Should he have kept his mouth shut? Is Stinky dead because of him?

He goes out to water the garden and looks across at Stinky's house. The only thing he has to look forward to is the ripening watermelon he's been carefully tending. With Kitty at his side he has nurtured the last two. He can't wait to bite into a slice. That morning, like every other morning before school, he goes out to check on their progress.

"Majka! Majka!" he yells, running inside. "Did you pick the watermelons?"

"What are you talking about?" his mother says, wiping her hands on her apron.

"They're gone. My two watermelons are gone." Dimitri bites his bottom lip in despair.

"What?" Her eyes narrow.

"Someone has stolen them."

In the village square, Dimitri eyes Vassili. He's never liked him since he sniggered on the first day of school when he'd been sent home for speaking Macedonian. Now he's sitting under a tree eating a slice of watermelon.

"Where did you get that?" Dimitri demands, his anger growing.

"Get lost, Bulgari," Vassili says, slurping without looking up.

"Where did you get it?" Dimitri yells.

"I don't have to tell you, Bulgari Boy," Vassili smirks before wiping the juice dripping down his chin with the back of his hand. "But I can tell you it's delicious. Now stop bothering me."

"Stop calling me that. I don't like it."

A group of children begin to gather. Rage builds in Dimitri – for his father, for his mother, for his hunger.

"I think you stole that out of my garden. I think you're a thief."

The other children murmur.

"Watch who you call a thief, Bulgari."

71

"Someone stole our watermelons. And you're eating a piece. No-one else has watermelon."

Vassili wipes his hands on his grubby shorts and stands. He's a full head higher than Dimitri. The other children stand behind him – the bravery he'd felt slips away when he sees the older boy's clenched fists.

"Get lost."

"My mother says it's the Partisans. Everyone has food missing," Lazo says, pulling on Dimitri's sleeve. "We lost our pumpkins the other night. Come on, let's go."

***

The next day, Dimitri spies someone at the end of his street. He recognises the stoop of the old man and runs, yelling, "Dedo!"

His grandfather looks exhausted as he enters the house. Blisters line his lips and unkempt grey wisps hang off his head. His grey stubble is almost lost in the deep lines of his face.

Dimitri and his mother wait while Dedo drinks and eats what little they have. When he's finished he talks. "I found people who had seen them. They were used as human shields against the Partisans. Eleni was shot dead."

His mother gasps.

"They moved them on after that and they worked building roads. One woman told me she'd given them blankets and food. I walked from village to village. We aren't the only ones. Some had all the men rounded up and taken. Then, I found him in a jail in Solun waiting to be shipped to one of the islands."

"Did you see him? Is he ... is he all right?"

His grandfather looks away and stares at the table. "I ... I only saw him briefly – through a wire fence. I yelled out to him. I think he saw me." His grandfather reaches to touch Dimitri's hand gently. "He looked all right." But there is something unconvincing in his speech.

His mother sits quietly at the table, her hands clasped in front of her. Dimitri waits for her to say something, but she remains still.

"Dedo. Will he come back soon?"

"No, son. Not for a long time. We must learn to get on without him. Now I must rest."

Fresh tears slide down his mother's cheeks and she dabs at them with the corner of her apron.

13

Wasting Water

Jim runs the tap in the kitchen and fills a glass before taking it back into the lounge. He sinks into the couch and feels something jutting into him from behind the cushion. He pulls it out. It's the framed photo of his father when he was in the army.

"That's what got me started," he says out loud to his father's photo. "Why am I remembering all this stuff and not what I've got to do on Wednesday?"

He looks for the remote control and spies it on the coffee table. He turns the channel but he feels the stare of the photo. He doesn't want to go back there again – to that time, to that place. He turns the photo over and this time hides it under the couch. He's spent his life blocking out painful memories.

"Right. Time for bed," he says out loud as he picks up the remote control and presses the off switch. Silence. No, there's another noise. He listens carefully. All he hears is a pulsing beat in one ear, and a whistle in the other. The more he strains to listen, the louder the noises become.

"Damn it," he says.

He heaves himself up and listens again. It's not in his head. He picks up his empty glass and takes it into the kitchen.

"Blast!"

The tap is running and he leans across to turn it off before plonking the glass in the sink.

"All that wasted water. How am I going to make up for that?" he says to the tap. Then thinks before saying, "I won't have a shower in the morning. That'll do it. In the village we only washed once a week. There was nothing wrong with that." He sniffs his underarms and nods.

Pleased with himself, he undresses. Pulling back the covers, he straightens the pillows in a line down the middle of the bed, like he does every night. He sleeps better thinking she's still there.

He turns out the light and all he can hear is the pulsating beat in his ear, which he finds oddly comforting.

Then he remembers and smiles. "It's the doctor's appointment on Wednesday."

14

The Proclamation

April, 1948

On any other day, bells ringing throughout the town would call the villagers to a church service or a meeting in the town square. Except on this day. On this day, the peels persist like cries of anguish and never stop. On this day, the bells are joined by many mothers wailing for their children.

Dimitri's house is no different. His mother, white as a ghost, paces the floor.

"It can't be possible," she says.

"Majka. What's happening?" he asks.

He knows it has something to do with the visit earlier that day. His mother had sent him to a friend in the next street to collect a bag. On the way back, he'd seen two soldiers step inside his house. Trembling with fright, he hid close by and waited for them to leave. He heard one of the men say, "In the name of the mother of our great nation, Queen Frederica, you will do what we say or your house will be burned to the ground."

He'd heard about the Queen. A few months before, the villagers had gossiped about how brave she'd been. Dodging the fighting, the Queen had crossed a shelled bridge into Konitsa, and was so horrified at the state of the orphaned children that she'd organised for them to be evacuated in the middle of the night to homes in the south – right under the noses of the Partisans. She'd set up a relief fund for Northern Greece. Dedo had ranted and raved when he'd heard her decree. "She expects everyone in Greece to give up a day's pay to her stupid fund. If only I could get a full day's pay. Don't expect us to ever get anything from her. She's only lining her own pockets."

His mother pulls him to her and holds him tight. The swell of her belly pushes against him. "Majka?" He waits for her answer but she stares out of the window. Her lips, set in a hard line, quake silently. Bubbles of panic gurgle from his stomach to his chest. It had been more than several months since the soldiers had taken his father. Holding him tight she begins to tremble. "Majka?" Is she worried about the bombing that's started and is worse than before? Is she upset that there's no food and no Tato?

Finally, pushing Dimitri from her, she walks to the window and turns to his grandfather as if her mind has been made up. "You need to do something. He's not going. I don't trust them."

Dimitri feels invisible, unable to read the source of the distress.

"It's not safe. He must go," Dedo says. "What choice do we have? It's only going to get worse. The sooner he goes the better off he'll be. There's no other way."

"What about the Partisans? They're taking them too."

"This way he'll go south. If he goes north with the Partisans, then it's into another country, another language and who knows where he'll end up."

His grandfather squats in front of him. His grey whiskers wobble across his wrinkled face when he talks. For the first time, Dimitri notices a hair hanging from his nostril. "Dimitri, you know how there's been a lot of fighting in the hills and it's heading toward our village. The government soldiers tell us that all children must be evacuated."

His stomach churns and tightens. "But Dedo, I want to stay. What if something happens to you?" A guttural sob escapes his mother's lips.

"Nothing will happen to us. Your mother can't travel yet because she's expecting your new baby brother or sister any day now, and I have to stay to help her. After the baby is born, I'll find Tato and we'll come and get you."

His eyes implore Dimitri to listen and to understand. But it's his worst fear – instead of his family disappearing, it's to be him who leaves.

"But I want to see the baby. I want to stay with Majka and you. I can help."

His mother wails. He can't fight the tears and the rising panic.

"Listen. All the other children in the village are going too. You're almost ten. It won't be for long. Just until we can come and get you." Dedo turns to his mother. "See how you've mollycoddled him."

The words, *it won't be for long*, echo in Dimitri's head. He wipes his face with the sleeve of his old jumper and takes a deep breath. The bombs scare him more than anything. "When do I have to go?"

His grandfather smiles in relief. "Good boy. You leave tomorrow morning."

Dimitri gulps and stares at the dirt ingrained in his toenails. The scratches on his feet are all but healed and the bruise on his shin has turned yellow. He thinks of the day when he skidded in the dry dust with Lazo chasing him. A bush stopped his run. It had been a good day.

"Where am I going?"

"We don't know."

His mother wails.

"Shut up, woman! You're not helping," hisses his grandfather.

***

The next day when he wakes, there's a dull ache in his stomach, but whether from hunger or anticipation he doesn't know. This is the day he leaves. Somehow he knows his life will change but has no realisation of how much. He almost feels excited until he sees his mother's swollen dark eyes stare

79

at him while he eats an olive for breakfast. She says nothing while Dedo collects a small bag stuffed with food and clothes. The other cases still sit next to his parents' bed. They had planned to leave the day after his father had disappeared.

Dressed in a shirt and shorts,his mother scrubs his face so hard he protests, "You're hurting me." Awkwardly, she lowers herself, covering his face with kisses and clings to him so tightly he can barely breathe. "Don't forget me," she cries.

Dimitri hugs her tightly and stifles a sob. "I love you, Majka. I'll see you soon."

15

The Beginning of the March

Clutching his small cloth bag and a jacket, Dimitri joins fifteen scrawny, shoeless children in a line at the front of the church to wait in the early dawn. Most are Macedonian but five are Greek children from beyond the village. They fidget and scratch. For some, the lice are the only things that have eaten that morning. Parents gather close by. Some quietly sob. Many can no longer feed their children. Two women clutch toddlers. The sound of distant shell-fire is never far away and this is what they fear the most. It's best, they whisper. At least Dimitri's mother has left her crying at home.

A canvas-covered truck arrives. Two women, each wearing a plain brown dress, jump down and stand in front of the crowd. Three soldiers, guns slung over their shoulders, lurk nearby.

The taller woman coughs. A large mole sits on her chin and dark strands of hair tumble out of her bun. She stares into the faces of the crowd. "As you know, the Partisans have been kidnapping our children and sending them across into communist territory to be turned into soldiers. In the name of the First Mother of Greece, we will take your children to the Paidopoleis, set up around our country with money raised from the Queen's fund. You have nothing to worry about. We will protect and look after your loved ones as if they are our own." She pauses and searches the faces, expecting objections, but there are none.

"When I call out your names, board the truck in an orderly fashion," the younger woman barks. Her plaited hair is wound around the nape of her neck. Her face is tanned but Dimitri can tell she is joyless.

The toddlers are called out first and the soldiers wrench them from their sobbing mothers' arms and hand them to the tall woman. The rest of the names are called out one by one until finally Dimitri hears his name.

Quickly hugging his mother, he climbs into the cool darkness of the truck. Guilt settles next to the excitement he feels, as he squeezes in beside Lazo on the hard wooden bench. He notices with satisfaction that Vassili, clutching a small bundle, looks frightened.

"Risto, Risto," a mother of one of the toddlers screams. A soldier pushes her back. "He's too young. He needs his mother. What will he do without me?" She begins to run to the truck but the soldier is quick and strikes her hard with his fist. Everyone is too frightened to go to her as she lies sobbing on the ground.

The young woman climbs into the truck saying nothing to the children who silently look out. A couple of girls begin to cry. Risto sits on the lap of the older woman, sucking his thumb. The engine cranks to life and pulls away. The back of the truck is open, framing their parents who begin to run behind calling out and crying in the cloud of dust.

"Dafina, Majka loves you. Come back to me," cries out one woman.

"Elena, remember your mother. Don't cry. You'll be home soon," yells another.

"Vassili, be careful," shouts one. "I'll come to get you as soon as I can."

Anguish is on his mother's face but she doesn't cry. She stands still in one spot, forlorn and sad, until Dimitri can see her no more.

It's a noisy, bumpy ride. One small girl begins crying. "I want my mother." The older woman holds her in her lap with Risto and comforts her.

"I wonder where we'll go?" Dimitri says to Lazo.

"My father says we're going south. He says we'll go to school and get lots of food."

Dimitri rolls his eyes. "I don't want to go to school."

"I heard there'll be more food than we've ever seen before," a girl says quietly.

Dimitri brightens at the prospect and imagines roast lamb and potatoes. His stomach growls.

After travelling for an hour, the truck bumps and jumps about as they veer off onto another pockmarked road. The children cling on to whatever they can until they reach a small village.

The women get out. "Stay here and don't move. Any of you," says the older woman as she allows children who need to relieve themselves to get off, one by one.

They peer at burned-out buildings.

"Whatever happens we have to stick together. Right?" Dimitri says getting back into the truck.

"Right." Lazo punches Dimitri's arm lightly.

"This is a treat," says a girl. She lifts a toddler and puts her into the truck before helping another small girl. Then she climbs in. "Aren't we lucky?"

"I don't know if you're lucky. Where do you think you're going?" asks Dimitri.

The girl, who could have been eleven or twelve, smooths down her ragged dress. "That lady out there said she'd give us a lift. We're going to my aunt's place in the next village. It takes a long time to get there," the girl says. A couple of boys snigger. Her large brown eyes take in the rest of the children and her face changes expression.

"Where are you all going?" she asks, frowning.

"You're not going to your aunt. You're going to a Paidopoleis, just like the rest of us," Lazo says.

"What do you mean? What's a Paidopoleis?" The girl looks wildly around and clutches the two younger children to her. She moves to get off the truck but she's too late – the women have jumped back in and the truck has begun to move.

"It's an orphanage set up for children like you to escape

the war. Find yourself a seat. You! Squash up and let these children sit down," the older woman commands.

"But you said you were taking us to my aunt," the girl says, refusing to sit. Dimitri is sure she's going to fall over as the truck lurches and groans up a hill. But she obstinately stands. "Stop the truck. We have to get off. I have to take my sisters home. My parents won't know where we are."

"Sit down!" the older woman yells. "All children are being evacuated and your parents know that."

"But…"

"SIT DOWN NOW!"

The older girl jumps and her younger sisters begin to cry.

They quickly squeeze into a space on the floor. The toddler climbs onto her sister's lap, pushes her thumb into her mouth while her sister quietly sobs.

***

After what seems like hours, the truck stops and the children who had fallen asleep awaken. The driver slams the door and his heavy footsteps crunch on the stony road toward the back of the truck.

"Stay here," the older woman commands. Jumping down she speaks quietly to the burly driver who is smoking and pointing toward the mountains. The younger woman watches them too.

The birds have disappeared and it's eerily quiet. Even the crying children have quietened. They watch and wait.

The older woman walks toward them.

"Take out all the food you have in your bags and put it in a pile here," she says to them. Pickled tomatoes, bread, cheeses and olives are made into a small pile on the floor of the truck. The younger woman puts most of it into a striped blue and red bag.

"Everyone out!" Eighteen pairs of grubby legs pile off the truck. The children mill around and stretch.

"Girls to this side of the road, boys to that side," the older woman yells loud enough for her voice to echo.

The mountains loom ahead. Behind them the dusty road winds its way around a flat, dry landscape.

Each child is given a tiny ration of food while the two women take control of the rest.

"Why do you think we've stopped?" Dimitri says.

"I dunno. But I'm glad," Lazo says. "I was feeling sick in there."

"All right, children, gather your things. We walk from here."

Dimitri feels a stab of fear and looks in bewilderment at Lazo.

"Why aren't we going on the truck?" Vassili asks.

"Because we have to go back and get more children. Do as you're told. If the Partisans get you, they'll make slaves out of you? When their food runs out they cook and eat children like you. Now get into line. No more questions."

The children look in fright and one of the smallest cries, "I don't want to be eaten."

"This stinks," Vassili grumbles. "I'm not going. I'm going home."

A look passes between the women. The older woman rolls her eyes skyward and drawls, "There's always one."

She signals the truck driver with a nod. Grinding the end of his cigarette into the dirt, he strolls over to Vassili, cuffing him so hard across the head that he sends the boy sprawling. "You'll do exactly as you're told if you know what's good for you. As for the rest of you, let that be a lesson."

The younger woman glares, daring the frightened children to speak up. "Any more complaints?"

There's silence, except for Vassili's sniffing as he picks himself up from the dirt. A line of blood trickles down his leg and small stones have left indentations on the dusty skin of his knees.

"Vesna is in charge and you'll do exactly what she tells you to do. Or else."

Dimitri looks at the woman. She stands tall and defiant, daring someone to say anything.

"Stay to the foot of the mountains. The government forces have this whole area under control so you should be fine. Good luck!" the driver says to her.

She nods, but Dimitri notices Vesna move stiffly as she gathers the bags together.

The older woman and the driver climb back into the truck, and Vesna counts the bewildered children as they watch the truck turn around and disappear down the road they'd come from.

"You!" Vesna's voice fills the air around them. "What's your name?"

"Vassili," he says sullenly.

"You go to the front where I can keep an eye on you. Everyone else march in single file along the road behind him. When I blow my whistle you will listen carefully for my instructions. Let's go!" Vesna yells.

The high pitch of the whistle pierces their ears and they move forward.

There's no chance to talk as they trudge in the unseasonal spring heat along the dusty road. No vehicles pass. Eighteen children aged from two to thirteen in single file march toward the foot of the mountains, hoping they're not found by the Partisans or the soldiers.

After a while they stop in a clearing along the roadside. A brook babbles nearby and Vesna lets them sink to the edge to drink.

"You two. What's your name?" Vesna snaps.

"Lazo."

"Dimitri."

"Right. Vassili, take these boys with you and find firewood. Don't even think about running off if you know what's good for you. There are vicious people and giant bears out here who will do far worse to you. Now GO!"

In the growing dusk, the three frightened boys set out into the forest to look for wood.

"We're not heading south yet," Vassili says.

"Yeah we are. They told us," Lazo says.

"Look at the mountains. The border's over the other side."

Dimitri stops and stares at the mountains too. The snow, yet to melt, gleams in the sun.

"Is it that close?"

Vassili says, "It can't be far. I don't know about you but I'm getting out of here."

"You can't. How will you find your way?" Dimitri says. He and Lazo, their arms laden with wood, stare at Vassili.

"And what about the bears?" Lazo says.

Dimitri remembers the stories his grandmother told him about the bears eating the goats in her village when she was small. He'd never seen one but they all knew they were out there.

"There aren't any bears. That's just superstition. When the moment comes, I'm going."

"Why don't you go now then?" Lazo stops picking up wood and confronts Vassili.

"It's not the right time," he says.

"It's only Vesna against eighteen of us. You could outrun her easily," Dimitri says, warming to the idea. "Where will you go?"

"I'll take my chances with the Partisans," Vassili says. "My older brother's up there somewhere and I aim to find him."

"So what are you waiting for?" Dimitri asks.

"Yeah," Lazo says.

"I'll go. Just not now." Vasilli continues to collect wood and looks around him, uncertain.

"Maybe we should take our chances and go with you," Lazo says.

"I didn't ask you, Bulgari," Vassili says. His lip curls into a sneer.

Lazo drops the firewood and leaps on the boy. For the second time that day, Vassili lies sprawled on the ground, wood strewn around him, this time with Lazo on top clenching his fists.

"What do you think you're doing?"

The three of them jump up to see Vesna with her handgun poised.

"Get up. Gather that wood and come back right NOW!"

The boys scurry to collect the wood before marching in front of Vesna's pointed gun. Dimitri begins to tremble as he places the wood down.

The fire soon roars to life as the sun slips behind the mountains. Dimitri glances at a small girl who is rubbing her face. There's a large red mark on her cheek. Coughing and spluttering, her eyes are red and swollen. Two older girls tear off small chunks of stale bread and hand them around while the group sits quietly by the campfire.

After eating in silence, each child finds a spot on the hard ground and, using what little belongings they have as pillows, try to sleep.

Dimitri curls up to keep warm. The cool dew rests on him like a blanket. This is the first day. His grandfather's voice – it won't be for long – rolls around and around in his head. Why didn't he ask him how long? Isn't a day long enough? He squints at the stars in the cloudless sky and wonders what his mother is doing. What of his father? Is he looking at these same stars and thinking of Dimitri? He blinks back tears and rolls over to face Lazo, who is sniffing. In the dying light of the fire, his cheeks glisten. Noises come from the rest of the children too; sobbing, sniffing, coughing.

"Stop that racket!" Vesna snaps. And soon all fall into an exhausted and fitful sleep.

***

It's still dark when they're woken by the shrill sound of the whistle.

"Get up! We have to go. Quickly!" Vesna shrieks.

"What I'd give for a full slice of fresh bread just out of the oven, with salt, cheese, tomato and a glass of milk," Lazo says.

"Silence," Vesna yells, clipping Lazo on the side of the head. "Let's go. In single file behind Vassili."

"Some Queen's fund," Vassili mutters quietly. "If this is saving us, I'd rather go with the Partisans."

"Vassili! Follow the road," Vesna hisses.

"What road?" Vassili grumbles. "I can hardly see in front of me."

Soon, they reach the top of a rise. A dog appears from the bushes and barks furiously at the group, frightening some of the small children who begin to cry. The mountains loom ahead of them like a shadow in the moonlight. A small girl cries inconsolably and the dog barks its farewell. The older girls try to comfort her but it's no use; she cries like they each want to – for her mother, her father, her own bed, a full stomach, for her childhood's brutal end. And the dog barks once more, as if in sympathy.

16

16

Peppy

The bark is incessant, and Jim can no longer stand it. He's already pulled the pillow over his head and now he sticks his fingers in his ears until all he hears is his own breathing. Then, the faint sound of the bark breaks through again. He hasn't always hated dogs, or their bark. Just tonight. This long night of disturbed memories reminds him.

"What the hell is that infernal dog barking at?" Jim mutters. "How can anyone get any sleep?"

He slips out of bed and hitches his white y-front underpants up over his round ball of a stomach. He debates with himself about whether to dress but the bark from the dog seems more urgent. In bare feet, he thumps to the front door and opens it, where the barking is even louder.

He unwinds the hose next to the bottom of the front steps and turns it on. Satisfied the water's flow is stopped by the trigger, he walks up the driveway until he reaches the footpath and peers into Ian's front yard. Peppy, the border collie at the gate, falls silent and happily wags his tail.

"Stop barking, you mongrel," Jim hisses.

Peppy responds by barking his greeting and that's enough for Jim. Pointing the nozzle, he pulls the trigger, releasing a powerful squirt and hitting the dog in the snout. Peppy yelps and runs back to the shelter of Ian's front verandah.

"That'll teach you," Jim says, releasing the trigger to stop the water.

"That'll teach who?" a voice behind him says.

Jim swings around to face his next-door neighbours, Ian and Flo standing on the footpath in front of their driveway.

"Oh, it's you," he sneers. "Is that your dog?"

"You know it is," Flo says.

"It's been barking for hours."

"What did you do to him?" Flo asks. Her hands are on her hips as she leans forward threateningly. "You keep away from Peppy."

"How is a man expected to sleep when your dog barks incessantly? And what are you doing in the middle of the night? If you were home, it wouldn't bark."

"Jim, it's only nine o'clock," Ian says calmly. "With daylight savings, it's barely dark.

"If you've hurt our dog ..." Flo snaps as she races to the animal.

"I'm sure Jim didn't hurt Peppy," Ian calls out. "What *did* you do?" he asks.

Jim suddenly feels chilled. By now other walkers have gathered.

"He's soaking," Flo yells out. She coos over Peppy.

Everyone stares at Jim.

"I hosed him. Now, if you'll excuse me, I have to get to sleep." Jim turns abruptly, cursing himself for not having checked the time. He mutters about wasting perfectly good water on the mutt.

He rolls up the hose, turns off the tap, then stamps up the steps without turning to see if the crowd has dispersed.

"I don't care. It's not as bad as what she did to you," he mutters to the photo of Anna next to the clock in his bedroom. It's nine fifteen. "Damn it! Why didn't I check?" he says to the picture. She would have stopped him. They would have watched a movie or sat up talking. Or they might have been walking with Ian and Flo. He can hear Anna's voice telling him that it wasn't Flo's fault. That he shouldn't be so cross. If his beautiful wife were here, he wouldn't have been in bed listening to the dog next door. He wouldn't have been remembering.

Hearing voices, he sneaks to the window, pulls the curtain across and peeks out at Ian, Flo and the others still milling around on the footpath.

"Blast!" Don't those people have anything better to do than stand around gossiping all night? He has a good mind to march out there and tell them all to piss off.

His fists clenched tightly, he races to the front door, then, remembering, goes back to grab his bathrobe. He swings the door wide and opens his mouth to yell. But whoever was there has moved on.

He furiously slams the door shut and paces up and down the hallway. What busybodies the neighbours are. They patrol the streets in the middle of the night, gossiping at the tops of their voices, making nuisances of themselves.

They'd tried to get him to decorate his house with lights at Christmas. The whole street was in competition with each other. Each year every house added more decorations. Ian was the worst. He had a blow-up Santa coming out of his chimney and reindeer on his lawn. You could hardly see the house for the lights.

He wasn't having any of that nonsense on his house. His parents had been too poor to celebrate Christmas. Anyway, name days had been more important, except he could never remember the date for his. Still, he'd turned away from it all – his country, his culture. It had treated him badly and he hadn't looked back. Until now.

Except for Helen. They'd celebrated for her. Anna did it all. She put up a Christmas tree and they showered her with presents. Anna and he should have told her together but the time never seemed right.

17

It Won't Be For Long

They stumble wordlessly in the dark in single file. Older children hold the hands of the younger ones. The line of whimpering children stretches ahead as Lazo and Dimitri allow others to pass them as they slip back toward the rear. The sky is clear and a half moon has risen above the mountains, giving enough light to see their way.

"No talking!" Vesna yells.

Dimitri holds Risto's hand, who is barely old enough to speak. He cries inconsolably and walks so slowly that Vesna lifts the toddler onto Dimitri's shoulders. Risto, stinking of stale urine and faeces, is light at first, but his hacking cough threatens to dislodge him. Dimitri's misery worsens with the fear that the pus-filled sores on the legs of the child will burst against his neck. Except for the coughing from Risto and a little girl with Lazo in front, they march silently in the cool, moonlit night. There is no sound except for the weak thud of their footsteps.

Dimitri chants Dedo's words in his head in rhythm to his own steps. *It won't be for long, it won't be for long, it* won't *be for long*. He takes himself to a place where he skips stones with his father. Kitty purrs against his leg and he throws stones at the birds. He was good enough that his mother sent him out to catch birds to eat. What he would give now for bird stew. His stomach rumbles and his thoughts switch to Kitty. He can't stop the tears sliding down his face when he remembers. Poor Kitty. He shakes his head. He'd had no dinner that night. His mother had said that was all there was. But he couldn't bring himself to face the bones floating in the soup. Dedo had said, "Come on, boy. It's delicious."

It won't be for long, it won't be for long. Risto has fallen asleep. Warm liquid oozing down the back of Dimitri's neck and back horrifies him. The child, a deadweight, begins sliding off his shoulders. Dimitri tries to push him up but eventually he stops and the chill of his wet back spreads through him.

A couple of girls behind him grumble.

"Get going."

"He's blocking us."

"You could at least help," Dimitri grumbles. "He's sliding off my shoulders."

But the girls walk around him. Only Lazo stops. He holds the hand of a small girl who is too big to carry and scratches his head hard.

"No talking and no stopping. Keep going," Vesna hisses as she straightens the sleeping child on his shoulders.

On they trudge. Dimitri imagines Dedo snoring in his chair. His mother bent over the mending. Skipping the stones across the river.

Clack, clack, clack. The pop of gunfire. Dimitri's heart thumps hard in his chest. Then a dull thud booms in the distance. A lurid red light fills the night sky and the smell of smoke stings his nostrils. Then silence.

"Hurry, children. Hurry!"

There's panic in Vesna's voice and they move even faster. She pushes past Dimitri to the front. "Hurry! This way," she screams as a shell explodes; closer this time.

It won't be for long; it won't be for long.

"He's slipping," Dimitri screams into a wall of noise. "I can't hold him." But no-one hears.

Clack, clack, clack. Another screaming shell. A tree in front of them explodes. The children scatter and dive into the undergrowth as they'd been taught. Get under a table. Hide in a hole. But where is safe? Another bomb lights the sky. A roar explodes in Dimitri's head.

Regaining consciousness under a blanket of dirt and dust, Dimitri rubs his aching head. The sky is alive with light but he hears nothing except for his own breathing as if he's in a well shaft. Pushing a finger into his ear, he wiggles it around and coughs. The air is sharp with the smell of burning flesh. He's groggy but aware of lying on something soft yet warm and comforting. Lying on his back he peers up at the sky and wonders where the stars have disappeared to. His throat burns and he coughs again from the thick smoke. The trees are in flame around him and heat burns into his face. He knows he has to get up.

Suddenly, he is hauled to his feet. Another explosion. Lazo's face glows from the flames – he mouths a silent scream. Dimitri's legs wobble as he and Lazo sprint into the undergrowth. They scramble blindly past branches that scratch and claw at their arms and legs. Stumbling, they run; sucking in burning air. And they run until they can run no more.

18

What's in the Bag?

Warmth from a ray of sun on his face nudges Dimitri awake. He's landed in a peaceful place where the air is sharp with the fragrance of honey and stale smoke. A pigeon perched on the branch above him swallows a worm. He thinks he hears the faint song of another but the buzzing is still in his head. His scalp tingles with the crawl of lice and he scratches until blood collects under his fingernails. Swallowing hard, the lump in his throat burns as his tongue glides over his flaky, dry lips.

Lazo is curled in a ball near him. A spider's web stretches from the top of his head to the bark of a tree. His clothes are crusted black with dried blood and Dimitri wonders if he's dead. Rubbing his stinging eyes, he sits up.

Memories of the night flood his mind. The bombs. The whiff of gunpowder and choking smoke, still in his nostrils, overpowers everything. High-pitched pops like firecrackers.

He begins to tremble when he remembers screaming. He tries now – nothing. He coughs and attempts to work enough saliva to soothe the sting.

"Lazo," he whispers hoarsely. He swallows again. "Lazo! Wake up." But his friend doesn't move. One, two, three, four … the sound of his heart pounds in his sore ears. The saliva works. "Wake up!" he shouts, leaning over to shake him. The birds cry out to one another at the intrusion.

Dimitri lets out the breath he's been holding when his friend moves, then stretches.

"You look awful," Lazo says.

Dimitri forces a grin. For the first time he notices his feet are covered in dirt and his legs are streaked with dry blood.

"So do you."

"Are you all right?"

"I think so. I can't hear much and my head hurts." It's then that Dimitri realises his body aches as well.

"Me too."

He gets up from his bed of sticks, ferns and dried leaves, and scratches. "Where are we?"

"Dunno. I just ran." Lazo slaps a bug from his arm and moans as he lumbers up.

"What about the others?"

Lazo shrugs and shakes his head.

"You were lying on Risto. I think he's dead. I didn't stop to see what happened to everyone else."

Risto. Sitting on his shoulders, asleep. Dimitri had forgotten the small boy in his care and remembers his distraught mother. He should have looked after him better but he can't think about him now.

"Lazo, do you think we should go?"

"Where?"

"If we find the road we can find our way home."

"Where do you think the road is?"

The boys look around. They can just make out the mountains through the trees – they're closer than before.

"If we walk in that direction maybe we'll get to the road."

"Let's go."

With the mountains behind them, they trudge towards where they think the road might be. The trees shelter them from the sun. Dimitri licks his lips. It's been hours since he's had water or food and his stomach rumbles. A breath of wind springs up, swaying the branches above. The brook where they'd camped upstream the night before gurgles just feet from their path, hidden by thick bush, but neither boy can hear or see it.

Dimitri stops first. "Let's rest a bit."

"We must be close," Lazo says. "The mountains are further away."

Dimitri nods. He feels braver when they're together.

"I'm so thirsty," Lazo says.

"Me too. When we get to the road, we can follow it back to the stream where we camped." Dimitri's not sure but it's the only plan he can think of. "Come on."

The sun high in the sky, they push on through the undergrowth but progress is slow.

"I don't feel so good," Dimitri says after a while. "My throat hurts."

Lazo bends over and holds his stomach. "Yeah, me too. I'd do anything for water or some soup, or a chunk of bread or ..."

"Shut up. I'll hit you if you don't stop," Dimitri says. "I think we're going around in circles."

"Let's have another rest."

They slump under a tree. Dimitri's eyes sting and his bare feet and legs are cut and bleeding. He thinks of home – being in the comfort of his mother's arms. Her laugh, her smile, and her kisses. He blinks back the tears, takes a deep breath and gets up. "That's enough. Let's go."

They walk on a little further, not sure when to give up. Neither of them can tell how long they'd run the night before – terror had propelled them.

"Look! I knew it wasn't that far." Lazo grins and points.

Stumbling onto the dirt road, Dimitri desperately hopes it's the one they'd travelled on the day before.

Shading his eyes with his hand, Lazo scans the road. "This is it. I remember the rise back there."

"It was dark. How could you remember that?"

Lazo shrugs. "I just can."

Stale smoke wafts over them as they follow the road.

"It's definitely the road. Look!"

In front of them is a crater the size of a large table. They step around it. Pieces of shredded clothing flutter off a bush. Flies buzz and crows are gathered on something. Their eyes follow another piece of clothing and they see the headless body of a woman lying on her back. A crow looks up from her head nearby and peers at them. It's Vesna. Lazo runs at the crow but Dimitri's empty stomach heaves.

Next to Vesna's severed head is Vassili. His legs are gone. The girl with her two sisters have died in one another's arms.

They step carefully around a larger crater. More limbs and remnants of flesh litter the ground.

"That must have been the bomb that blew up in front of us," Lazo says quietly. Risto lies on his back in a ditch, half his head is missing. Dimitri remembers a hot, powerful wind had lifted him off his feet. Screams. Wetness down his legs. The bitter smell of blood. His stomach heaves as if it is trying to expel what he's seen but all that comes out is bile and bitterness.

Dimitri slumps to the road and howls, and so does Lazo. Their only company is the flies, the crows and dead children.

After a while, they wipe their faces with scraps of their dirty and torn shirts and lie on their backs in the middle of the road to stare at the cloudless sky – too tired and distraught to care about what to do next. Then Dimitri spots something in a tree above them.

"There's the bag of food. Can you reach it?" Dimitri says, jumping up. "Can you see it?" It dangles precariously on the end of a branch. There is no mistaking the blue and red stripped bag among through the leaves. "Come on. We can reach it."

Lazo scrambles to his feet and jumps, but it's too high.

"Climb on my back so you can reach the branch," Dimitri says.

"Keep still!"

"I'm trying." Dimitri sways under Lazo's weight. "Can you reach it?" But Lazo is too heavy and Dimitri buckles under his friend and they sprawl on the ground. Face to face with someone's severed arm, they both spring back.

"Come on. Try again," Dimitri commands, licking his dry lips. He focuses on what's inside the bag, knowing that it's food and water.

"Stop moving. I'm trying to get it." Lazo's knees burn into Dimitri's back and when he feels he can hold him not a second longer the weight lifts from him. Lazo is perched on top of the branch grinning, then carefully inches forward, unhooks the bag and drops it down.

Dimitri catches it and eagerly opens it.

"Hey! Wait for me," Lazo exclaims as he swings down to the ground.

He sees Dimitri's crestfallen face. "What's the matter?"

"There's nothing in here. See." The bag is filled with clothes. "I thought it was the bag with the food. There must have been two of them."

"Let's find the other one," Lazo says. They search the trees around them, some are black and burned, but there's nothing.

They have to go back to the dead bodies. Searching nearby bushes, they try to shield their eyes from the carnage, the birds and the flies.

"Maybe Vesna has it on her back. Let's check," Dimitri says.

They tread carefully around the bodies and limbs until they reach her. Under her body is another blue and red stripped bag.

"I'm not touching her."

"Ugh. Her head's looking at us." The head nearby is on an angle and her face is strangely serene. She gazes at them as if she's resting after a picnic but surprised by something she's seen.

Lazo moves first and tries to push her with his foot.

"You can't kick her."

Lazo crosses his arms. "How else are we going to get the bag off her?"

Dimitri brings out a jacket from the bag he's still holding "I can't touch her while she's looking at us." He spreads the jacket over the severed head. "There. You push her up and I'll grab the bag."

"No! You push her up and I'll get the bag," Lazo says, his eyes flashing in anger.

"You've already touched her so you have to do it. Stop arguing. I'm hungry."

"I'm not that hungry." Lazo moves to the other side of the crater and sits.

Dimitri sighs and walks over and sits next to him. "Imagine it's one of the goats back home. It's just a lump of meat. You push her up and I get the bag. Then we get far enough away from here and have a feast. Remember there were pickled tomatoes, olives and bread."

Lazo grumbles. "You mean squashed bread." He gets up. "Let's get this over with."

"Okay, now." Lazo pushes Vesna with all his might and the body moves to one side. Dimitri manages to get a strap off one shoulder but not both.

"Now for the other side."

"Ugh. Look at it!" Lazo says. "I don't want to touch it."

With his hands on his knees, Lazo dry-retches. The other side of Vesna's body is mangled. Bones, sinew and muscle are exposed to the flies who have settled.

A sour smell reaches Dimitri's nose and he heaves until his stomach aches. Finally, he straightens to stop the dizziness. Staring at a bird in a nearby tree, he tries to focus his mind on the food. It sings in his mind. *Olives, tomatoes and bread. Olives, tomatoes and bread.* Then he finds a large stick. "Use this."

Somehow, Lazo manages to push Vesna high enough for Dimitri to yank off the strap and pull the bag out from beneath her. Then Lazo runs to a nearby tree and heaves.

Now that Dimitri has the bag, he's scared to open it. He drops it and looks from Lazo to the bag.

"This is the bag. I'm sure of it." He picks it up again. Except for dirt he's relieved there's nothing of Vesna on it. "Let's go," he says, breaking into a run, and he hears Lazo running close behind. They zigzag around the craters and pass the bodies without looking until Lazo stops.

"Dimitri!" he yells.

Dimitri stops and turns around. "C'mon."

Lazo cocks his head. "I think I hear something. My ears are better."

"What do you mean?"

"Listen."

"I can't hear anything. Let's go. We've got to get out of here."

"Wait!" Lazo dives into the bushes.

"Come back!" Dimitri shouts. Standing in the middle of the road, he feels alone and frightened.

"Lazo! If you don't come back, I'm going without you! Stop playing around."

When Lazo doesn't return, his stomach jangles with nerves. His legs twitch and his hands sweat. Several black crows circle and descend on the carcasses.

"I mean it. I'm going." He turns and sees the dirt road stretch ahead of him. He remembers what he'd said to his friend. *No matter what happens we stick together.* Lazo had pulled him to safety. He can't leave him now. He turns his back on the road and plunges into the undergrowth.

But he's suddenly confronted by his grinning friend and a small child. "Look who I found! Dafina!"

It's the girl whose hand Lazo had been holding before the bombs fell. Her dark eyes, still full of fright, stare blankly at the two boys. She seems unscathed except for a scratch on her forehead and dirt and leaves tangled in her hair.

"She was coughing. That's what I heard."

"All right. You'll have to come with us." Dimitri shivers

when he looks at the girl and wonders if he's capable of looking after another child. This one looks like she's barely five years old.

Dafina says nothing but allows herself to be led. The three children set off on the dusty road toward what they hope might be home. When they're well away, they sit beneath a tree to enjoy the feast.

Opening the bag, Dimitri brings out another jacket, his heart sinking. "This is my jacket. How did it get in there?" he says. "The food must be right at the bottom." His heart thumps with hope.

"Just tip it out," Lazo says impatiently. Dafina stares blankly ahead.

The contents spill onto the grass. There's a half-full bottle of red wine, a slice of bread, nuts wrapped up in a newspaper cone and another jacket.

"But this was the food bag," Lazo cries. "Where's the rest of it?"

"This is it," Dimitri says. "Open the wine. Lucky the cork is half out."

They divide the slice of bread into three. Lazo counts the nuts. There are twenty.

"Let's have three each and save the rest for later," Dimitri says, opening the bottle of wine. He sniffs it and hesitates. It smells off. The others are watching him. They're thirsty too. He takes a swig and stifles a cough as its sour taste fills his mouth. He wipes away the dribble on his chin.

"Well?" Lazo says.

"My grandfather makes better wine than this." He feels a warmth come over him.

He passes it to Lazo. "It's better than nothing." Lazo gulps some down and passes it to Dafina, who makes a face as she drinks before spluttering and coughing. "What do you think happened to the rest of the food?"

"Dunno. There was a lot more food when we got on the truck." The bottle is passed around and Dimitri tries hard to hide his disgust at every mouthful.

"Maybe the truck driver and that other woman took it."

The girl becomes animated. "There was another bag." And her hacking coughs starts up again.

"Could the food have been in the other bag?" Lazo picks up a twig and draws in the dirt.

"I saw them take it," she says, gasping for air.

"So you can talk?" Dimitri watches as she curls her legs under her.

She nods and lowers her eyes.

"How old are you?" Dimitri asks.

"I think I'm eight," she says.

"You're little," Lazo says.

"Girls are small in my family." She coughs and turns pale, then suddenly gets up and runs into the bushes where they hear her retch.

"That happened to me once. My father was drunk and gave me a whole glass. I wouldn't have any for days after that." Dimitri touches his hot face and closes his eyes.

"It only happens if it's off," Lazo says, yawning.

"It doesn't have to be off," Dimitri says.

Dafina comes back wiping her mouth with the back of her hand. Lazo is already asleep and Dimitri is settled with his jacket under his head. Closing his eyes, he makes a picture of his mother sitting at the table peeling potatoes. She turns her head painstakingly toward the window as if she is waiting for something. For his father, for his grandfather? He'll never know.

Dimitri wakes to find Dafina coughing violently. He's surprised to see how far the sun has sunk. "It's getting late. Wake up. Let's try and find the brook and stay there for the night. It can't be too far."

Picking up the two bags they set off.

19

Water and Cheese

Jim rubs his belly. He doesn't feel good.

"Blast that cheese," he mutters, padding into the kitchen.

Pain travels up his oesophagus and as he leans against the kitchen sink, a loud belch escapes.

"That's better," he says, before farting. "Better out than in."

He fills a glass of water from the tap and gulps it down fast, as if he's not drunk in hours. He's always hated dryness in his mouth.

He turns off the light, checks the front and back doors are locked, before going back into his bedroom. Looking at the vacant spot on the large bed, he sighs.

"I wish you were here," he says, flopping onto the bed. "It shouldn't have happened. You shouldn't have left me."

Rolling from one side to the other, he gets no relief. His stomach swills with water and a slow burn settles in his chest.

Getting up, he goes back to the kitchen and rummages in the drawer for his medication.

"This will sort it out," he mutters.

He checks the doors are locked, then peers out the window again and groans. Another dog is barking.

20

I Could Eat a Herd of Goats

Lazo has the best hearing of the three and hears the running water before he sees it.

"That way," he says.

By the time they reach the brook, the sun has almost sunk behind the mountains and a chill settles over them. They find the remnants of last night's camp, then scurry for wood. After finding matches in one of the bags, Dafina manages to light a fire. Winter is not over and they shiver inside their jackets.

"Did you live in our village?" Dimitri asks.

Dafina nods. "I lived with my mother and my twin sisters. My father was murdered. They … they hanged him from a tree in a field outside the village." She begins to cry quietly in the awkward silence.

Dimitri remembers. He thought it was a scarecrow and for a dreadful moment he wants to cry too. It was at the war's beginning when the Partisans were trying to force men to join them. The man's feet had been cut off and he'd been left to hang so that everyone could see. It sent fear through the village and everyone assumed the Partisans had done it.

"Were your sisters on the truck?" Lazo asks, holding his hands out to warm them by the fire.

The flames reflect in her tear-filled eyes. "They died a little while ago. We didn't have enough food for them, my mother said. That's why they got sick. The twins are gone and without me..." She stares blankly into the fire and is somewhere else.

Lazo throws a piece of wood onto the fire, sending sparks into the cold night air. Pulling his jacket around him, Dimitri rocks back and forth ever so slightly then begins to hum. Lazo follows and then Dafina joins in to hum a tune their mothers had taught them.

Lazo grins. "We're good enough to sing at the next dance."

Dimitri and Dafina smile too and they huddle closer to keep warm, sitting in silence in front of the flames.

"There's bread in this pocket," Dafina says suddenly. They frantically turn out the pockets of all the jackets. Nothing. Dafina's crooked white teeth gleam in the firelight as she divides the piece equally, and they gratefully eat but it does little to stifle the ache of hunger.

"Anyone for wine?" Lazo asks, grinning.

"Throw it out so we can fill it with water for tomorrow." The wine had made Dimitri feel sick but he isn't going to admit it.

They try to sleep, but the pop of gunfire in the distance

starts up and frightens them. The fire comforts them; like the sound of dried leaves being crumpled under their feet and reminds Dimitri about the mounds of leaves he'd waded through like an explorer; of throwing them high in the air to drift away with the wind.

"I could eat a big bowl of chicken soup right now," Lazo says, interrupting his thoughts.

"I could eat a whole chicken," Dimitri retorts.

"I could eat a herd of goats," Dafina says. They can't help but laugh and it feels good. "Once when I was small…"

"You're still small," Dimitri grins.

"When I was smaller, I ate a whole leg from a goat. My mother cooked it over the coals. My job was to turn it over slowly while she sprinkled rosemary and lemon over the top."

"Mmm … sounds good," Lazo says sleepily.

"You couldn't have eaten a whole leg on your own," Dimitri says. The sky lights up and they hear a booming sound in the distance and huddle closer.

"Are you calling me a liar?" she asks fiercely. "I ate it, so there!"

Dimitri gets up to cover the dying fire with dirt. "Just in case." He comes back to the huddle. "It sounds like it's getting closer." Dimitri shivers, but not from the cold.

The other two have finally fallen asleep but Dimitri lies awake, on guard. A breeze springs up and the tree above them sways. The stars have disappeared and the night is dark. He searches the shadows. Is someone there? He thinks he can hear heavy breathing. Or is it the buzzing in his ears? He fixes on a bush. It rustles. He imagines it's a man crouched with a long stick in the air. Could it be a rifle? He closes his eyes. The moon sneaks out from behind the heavy clouds and lights the area. He opens his eyes and lets out the breath he's been holding. It's just a bush after all.

***

Dimitri wakes the next morning to light drizzle. Cocking his head, he tries to listen. The shelling has stopped. The buzzing in his ears has lessened. He knows his arms and legs are part of him but without moving them he floats. He feels safe when he's like this, as if he's a bird. Dafina moans and the ache of his body comes back to him. Lazo stirs and stretches.

Yawning, Dimitri hauls himself up. He's determined that they'll make it home. That he will see his mother and grandfather once more. And when he's strong enough he'll search for his father and find him, too.

After washing their faces, they spread out the remaining eight nuts and eat one each before Dimitri puts the rest in his pocket. The brook rolls over the rocks, minding its own business, oblivious to the world around it and they drink as much water as they can.

"Let's go," Dimitri commands. He hands one bag to Lazo and he takes the other.

"Why do we need to take these? There's no food and we're wearing the jackets," Lazo says.

Dimitri shrugs. "Let's leave them then."

"What about when it gets hot? We can put the jackets in the bags. Who's going to carry the water?" Dafina frowns.

"Oh yeah," Dimitri grumbles as he picks up the one he'd flung on the ground.

"I can take one," she says.

Lazo laughs. "It's as big as you."

Her eyes flash in anger. She snatches the bag off Lazo. "I may be small but I'm strong."

"All right, all right," Lazo says.

"You can take mine." Dimitri grins. Lazo punches him in the arm and they run after Dafina, who's already started walking.

They're hopeful. Maybe it's because the sound of the war has stopped and they're on the road, heading home.

"How far do you think our village is?" she asks, coughing between breaths. Both boys shrug as they set off.

21

The Cough

Starving, Dimitri stands with Dafina and Lazo in the middle of a dirt road and studies the countryside. The mountains to the north and south and the valley before them are covered in a pearl-grey murk. They decide to walk west to get home. Sidestepping the craters, they pass charred, limbless trees. They explore a burned-out, abandoned farmhouse in a blackened pasture, but find nothing of use. Dimitri feels exposed on this sunless day. It begins to rain again and he pulls his coat tighter. A plane flies high above. Then another. He picks up a stone and throws it defiantly into the air. "Go away," he yells.

All three throw stones at the planes until a rumbling noise sends them scattering into the undergrowth to hide. The ground shakes as the sound comes toward them.

"What is it?" Dafina asks. "What is it? We're going to die."

"No, we're not. Stay still!" Dimitri says, terrified.

"I'm scared," she whimpers. Her coughing starts up; it's thick, gurgly and hard.

Lazo draws his legs to his chest.

As it comes nearer, they shrink back from the rumble.

An army truck passes and relieved, they brush themselves off. But the pop of firearms signals the fighting is starting.

"We can't keep going," Dimitri says glumly. "We'll have to wait until it stops."

"But what if they bomb us?" Dafina asks.

"We can hear. It's a long way off." Lazo sounds convincing. "Let's stay here."

They huddle together under the green, leafy canopy, hoping for the rain to stop. Ears cocked. A plane thunders above them, circling lower. They hold their breaths until it has gone. *Pit, pat* of raindrops falls on the large leaves and the boom of shell-fire seems far away.

Dimitri drops off to sleep. He wakes to Lazo and Dafina whispering. They're talking about what they'll eat when they get home. Only, they've already forgotten that there is none of the food they want at home; what they're remembering now is in their past. Dimitri doesn't have the heart to tell them. He just wants to be in the safety of his mother's and father's arms. To talk to his Dedo. To throw stones and play with Lazo. He's so tired of all of this.

After a while the rain stops and so does the fighting. They have no idea of the time but decide to set off while it's still light. They stay off the road in case they need the shelter of the undergrowth.

"Why didn't you go to school?" Lazo asks Dafina.

"I wasn't allowed to go. My father thought school was a waste of time for a girl. He said I needed to help with my sisters."

"That's stupid. My sister went to school."

"Where is she now?" Dafina coughs.

"She's somewhere in those mountains. She was forced to go with the Partisans. She's much older than me. She's sixteen." Lazo drags a long stick behind him.

"She's probably helping them a lot," Dimitri says, sensing his sadness.

"I think she's on the right side," Dafina says. "I think we were lucky to escape back there. The Fascists are bad, so my father used to say."

"But didn't the Partisans kill him?" Dimitri remembers his fear when the gun was under his chin.

"We never really knew. The Partisans were really nice when they came to our house. And the Fascists said they'd burn our house if I didn't leave."

"The Partisans weren't nice to my family." Dimitri throws the stone he's been holding with such force that it cracks against a blackened tree.

"Or mine," Lazo says. "The whole lot are awful."

They reach a rise. The shape of a village below them reminds Dimitri of the stone fortresses the boys made in their play long ago. He doesn't notice the absence of smoke from the houses. They hurry towards the nearest one. Maybe someone can help them. Perhaps there's food.

Bomb craters are everywhere. The first house they come to is a shell; the roof caved in and empty. The next house is the same. Rubble piles high where several houses once stood. A misty rain begins to fall and in the dying light it's clear the village is deserted.

"Now what do we do?" Lazo says, slumping against a wall of rubble.

Dimitri is quiet. His hopes are dashed. His clothes are damp and his feet are cold and caked in mud. He listens, for something, anything, but there's nothing. The wind rustles the leaves of the few remaining trees and somewhere a door or a window creaks.

"Don't be so glum. We can stay here tonight." Dafina looks earnestly from one boy to the other. Her hacking cough starts up anew. "Maybe there's food in some of the houses."

Dimitri brightens. "Yes. Let's look."

They split up and hunt.

Dimitri hears Dafina's yells first and finds Lazo. They run through the village, hoping she's found food. Their hollow stomachs ache but there's no use complaining.

She waves from the doorway of an old stone house. Paint peels off the blackened, broken windows. "Look what I found!"

They follow her into a corner of the house that's still standing. On a bench sit three dirt-caked carrots and a bottle of pickled tomatoes. The boys look at each other and smile.

"Dinner!" she exclaims. "And a big soft bed out of the rain. I found a well out the back so there's plenty of water, too."

Lazo can't help himself. He runs and jumps onto the bed while Dimitri runs around in a circle and whoops.

The front half of the room is in ruin but the back half is intact. Newspaper is strewn across the floor along with leaves, dirt and ash. Cups sit neatly on a shelf above a bench. A half-torn curtain hangs limply alongside a small grubby window. The fireplace, surrounded by blackened bricks, is filled with ash. A large pot lies on its side as if it has rolled away in a hurry. The cupboards are bare except for some plates and a saucepan. In a dark corner, Dimitri spies a bottle with a few olives inside.

They don't risk lighting a fire, so they eat the carrot with the olives and the pickled tomatoes in the dying light of the day.

"That was good," Dimitri says, drinking some water.

"That was the best carrot I've ever had," Lazo says. "Where did you find it?

"In the garden," she beams. "It was hidden under a bush. Must be the last of the crop."

"I don't suppose there was anything else?" Dimitri stands up and pats his stomach as if it's full.

"I didn't see anything. We can look again when there's more light." Moving to the window, with her back to them, she coughs a fine mist of blood into her hands, which she wipes hurriedly on her dirty dress.

Dimitri sees it and frowns. "Your cough is bad."

Holding her hand over her mouth, she coughs again. "I'm fine," she wheezes. "I wonder where we are?"

"Dunno. But I hope this road takes us home," Dimitri says.

"What if our village is like this one?" Dafina asks. "What if everyone's gone? What then?"

"They'll be there. They've got to be." But Dimitri's confidence wavers. "We better get some sleep." He thinks about what Dedo said before he left. The reason they were put on the truck was because the fighting was heading for their village. A shiver of uncertainty runs through him. What, if after all this, their village is like this one?

A shadow passes across his friend's face and he knows that Lazo doesn't believe him.

"Everyone will be there, Dafina," Lazo says. "There's no place else to go."

Cold and darkness creep through the house and they're comforted by the steady fall of rain. With no other sound to alarm them, they drop their guard, climb into the bed and fall into an exhausted asleep.

***

Dimitri wakes first. He's sure their luck has changed. After all, they'd found shelter and food and surely the worst is behind them. Light is forcing its way across the cottage. The rain has stopped but when he peers through the window the sky is still overcast. Then he hears a noise. He listens again and thinks he hears voices. Is it in his head? Lifting himself on his elbow, his yellowed pillow lies limp and dented like a half-empty sack and he hears it again.

Gently shaking Lazo awake, he puts his finger to his lips. Dafina's eyes open too, then widen in fright.

124

"Do you hear that?" Dimitri whispers.

Crawling on his hands and knees, Dimitri makes his way to a window and peeks through it. He shivers, then crawls back. "It's men with guns," he whispers. "They're heading this way."

"Partisans?" Lazo whispers.

"Probably," Dimitri says.

Dafina is out of bed looking wildly for a place to hide. She dances in one spot, not knowing what to do; there's no way out without being seen.

"Quick! Under the bed," Dimitri hisses. Lazo is under first but Dafina still dances about on the spot. Dimitri grabs her arm and drags her and their bags under the bed. Trembling, they wait.

Dimitri hears the muffled sounds of the men and then a laugh.

Being as still as they can, the voices move along the street. The men search the houses, just as they'd done the day before and the sound of footsteps gets closer. One set reaches the doorway. The clump of heavy boots echoes across the wooden floor to the bench then turns toward them leaving a trail of dirt across the floor. The bottom of the man's pants, wet with mud is close enough for Dimitri to reach out his hand to touch them.

Dimitri is certain the man can hear his heartbeat – panic courses through his body. In the dull light, he glances at Lazo and Dafina, whose faces mirror his own terror. Dafina's hand is clapped over her mouth to stifle a cough. Her eyes bulge, wild with fear. The man walks away from the bed to the window, then moves toward the door. Dafina looks as if she'll burst. Just another few minutes and the men will leave. Then they'll be free. Her body shakes. Don't make a noise. Stay still.

"In here," the man calls out. The boots return, their toe caps inches from Dimitri's face. Another person enters.

"Someone's been here. The bed's still warm. Feel that? Anything out there?"

"Nah. Maybe they've gone."

"But not too far, eh."

"We'll get them. Don't worry."

The footsteps begin walking away and Dafina explodes with a wild hacking cough. Dimitri closes his eyes, knowing it's over. The footsteps walk back toward the bed and a boot kicks the frame.

"Come out of there. Now!"

They can do nothing else but obey. Dafina whispers, "Sorry" and begins to cry.

She coughs noisily and is the first one out. Then Lazo, followed by Dimitri, scramble out to face the muzzle of two rifles.

Two men stare at them and lower their guns.

"What have we here?" says one man, smiling. One of his front teeth is missing but he has a kind face.

"Please, sir, don't eat us," Dafina says, shaking.

The men laugh loudly.

"Eat you?" the other man says. Shoving his long fair hair

out of his eyes, he frowns. "We're not going to eat you. Who told you that?"

"The soldiers told us," Dimitri says, shaking like a leaf.

"Where do you come from?"

They told them the name of their village and what had happened.

The fair-headed man says, "I'm Kostas and this is Zisis."

"I'm sorry but they're bombing all the villages. Just like this one," Zisis explains.

"We better get you out of here before the militia come back." Kostas glances out of the window chewing on his moustache.

"Come. We'll take you somewhere safe." Zisis holds out his hand to Dafina.

"Please, do you know where my mother is?" Her voice catches.

"And mine?"

"And mine too?"

Kostas places his hand on Dafina's head and shrugs. "We don't know."

22

The Fight with the Mosquito

The alarm shrills on the bedside table. Set for six thirty, on the loudest setting, Jim rubs his stinging eyes. Another rough night. Throwing on a worn-out bathrobe, he heads to the bathroom, where he fills the basin with a container of water from the bath and splashes his face. Staring at the mirror, he wonders where the years have gone. He runs his hand over grey stubble and picks out the shaving cream from the cupboard and notices a wayward hair hanging out of one nostril. "Why does hair grow there instead of on my head?" he says out loud.

Something buzzes around his ear and flies in front of his face. He swipes at it, but misses. He grunts, remembering his daughter's words, *get rid of the water*. The thing lands on his arm and he slaps it, smearing insect and blood. He peers at it. A mosquito? Is Helen right? Mosquito larvae in the bath?

Squinting into the bathtub, he can't tell if there are things floating. He grabs his glasses and lowers himself carefully to his knees and peers into the water.

Grains of dirt have settled onto the bottom and the beginnings of algae are forming on the water's edge, along with things that wriggle. He rests on his haunches and another mosquito buzzes past his nose. He peers up to the light and sees a squadron of them flying like fighter bombers across the ceiling and toward him. Plunging his arm into the cold water, he finds the plug and pulls hard. The water and the larvae quickly swirl into the hole.

"Now for some spray for the rest of you buggers," he exclaims, scratching.

He tries to pull himself up but struggles. His legs seem to be caught under him. He slides onto his bottom to pull his legs out and leans against the bath. He stops to scratch the growing lump on his arm where the mosquito bit, then hauls himself up to sit on the edge of the bath. He searches for something to hang onto, but as he swings around he loses balance. Sliding into the bath, he bangs his head on the tap and passes out.

23

Climb to Base Camp

Dimitri wonders what would happen if they refused to follow the men silently out of the village. Where are they going? Must they blindly trust them? The men seem sympathetic to their plight. Partisans are evil, the soldiers had said. But these men seem preoccupied with things other than them.

Instead of being scared, Dimitri wrestles with anger and disappointment at Lazo and Dafina. He knows he shouldn't be, but they'd been close to getting home. If Lazo hadn't found her, they wouldn't be marching behind these men to an unknown place. If Dafina hadn't coughed, they might never have been discovered.

According to these men, his village could be gone. How will he find his mother, father and grandfather now, and how will they find him? What if he'd never spoken up about Stinky Spiro? What if he'd got the Rakia that night? The Partisans might have left before Stinky saw them. What if they'd left before the fighting had started, just like his mother had wanted? So many what ifs race through his mind until his anger dissolves as he drags his feet.

"We rest here," Kostas says, stopping. They are close to the foot of the mountains and rest next to a stream. "We will have something to eat and drink."

It's the first bit of good news for the weary children.

Sitting on a rock, Zisis digs inside his knapsack and brings out bread, which he breaks up. "Here!" he says, offering a small piece to each of them. The children sit quietly on the ground and eat.

"Don't look so worried," Zisis says, laughing. "Look at them, like scared mice."

Dimitri notices his friends are as despondent as he is. Dafina's eyes are red and swollen and her face is smeared with snot she hasn't bothered to wipe away.

"If we take this path, we should get to base camp by evening," Kostas says to Zisis.

"It'll be hard going but it's the quickest way."

"When we get to base camp, I promise you the food will be a bit better," Kostas says to the children. "And you'll be looked after. And safe. But we have to go a different way. Up and over those rocks. It'll be hard. Do you think you can do it?"

The children nod.

"Will my mother be there?" Dafina asks.

"Perhaps. There are a lot of people fleeing," Kostas says, getting up. "But we don't know."

Kostas slings his rifle across his shoulder and leads the way. They're climbing through the undergrowth when gunshots pepper above them.

"Duck behind this rock," Zisis says, pulling the rifle off of his shoulder.

The men are poised, just like Kitty before pouncing on her prey. They stalk away and out of sight. Dimitri trembles in terror. Shots are fired again. Dafina sticks her fingers in her ears and clenches her eyes shut. More shots. *Ping, clack, ping.* Is this where it ends, Dimitri wonders?

Then, as suddenly as it started, the firing stops.

Where are Kostas and Zisis? How long should they wait?

"Should we keep going up the mountain and try to find their base camp?" Lazo whispers.

"Yes. It's safe there. Kostas said we'd be looked after." Dafina, trying not to cough, is shivering. "Or maybe we should wait a bit longer for them to come back."

"They might be dead. I think we should try to get to our village and see for ourselves. Maybe they lied. If it was bombed, our families might have escaped; they might even be back now," Dimitri argues.

"But what if there's more gunfire? Or shelling? Shouldn't we stay a bit longer?" Dafina asks.

Lazo scratches his head, his face uncertain as he stares at Dafina. Dimitri knows what he's thinking. She might not be strong enough to make it home. Her eyes widen as if she's listening to their thoughts.

"Go without me. I'll be all right. They'll get me to safety."

A Perfect Stone

Without another thought, Dimitri stands up. He's made a decision – he is going with or without them. He needs to go before he has a chance to think; to change his mind.

"Dafina, we're not going without you," Lazo says.

"She's right. We have to go now." Dimitri goes to move but Lazo holds his arm in a vice-like grip.

"We made a pact, Dimitri. Remember? Whatever happens, we stick together. And I'm not leaving Dafina."

They hear rustling. Their panic fades when they see the two men.

"Are you all right?" Kostas asks.

They nod.

The men look pleased with themselves.

"Let's get out of here." Zisis wipes the blade of his knife on a tuft of grass growing on a rock, then onto his pants, leaving behind a faint red smear before he tucks it away in his belt.

Dimitri isn't shocked to discover how easily he's abandoned his escape plan – that in truth he just wants someone to look after him and to feel safe again. He knows Lazo is right and wonders if he really is the boy who would have left them and ventured off by himself.

They trudge up a rugged slope. What was once a path is marked with holes, slips and bush. Treading carefully, they puff and pant as they climb. Dafina's cough is getting worse and she's slowing them down.

Kostas waits for her. "Let me carry you," he says, scooping her up in his arms. Dimitri looks after her in envy. His feet and legs sting from the cuts and scrapes from the rocks.

133

The going is so steep in parts that they hold tufts of grass or branches to stop themselves from falling. The men help the children, holding their hands to pull them up over large boulders.

"Let's rest here," Kostas says, puffing. He sets Dafina down carefully and stares at her, frowning. "You may be little but you've got a ferocious cough." Her large eyes seem to have sunken into her small pale face. Her dress is dirty and ripped, and she's covered in old and new scratches and bruises. Lying on his back with his hands behind his head, Dimitri says nothing as he stares at the overcast sky.

They take sips of water from a canister that Zisis hands around. They're high enough now to see the valley stretch below them. They hear the faint sounds of gunfire, which has moved further into the valley. A spiral of thick smoke works its way up from another destroyed village.

"We're winning the fight," Kostas says, shading his eyes from the sun that has come out for a moment. He gestures at the valley spread below them. "Soon that will belong to us all. We will be free and life will be better than you ever imagined."

Dimitri wonders who they'll be free from. He wants desperately to imagine a better life. To be with his family again. To have a home; to be safe and never hungry. Is that what Kostas means? But he says nothing. The image of the misty grey valley etches itself into his mind. As he gets up, he wonders if he will ever see home again.

"Come on." Kostas hauls Dafina onto his shoulders and

pushes on up the rocky slope. Higher and higher they climb, puffing. Finally, as the day begins to fade, they reach a well-worn path.

"Not far now," Kostas says. The going is easier and flat as the path winds its way around the mountain. At times the edge plunges down to an abyss of bush and rock. Dimitri dares not look down. He, like the others, is exhausted and starving.

"Kostas, Zizis, where have you been? We expected you hours ago," a big burly man yells out. They reach a clearing. Dimitri stares at the people who are milling around the entrance to a tent. There are other tents behind it. He watches the women bandaging the injuries of several men.

"We got into a skirmish with two of them who came off second best," Zizis says with a grin.

The burly man with a cigarette hanging limply from the corner of his mouth nods approvingly. "That's what's to be done even if it's two at a time."

Dimitri gulps in fright. It's the same man who'd been in his house demanding Rakia. Head bowed, he hides behind Zizis.

"And who have you got here?" the burly man asks.

Kostas gently puts Dafina down to shake the burly man's hand. "We picked them up out on patrol. This one's sick." He places his hand protectively on Dafina's head. "I better take them to Olga. See you later."

"Stay safe," Zizis calls out to the children as they follow Kostas to a tent. Dimitri turns and watches him disappear.

Wide-eyed, Dimitri takes in the piles of guns and the smell

of cooking. They step into a large tent filled with other children. Some are lying on the floor; others are on canvas camp stretchers.

"Stay here," Kostas commands. He walks amongst the children until he reaches a pretty blonde woman who is rubbing the head of a child. He kisses her on both cheeks then talks to her. She looks across, nods and walks toward them.

"Hello," she says, smiling. Her teeth are white and her eyes are blue and friendly. "I am Comrade Olga and I'll look after you. You're safe now. Think of me as your mother. Kostas tells me that you've hardly had anything to eat. You must be starving."

They nod.

Olga looks them over and sees the scratches on their feet and legs. She bends down to touch Dafina's forehead and looks at her face. "What's your name, little one?"

"Dafina," she replies, coughing.

"It's all right, Dafina. We'll look after you. How are you feeling?"

"I'm okay," she says, blinking.

Dimitri is not sure. She's not his mother. Why does she call herself that? He glances at Lazo, who has a dopey grin on his face. His friend tells Olga who he is and acts coy when she tells him how big he is for his age. Dimitri wants to hit him, to shake him, to scream at him. But Lazo seems to be in a daze.

Then she turns to him. "And what is your name, young comrade?" she says, dazzling him with a smile. He feels calm for the first time in a long time. "I'm Dimitri, Comrade Olga," he forces. She touches his shoulder and looks deep into his eyes, as if she's looking into his soul to see what kind of boy he is. Would she see a selfish boy who'd been ready to abandon his friends only hours ago? Or would she see someone who was weak and wanted desperately to take his life into his own hands but couldn't?

"Dimitri, I can see you have very special qualities. You're safe now and we'll take a look at those scratches. Let's get something for you to eat." Dimitri follows, desperately wanting to believe her.

24

It's for the Best

Dimitri almost faints when he sees a morsel of roasted goat, a small square of cheese and bread on a plate in front of him.

"This is the best meal I've ever had," Lazo declares, with his mouth stuffed with everything from the plate.

Dimitri nods in agreement and savours every small morsel. One goat between scores of children and adults doesn't stretch very far. It doesn't fill his empty belly but Dimitri is so exhausted he can barely keep his eyes open.

After dinner they're separated from Dafina, who is taken to a tent filled with girls. Lazo and Dimitri find themselves in a tent occupied with boys who are scratching, burping, farting and crying. Their feet and legs are checked and the blood washed away with wet cloths before they fall asleep on the ground almost immediately. Deep and dreamless. But not for long.

"All right children, it's time to get up," Olga says, banging a spoon on a saucepan lid.

Dimitri opens his eyes to see a lantern light bobbing around the tent. It's still dark. Shadowy figures shake each child awake. Yawning and rubbing their eyes, they struggle to get up. Crying can be heard from a tent nearby.

"Where are we going?" Dimitri asks a boy next to him.

"I don't know," the boy says, yawning. "This is what we do. We move from place to place at night and rest in the day so the blackbirds don't see us."

"Come along," says a woman with a young child clinging to her hip. She's holding a lantern and nudges the boys out of the tent. "Follow me."

Another woman appears with the girls.

The clearing is filled with moonlight and children and they soon move off. It's cold and some have no jackets. Dimitri is thankful for his. The horror of the last march is fresh and alive in his thoughts, and now they're marching again in the dark to somewhere further from home.

He tries to count the children ahead of him but stops at twenty. What comes after twenty? he wonders. His schooling had been so interrupted that he's forgotten how to count properly. The school opened and closed as frequently as it rained. He can hardly remember the teachers, many of whom ran off to join the Partisans or were forced to fight with the Fascists. He can write his name and a few words but his reading is dreadful. He wonders if he will ever go to school again.

Walking two or three abreast, away from the camp, there's a dull murmur of chatter and crying from the smaller children. Luckily, there's enough moonlight to show the way and no cliff edge to be wary of. The women keep the stragglers going. When will they get there? What will it be like? Dimitri tries not to think of his mother, yet she pops into his thoughts. Perhaps she's waiting at their destination? Waiting and crying for him. He imagines her in her apron and scarf searching each child's face until her eyes rest on him. Her lovely smile, calling his name over and over, holding out her arms, and he lets his imagination romp off like a new puppy.

"Dimitri, Dimitri! Lazo!"

Dimitri hears coughing and immediately recognises the voice. He calls out, "Dafina! Where are you?"

"I'm back here. Hold up your arm so I can see you," she shouts between coughs.

With his arm in the air he feels her small, cold hand on his back. "Can I walk with you?" she asks.

"Sure you can," Lazo says, putting his arm around her.

"Keep going, children," a voice calls out.

Dimitri is glad Dafina is there and slides his arm around the other side of her.

"I'm really sorry," she says. "About giving us away."

"It doesn't matter now. Our village is probably gone so we've nowhere to go except with this lot." Lazo rubs his eyes and pats his stomach. "At least we got something to eat," he says. "Maybe there'll be more."

"And when we get over the border, we'll all be safe."
Dafina coughs again.

"Is that where we're going?" Dimitri asks.

"That's what Olga said. We have to climb the mountains
then cross the border to safety," she says with hope in her
voice. "Isn't she wonderful?"

Dimitri shrugs. "Yeah. But she's not our mother. None of
them are."

"One of the girls told me Olga lost her husband and two
children when their house was shelled, and that's when she
joined the Partisans. She takes groups of children like us over
the border to safety."

Then what? Dimitri wants to say, but doesn't. When they
cross the border, what will happen? He thinks again about
turning around and going back. It wouldn't be far, he
reasons. He could steal some extra food and find the path
back. With so many children here he knows he won't be
missed. He makes another plan, quashing any thought of
what he'll actually find when he gets home.

It gets colder and the going rougher. Down a gully, they
scramble up and over rocks. In the moonlight, children are
spread across the side of the bare mountain like a line of ants.
Each of the women carries at least one child. A large woman
has a crying baby on one hip and a toddler on the other. It's a
path of despair, fear and tears.

"Vangelia, you should not be crying. You are a soldier. Be
brave now," Dimitri hears a voice say. Turning around, he
sees a young woman with a child on her hip being comforted

by another woman. If a grownup is crying, what hope do we have? he wonders, and he continues to plan his escape. It must be now while it's still dark, he thinks.

"I don't want to go over the border. I'm going home," he whispers to Lazo and Dafina.

"I'm coming with you," Lazo whispers back.

"I don't think I can make it," Dafina says, coughing. "I'm staying."

"We want you to come too," Dimitri says. "We can look after you."

"No! What if our village is gone? I couldn't bear it. It's better here. I feel safer."

"But how are we going to escape?" asks Lazo.

"We'll hide behind a bush after the next bend."

They look at the path ahead, which is becoming steeper.

"I'll fall down as if I've fainted. That way they'll be helping me and won't notice." Dafina coughs and splutters.

"Thanks." Dimitri gives her a quick hug.

"If you find my mother can you tell her that I'll be over the border and … that I miss her?" She sniffs. "Be careful."

"We will."

Despite the cold, Dimitri's hands are clammy with nerves. They're almost at a bend in the windy path when Dafina coughs hard and falls in a faint. The two boys slip into the undergrowth while some of the women rush to attend her. Then they wait, crouched, for the last of the children to pass before they slip out and run down the path in the opposite direction.

"That was easy," Dimitri says, slowing. His feet and fingers throb with cold.

The path, littered with small sharp rocks, punctures their hard bare feet.

"Now it's downhill all the way." Lazo hops as if he's walking on hot coals. "Dafina will be all right. She has the mothers to look after her. It's for the best."

He's heard that before. His mother said it after Kitty went missing. It's for the best, she said, when Dedo left for days to look for his father. She'd whispered it to him in a hug right before he'd climbed onto the truck. But not everything is for the best, he thinks, as they make their way down the winding path that will hopefully lead them home.

"Did you take any notice of where this path leads to?"

Dimitri shrugs. "Nah! How many paths can there be on this mountain?"

"Did your plan think about the base camp and the men?"

"I didn't think that far ahead. We'll just hide when it gets light. We'll steal some food from the camp, and when it gets dark we'll follow the path down. So long as it doesn't go up we should make it down."

"That makes sense."

Dimitri is pleased with his plan. "Before we know it, we'll be walking back into the village. Our mothers will cry with delight."

"Yeah," Lazo says. "We'll be like heroes coming back from war."

"We'll be carried about the village as long-lost sons. They'll put a dance on for us and shower us with food."

"I wonder if there's any more of that goat left at base camp? We should try to steal some."

"Yeah, we should."

Their pace slows as they negotiate their way on the rugged track.

"Funny, but I don't remember this many rocks when we passed through here before," Lazo says.

"Maybe we were still half asleep. We're still going down so it must be the right path."

They scramble over a large boulder. "I'm sure that wasn't there before," Lazo says. He stops and stares while trying to remember.

"Come on. It's the right one. We haven't seen any other path. I'm sure the camp is just around that bend."

They see the torchlights too late.

"And where do you think you two are off to?" says a gruff deep voice.

One man grabs Lazo as he tries to run. Dimitri dodges another man and runs back up the path to the boulder. But the man is fast, too, and sprints after him, pushing him hard to the ground. The man pants next to Dimitri, who lies face down, winded. He feels himself picked up by the scruff of his jacket collar.

"Well, it looks like we got a couple of escapees," the man holding Lazo says. "Going in the wrong direction."

There are three men, each armed.

"Lazo and Dimitri. What are you doing? Aren't you supposed to be with the others?"

Dimitri jerks his head up to peer at Zisis.

"Do you know these two?"

"Yep. Picked them up down in the valley yesterday." He puts his hand on Dimitri's shoulder.

"We're going home." Dimitri is glad the men can't see his tears in the moonlight.

"Listen. Your home will be gone and your family has probably fled to safety somewhere," Zizis says. "It's better for you to go back to the other children. Let's go."

They march back up the path and then veer left. Dimitri realises they'd been going the wrong way after all – this path is worn down and less rocky.

"You're lucky we found you and not the Fascists. Do you hear that?" Gunfire and the dull thud of bombs are heard in the distance. Both boys cock their ears in alarm.

"If you'd kept going on that path you would have walked right into their hands. This is for the best, believe me."

The men walk so fast that the boys have to jog to keep up, and they eventually catch up to the group.

"We found these two trying to run away. Here you go," Zizis says to the woman at the rear. He nudges the boys toward her. She has one toddler on her hip.

"Thanks," she says.

"You can't go back," he says to the boys once more, and then the men disappear into the darkness.

Dimitri braces, expecting a cuff to the ear, or, worse, a

beating. The moment moves in slow motion and he's resigned to it. Instead, she says, "You will only be safe if you're with us. It's too dangerous on your own. Now run along in front of me. We'll stop for a rest soon."

The two boys run ahead before she changes her mind and quickly fall into the rhythm of the march. Dimitri cups his icy hands together and blows his breath to warm them, then pushes them into his pockets. Hunching against the wind, he realises he may never get home again.

The barren slope begins to change. They now wind their way through thick vegetation until at last they stop. The first of the sun's rays filter between enormous fir trees. As daylight spreads, Dimitri sees for the first time the mass of children. Maybe it's thirty, fifty, one hundred, he can't tell. But it's the most children he's ever seen in one place. While water is being given out, the boys search until they find Dafina, who's shocked to see them.

"Who knows," she says, "maybe it'll be better where we're going?"

Dimitri shrugs without hope.

"Sorry, my little ones," Olga calls out, "there is no food. Rest now."

But her words do nothing to subdue the cries of hungry, tired children, some of whom cough like Dafina. Dimitri watches everyone looking for a place to lie; some are lucky and find beds of damp leaves. Others lean against the trees and can only stare blankly ahead.

"Look!" shouts one boy, pointing to the sky. "It's a blackbird."

All eyes stare at the plane flying overhead. Like the others, Dimitri cringes and crouches under a tree, desperate to hide. The blackbird swoops and the roar of its engine echoes across the mountain, reminding Dimitri of the terror he's trying to escape.

25

Stuck

Jim is puzzled at first when he opens his eyes and sees a tap above him. Then remembers the mosquitoes. One leg is draped over the top of the bath and the other rests along its length. It's been years since he's had a bath, and no wonder, it's damn uncomfortable. His back is wet and his head aches.

"Now to get out of here," he mutters. Except, try as he might, he can't seem to leverage himself up enough without sliding back down. Then he spies the railing. Anna had insisted on getting it installed. He'd only agreed for her. He couldn't see the point of the expense in a bath they never used.

He stretches his arms but can't seem to reach the thing. He pulls himself to a sitting position and it's still not enough. "Why install these bloody things if you can't get to it?" he mutters.

Finally, he gives one last heave, reaches the railing and

hauls himself to his feet. Feeling dizzy, he closes his eyes. When no longer woozy, he gingerly steps out of the bath.

He picks up his watch on the basin – eight o'clock. "Damn!" He's late and he hates to be late.

Every morning for as long as he can remember he gets up and goes for a walk to buy the paper. He doesn't understand why everyone else has theirs delivered. It's important to walk. Mary at the shop always expects him. They chat for a few moments and then he goes to the bakery and picks up a vegemite scroll. Brian, the baker, and he talk about the football or the cricket. Brian is always keen to hear his predictions for the weekend and his analysis of the wins and losses.

He sighs. He would always head back by seven thirty in time to take Anna a cup of tea to have in bed and share the vegemite scroll. He'd give her the inner section of the paper while he took the outer pages. If it was sunny he'd sit on the verandah with his breakfast to study the sports section. Sometimes, he read quotes out loud to her. "Listen, love. *The selectors need to consider…*" But he stopped reading to her when she seemed to turn off. She preferred the fashion news.

Now here he is, scratching like a monkey and hardly able to get out of the bath. He rubs his sore head. His fingers are wet and sticky with blood.

After cleaning off the blood, he plods back to the bedroom. Anna's photo stares at him. "I know, I know," he says. "I'll get checked out. Stop nagging me, woman." He can hear her voice like it was yesterday. He throws up the doona and straightens the pillows. He smells hers before he places it next to his. He likes to breathe her in, even if her smell has faded. Sometimes he likes to lay some of the dresses she'd made on the bed to admire them. He's comforted by remembering her wearing them. Her figure thickened as she'd gotten older but she seemed to get more beautiful with age. He loved her in blue – it matched her eyes.

She used to make and sell her dresses to women in Toorak. She started with a shop in South Yarra and it grew from there. Now Helen runs it – the business empire, she likes to call it. Three shops are hardly an empire, my dear, he liked to tell her. "Dad, it's a global business. We sell more online than through bricks and mortar," she'd lecture. He enjoyed riling her.

Better to get this over with, he thinks, and dials the number of his doctor. The next appointment is at ten thirty, the grumpy receptionist says, telling him how lucky he is. Good, he thinks, he has time to get the paper and a vegemite scroll, if there are any left.

26

The Fight

Their rest is short-lived before they're up on their feet again, marching wearily and in silence through the forest. Snow lies in the cracks and crevices that the sun is yet to reach. As the sun's rays poke through the lifting fog, they walk out of the forest and onto a dirt road.

"Stay to the side," Olga calls out from behind.

"Are we nearly there? My feet are sore," a girl complains.

"Nearly there," Olga says wearily.

"I'm hungry," says another, crying. "Will we get something to eat?"

"I'm cold," says a shoeless boy dressed in shorts and a shirt.

"I want my mother," cries a small girl with matted hair and a dirt-smudged face.

We all want our mothers, Dimitri wants to scream, but all he does is look behind and glare at the girl. Beyond her he checks if the group of men are with them, but they've disappeared. Perhaps they're setting up to fire at the blackbirds, he thinks.

Soon they see a building ahead and then another. Their footsteps hurry and they soon find themselves in a tiny mountain village. A ripple of excitement runs through the group, and as they round the corner they merge with another group of children.

"Comrade Olga, what took you? We got here hours ago," a blue-scarfed woman calls out and waves. "Come this way." Olga hurries past the children and embraces her.

"Stavroula. Good to see you. All in one piece, comrade?"

"Yes. A couple of problems but nothing we couldn't handle. But the worst is yet to come," Stavroula warns, lowering her voice. She looks toward the craggy, snow-covered mountain peak looming ahead even though the sound of trickling water signals winter's end. "I'll see you later. My group, come this way."

Olga smiles wearily and leads them into a large barn, where the ground is covered with straw and smells of fresh dung. In one corner, half a dozen cows stand looking on in bemusement at the scores of tired children.

"Have something to eat and then you can rest," a woman calls out. She hands a sleeping baby over to one of the villagers and rubs her neck and shoulders. She looks exhausted.

On one side of the barn is a long table where the village women have set out jugs of milk, soup and bread. It seems perfectly normal for their village to be overrun with children at the crack of dawn. It appears they've been expecting them, and they share what meagre supplies of food they have with the children.

"Stand in a line," Olga calls out. "There's hot soup for everyone."

"Hot soup," Dafina whispers. "If I fall asleep while I'm standing, catch my food. Where's Lazo? He's going to miss out."

"I don't know," Dimitri says, looking around. "There he is ... at the back of the line." They giggle when they wave to Lazo, mistaking his glum face for envy.

"Dafina, why don't you go in front of me?" Dimitri says. She looks exhausted and winces with each cough. When she thinks no-one is watching, she quickly wipes the blood she spits into her hand onto her mud-spattered dress.

"Thanks," she says.

But a bigger boy pushes her roughly onto the ground and stands where she should have been.

"Hey!" Dimitri says, helping Dafina up. "She was there first."

The boy sneers and says in Greek, "I was there first and she pushed in."

"She did not. She's sick. Let her go first."

"Macedonian idiots should be at the end of the queue," the boy mutters, turning his back on them.

Anger pours out of Dimitri like lava exploding from a volcano. Without thinking, he leaps at the boy, pushing him to the ground. He drops onto him and connects his fists to the boy's rubbery round face. The boy twists beneath him, trying to ward off the blows but Dimitri keeps punching. Blood from his nose sprays as the boy is subjected to Dimitri's pent-up distress. His anger is so intense that he doesn't hear the noise of the other children or the boy's screams from each punch, or Olga's yells. He feels himself pulled off the boy by three of the women.

His anger subsides as arms encase his shaking body firmly in a hug. He hears, "It's all right, I'm here," whispered in his ear. It's Olga's voice. "There, there," she says. It's only then that he calms down. Looking over her shoulder, he sees blood all over the boy's face and some of the women helping him. The children stare at Dimitri and the boy. It's utterly quiet in the barn except for a bird's screech, which is as disturbing as nails on a blackboard.

Dimitri doesn't recognise himself and he closes his eyes, trying to shut out the stares. He hears words. *What happened? Did you see what he did? He shouldn't have done that. There's nothing to see. Get your food and sit down.*

He's prepared to get the punishment he knows must come. Holding his hand, Olga leads him to a corner of the barn, where she sits beside him on the straw. If he doesn't open his eyes, he won't see when the blows come. If he keeps them shut, he won't see her disappointment.

Olga speaks softly. "You'll need to apologise to him. There'll be no food for you now, I'm afraid." But there is nothing more. He's unaware of the boy being comforted or the murmuring children who continue to move in the line to be fed. He doesn't notice the worried looks of Lazo and Dafina, who sit quietly in another corner and watch him. When the tears stop, he lies down and opens his eyes. He watches a spider glide across its web, fastidiously building the outer edges. A bird flies into the corner of the barn and he follows its flight to a nest up high.

Having finished their sparse meals, the children are soon asleep. Olga hugs Dimitri close, like he's her own child. He feels her kiss on his forehead before she gets up and leaves him.

He dreams of his father. They're skipping stones across the river. At first the stones are small and perfectly flat. His father skips the first stone ... one, two, three, four, five, six, seven ... and it reaches the opposite bank. When it's Dimitri's turn, his stone only reaches halfway. After a few more tries, his stone reaches the other side. His father beams and thumps him on the back. The whole village has turned out to watch. He tries again but the more he skips, the bigger the stones become, until he can barely lift them.

"But, Tato, it's a big rock. It's too big to skip."

"Come on son," his father says. "Lift it. You can do it."

Then he wakes up. It's still light. Scanning the lumpy forms of sleeping children, he spies Lazo with his hands tucked under his head, then Dafina, who's sitting up. She smiles weakly at him, as if in sympathy. Then he remembers and his face flushes red. He should find the boy to apologise. He remembers the look of terror on the boy's face. Then he notices his hand and arms are still covered in dry blood, and he feels sick.

He hauls himself up to find a place to wash. The air is cold but the sun is out. He's told by one of the village women to go behind the barn, where he finds a dish of murky water. He shivers as he washes away the dried blood. When he's done he walks over to where a small number of children mill about outside a nearby building.

And that's when he sees her.

Her hair is short and straight with a bowl haircut. Her dark shorts, too big for her, are held up by a rope tied around her thin waist. Her eyes are the deep blue he'd seen only once before. The long sleeves of her oversized brown shirt flap when she throws a stone high in the air before cupping one hand to catch it. It's the girl he'd seen when he'd been kicked by the donkey. She'd called him a baby when he'd sat on his mother's lap. Maybe he was a baby back then, he thinks, but now he's become someone else. Someone he hardly recognises. The fighter, the escaper, the scavenger. A street urchin. That's what his mother called children in rags who begged in the large villages. He looks down at his torn shirt, his filthy shorts and his jacket. Is he now a street urchin?

The girl, sensing his stare, turns and stares back.

"Nice punching," she calls out, grinning.

"You saw that?"

"Everyone saw it. You showed that bully a thing or two." Suddenly, she throws the stone straight at him. He's about twenty feet away from her and her throw is good, but his catch is better. She smiles in approval.

"The punishment you're going to get is worth it."

"I didn't get anything to eat. I think that's my punishment," he says.

She raises her eyebrows. "You're lucky then."

Dimitri opens his hand and is dismayed to see that it's the same perfect stone he'd held in the doctor's office. It sparkles in the sunlight and he wonders if she remembers him.

"He's been thumping all the smaller children behind the mothers' backs. Didn't you hear us cheering? You're a hero, Dimitri."

"Huh?" He hands back the stone. "How do you know my name?"

"Olga screamed it loud enough. We all know your name. I told you, you're a hero."

He looks around. As children wake they come out of the barn toward him, smiling and nodding.

"Good on you, Dimitri," one boy says. Another waves and smiles.

"Oh," is all he can say. It seems he's gone from a nobody with one friend to somebody. When they see him, children go out of their way to pat him on the back. One wants to share a biscuit they've saved from home. It must have been precious to have lasted as long as it has. He politely declines. He doesn't quite know what to make of it, and he's beginning to feel better.

"Don't you want to know my name?" she says.

Should he admit that he's the baby?

"What is it?"

"Marika Anna Ginova. I have no family that I care for and I'm probably the only kid here who wants to leave. I never want to step foot in this country again if I can help it. I'm ten years old and this is my lucky stone that I found a couple of years ago at a creek next to my village. I'm the best marksman you've ever seen."

"Oh yeah? My friend Lazo and I are really good. I used to hit birds with stones to catch them for dinner."

"I could do that when I was four. I once hit my cousin in the head. See that tree over there? That's how far away he was." She points out a distance of over one hundred feet. He's doubtful.

"He beat me up afterwards but it was worth it," she says. "You don't believe me, do you?"

"Well, it's just it's a long way, that's all."

"See the white flower hanging off the tree there, next to the barn. I'll hit it."

Dimitri wonders where Lazo is to witness what seems an incredible feat, and he searches the yard that is filling with more children, but his friend is nowhere to be seen. Marika squints at the stone, then draws her arm back as far as she can. He doesn't see the stone fly through the air but when he looks for the flower it's gone. Marika turns and runs off to find her stone, leaving Dimitri with his mouth agape. He wonders how she'll manage to find it.

Then a long shrill whistle blows and he jumps. It reminds

him of Vesna and it makes him shudder. Olga again blows the whistle and calls the children together to eat. Facing the mush floating in the congealed milk makes him feel dizzy and nauseous but he forces it down.

Names are called out. He assumes it's for chores.

"Dimitri Filipidis!" yells a voice. Heads swivel to look at him and he catches sight of Marika's grin. She seems smug. Lazo doesn't look up from his bowl and Dafina is lying on the straw under a blanket.

"Yes?" He jumps up and is ready for his punishment of extra chores.

A young woman with kind eyes walks over to him and places her hand on his shoulder. "We have a message for you. From your mother."

"From Majka?" His hopes soar.

"She says you have a baby brother. She asked that you get this."

She hands him a jumper. He clutches it and holds it to his face. It smells of home and he hides his tears in it. Pulling the jumper over his head he hears his mother's voice, her laugh and smell – her special smell – garlic.

"How?" he asks. "Where is she?"

But she doesn't hear him as the woman calls out other children's names, and many receive items from home. Many cry when they get nothing.

"All right, children. We're staying here for the rest of the day. So, go outside and play while it's still light. But don't go too far away."

Instead of jumping, laughing and running into the yard, most of the older children wander aimlessly, stunned and bewildered. They miss their families; the ones who receive a parcel miss them all the more.

Dimitri searches for Lazo and finds him seated cross-legged on the straw by himself.

"Did you hear? I have a baby brother. Majka is alive and somehow she found me."

"That's nice." With his elbows leaning on each leg, Lazo runs some straw through his hands.

"What are you doing?"

"Nothing." He winds the length of straw around his finger until it turns blue.

"Are you going to come out?"

"What for?"

"To play."

"I don't feel like it."

"Are you sick?"

"Just leave me alone."

The words hang between them in the stillness of the empty barn. The sounds of play from children outside, waft in. Dimitri moves from one foot to the other, not knowing what to do or say. He stares at the top of his friend's unruly black hair and wonders why he says nothing about the fight. "All right," he says confused, glimpsing Lazo's wet face.

27

The Grumpy Receptionist

The waiting room is full of old people and small children. Jim stares at the television screen and the animated morning show host. He hates to wait and he hates queues – there's something about them that he can't bear. He picks up a magazine then puts it down. The morning show host says something about children drowning in the Mediterranean. He shudders and wants to turn it off but the remote control is with the grumpy receptionist, Tara. He looks at his watch – it's ten fifty – then glares at the large woman. Chewing gum with her mouth open, she's telling some poor sod the doctor will see him when it's his turn. Jim wonders why these people never seem to keep their end of the bargain. You make an appointment and when you get there on time they're never ready. He taps his walking stick on the floor, then notices everyone's stares, and stops.

Agitated, he tries to work his mind to think of something

else, to find anything to distract him from the monotony of waiting. He thinks unhappily about the water and the waste that gurgled down the plug hole. At least Helen will be pleased.

Looking at his watch again, he pulls himself up to talk to Tara. He's sure she knows he's standing in front of her, yet she's intent on making herself look busy, fingers flying across the keyboard. He clears his throat and at last she peers at him over her specs, raising her eyebrows as if to say, what now?

"How long do you think the doctor will be? I've been waiting for nearly an hour."

Tara clucks her tongue and glances at the computer before chewing vigorously on her gum.

"I'm sorry, but he's running late. There are two more in front of you. You should be thankful that he can see you at all today. I did squeeze you in. Would you prefer to come back tomorrow?"

Fat cow, he thinks. "Thank you, Tara, for being so patient with an old man. I think I'll stay." Turning his back on her, he mumbles, "I'll be buggered if I'll come back tomorrow. You're lucky you got me here."

His muttering raises heads in the waiting room, and he settles back into his seat as far away as he can from everyone else.

"Why don't you play with this?" a young mother says to her toddler. The child, sucking her thumb, decides to stand in front of Jim instead. Holding her doll, she stares at him, then coughs. He squirms in his seat while trying to watch the television. But he can't help but glance at the child. She doesn't move. He looks away. There, he thinks, you won the staring competition. She sneezes and a bubble of snot hangs from her nose. He's relieved when the mother comes to distract the child with something else. From the corner of his eye, she continues to cough and stare at him. He begins to fidget. A flash of a memory of another child coughing hard disturbs him. His hands clammy, he begins to sweat.

Don't be stupid, he tells himself. It's just hot in here. He's parched, that's all. Hauling himself off the chair he reaches for a plastic cup to get a drink from the water cooler, then everything goes black.

28

The Girl and the Stone

Standing in the doorway of the barn, Dimitri's gaze drifts across the yard. A group of small children forage for sticks to draw pictures with in the dirt. Some chase each other and their playful screams and yells temporarily push away their feelings of homesickness and fear. The older girls sit in twos and threes along a heavy wooden fence, which separates them from a steep slope of trees not quite thick enough to hide glimpses of villages in the valley far below.

Grim clouds darken the woods surrounding the small mountain village of unkempt stone cottages. The air grows colder and Dimitri is glad of his mother's jumper under his jacket. She must have known winter was not over.

He wonders what to do about Lazo. A mother tries to shoo him out but not before he hears her whisper to another, "I don't know what's wrong with that one. He refuses to go out." They stare at Lazo sitting alone, in the spot where Dimitri had left him, fiddling with a piece of straw.

"What did you think?" The voice is Marika's and her welcoming wide smile makes him feel better. She's alone, throwing her stone in the air.

"You're quite good," he says.

"Quite good? I'm actually the best."

"Maybe for a girl," he says, grinning.

They spend the rest of the afternoon sitting on the fence away from the others, talking. Like Dimitri, Marika is undersized. Her nose sticks out of shallow cheeks, but the intensity of her blue eyes is what he stares at when she speaks.

Besides their language, they have a lot in common. She'd grown up in a village just four kilometres northeast from his. Her tiny village was nestled hard against the mountains with a view to the valley. Like Dimitri, her early years were grim. Food was scarce. Dimitri tells her about his family, how much they mean to him and his desperation to get home. But he learns it's not the same for her.

"Have you heard of Mirka Ginova? Or maybe you've heard her alias, Irini Gini?" she asks.

"Yeah. She's famous. My mother used to talk about her all the time, how she tried to save the Macedonians and got executed for it."

"Well, she's my aunt," she says smugly. "She was my father's sister. She would have looked after me when I was a baby, but she was fighting the Germans."

"I never heard of a girl fighting in a war."

"Well, she did!" Marika jumps off the fence and faces him, fists clenched. "A lot fought the Germans. Girls can fight, you know." Dimitri is alarmed by the change in her and realises rage bubbles just beneath the surface. "Wanna see how?"

"Ah, no!" Dimitri says, staying where he is on the fence. He has no doubt she can use her fists. "Did your father die in the war too?" He's relieved when she jumps back onto the fence.

"I don't know." Marika flips the stone over and over in her hands. Her father, she learnt from her great-uncle, was tall and handsome with fair hair – he was shot and for what reason, no-one knew. She has no knowledge of her mother, but imagines she was like her, with dark hair and blue eyes, skin as white as snow and a kind smile.

"Wanna see something?" Her hand ducks down the front of her shirt and she pulls something from its hiding spot. It's a gold pendant. On the back is written, Marika Ginova.

"It's my mother's. I was named after her. When I was small I found it in a box under my great-aunt's bed but she caught me and beat me. But before I left, I found it and stole it." She fingers it tenderly. "It's mine anyway."

"Why do you have a middle name?" Dimitri asks.

"My great-uncle used to call me Anna. He liked it better than Marika." She stares into the distance and he knows she's somewhere else – back in her village.

They'd been talking so much that Dimitri hadn't noticed Lazo leaning in the doorway of the barn. When he finally sees him, Lazo scowls, then turns on his heel and walks back inside.

Dimitri tells her about Lazo and how he'd met him at school. Glancing nervously toward the barn, a part of him hopes Lazo comes out, but another part doesn't want to share this girl's friendship. He knows he should have left her and joined Lazo.

"We arrived yesterday, a few hours before you," Marika says. "I saw you coming up the hill. Your face seemed familiar."

"Did it?" Dimitri's cheeks grow hot.

"I was wracking my brains trying to remember where I'd seen you before. Then I remembered. I thought you tried to steal my stone."

His face burning, Dimitri glances at the barn door, willing Lazo to come out to save him. Has this girl feigned friendship only to humiliate him?

"Oh?" is all he can say.

"Yes. It was at the doctor's. You were on your mother's lap holding my stone."

Dimitri busies himself by picking at a large scab on his knee.

"Then you gave it back to me. I think I was a bit mean to you at the time. I thought it was gone forever, but you actually gave it back. I wanted to say thank you."

She grins and it shocks him that she's known all along.

"It was just about the nicest thing anyone has ever done for me." She tilts her face back and closes her eyes, as if she's waiting for a ray of the sun's warmth. She's not in the least bit interested in his reaction. Before he can think of anything to say, she suddenly jumps down from the fence and pockets her perfect stone.

"See you later," she says and wanders off.

***

Alone with his thoughts, he feels a tap on his leg. Two grubby children stand next to him. They're probably not more than five or six years old but it's hard to tell in a place where many children are small; where the size of the child depends on the amount of food your family could get. In a time of war there's no other difference. Their large, frightened eyes peer up at him. Covered in bruises and cuts they're the same as everyone else. One stretches his arm toward him and gently touches his hand with deformed fingers, making Dimitri want to recoil.

"Thank you," the child says, before running off, leaving Dimitri bewildered. Other children whisper and smile as he passes. Maybe Marika is right, he thinks. Maybe that boy deserved it. But he's still wondering about his punishment. Surely it's still to come.

He wants to talk to Lazo but can't find him and decides to look for Dafina instead.

In another barn he scans a sea of sick faces until his eyes land on her. She smiles weakly, then waves.
"What are you doing here?" he says.

"Nothing. They don't like my cough and want me to rest. It's been nothing but trouble for everyone. They won't even let me go outside with you and Lazo."

She looks so sad that he decides not to tell her about Lazo.

168

"It's not your fault you've got a bad cough. They just want to help. They're not as bad as we thought. At least they haven't eaten us like the soldiers told us."

"Not yet," Dafina says. "Still, I feel really bad about getting us caught."

"Forget it."

"I just want to go home. I want my own bed; my mother to cuddle me; her food. I want my dog. If it wasn't for me we'd be back." Tears well in her round sunken eyes.

He looks at her fiercely. "Stop it. Promise me that you'll forget it. There's no hard feelings. Really. Sooner or later we'd have ended up here. Our village is probably gone. That life has gone."

She nods before the coughs wrack her small body. The realisation of what he's said fills him with a fear that touches his heart like a piercing needle. His old life has truly gone and he's filled with dread.

The whistle blows and one of the women calls out, "Dinner time!"

Dafina and Dimitri line up for a small piece of dry bread. When Dimitri sees the boy, prickles of sweat break out across his back. The boy's face is puffed purple and red. One eye is so swollen that he can barely see out of it. Dimitri stares; he's done that. Ignoring Dafina's hand trying to pull him back, he walks over to the boy. He holds out his hand, but the boy shrinks back in fear as if Dimitri is a monster.

"I'm really sorry," Dimitri murmurs.

The boy blinks in relief and stares at the suspended hand.

The moment drags. The other children watch and wait in rigid silence.

The sound of the whistle interrupts. The boy blinks again and Dimitri suddenly lets out the breath he's been holding. Children begin swarming around them and Dimitri lets Dafina pull on his outstretched arm to lead him away.

***

Cross-legged on the floor by himself, Lazo chews on a piece of dry bread, spitting out stones into the dirt. He barely looks up as Dimitri and Dafina sit next to him. Marika, on the other side of the barn, laughs at something someone has said.

"There are more bits of stone and dirt in this than flour," Dafina sniggers. "I suppose you both had a good time playing in the sunshine while I was cooped up in that dingy barn?"

Lazo and Dimitri chew on their bread.

Dafina looks from one to the other, narrowing her eyes. "What's going on?" She frowns and stares at them. "Lazo?"

"Nothing."

"Yeah, nothing," Dimitri says. "You didn't miss much."

"Something's going on. You're too quiet."

Dimitri feels her gaze as he brushes an ant from his bread. Then he watches it scurrying around, hopeful for a crumb; too precious for even a child to waste.

"Well?" she says, before breaking into a coughing fit.

Dimitri's afternoon with Marika has faded away. The whistle pierces the barn and the children quieten.

"Attention everyone. We will be leaving later tonight," Olga says.

Lazo straightens, interested.

"Children, it will be a harder walk so you must listen very carefully to the mothers and do everything they tell you. Try to sleep now."

The lanterns are switched off and they lay where they've eaten; Lazo, Dimitri and Dafina next to each other. After the usual coughs, whispers and crying have stopped, Dimitri lies awake. After worrying about the boy he hurt, his worry turns to Lazo and he wrestles with a new guilt. He stares into his friend's hunched back and wonders what he's said and done to cause his hurt. Maybe he's disgusted with him for beating the boy. They haven't talked about it. The thought bounces around his head until he wears it out. Then he settles on only one thing – abandoning Lazo for his new friend, Marika.

An owl hoots outside. A cool wind whips up and blows in between the cracks of the barn to land on his bare legs, which he brings up to his chest. He's glad of his mother's jumper. Then he hears something else.

"Are you crying?" Dimitri whispers to Lazo.

He hears him sigh. "No!" Lazo sniffs.

"What's wrong?"

"Nothing. Go to sleep," Lazo whispers.

"I'm sorry about before," he says, not knowing what 'before' might mean but hoping his words will make everything right with his friend.

Lazo turns around and looks at Dimitri, his elbow under his head. "It's not that."

"What then?"

"I'm just sad, that's all. I'm allowed to miss my parents and my sister. I thought someone would know her; that she'd be here. No-one knows anything. At least you know your mother is alive."

Lazo rolls over, facing away from him. Dimitri puts his hand on Lazo's arm, hoping it might help. He feels ashamed he's given little thought to Lazo's older sister before.

"I'm glad you've got a baby brother," Lazo whispers.

"Me too."

Finally, they fall asleep, while they can.

29

Are Energy Efficient Lights Cheaper?

Stale peppermint wafts over him. Has he died? Is Anna here? Squinting, all Jim sees is grumpy Tara chewing gum, peering above him along with the rest of the waiting room. Closing his eyes, he hopes they'll all bugger off. Something heavy is thrown across him.

"Are you right?" asks a woman. Of course he's not right, he thinks. If he was, would he be on the ground? Some people are just plain stupid.

"Call an ambulance."

"Hey, I need that jacket. Tara, why don't you get a blanket to put on him instead?"

What he thought was a blanket is whipped off him, replaced by a real blanket, which is hotter and heavier.

"Is there a cushion?"

"How about a seat cushion? Will that do?"

Someone gently lifts his head then lowers it to sink into

a soft warmth, until he realises that someone's arse has been sitting on it. He tries to move but can't.

"That's one way to get in to see the doc before me. I might try fainting too!" A croaky voice nervously laughs.

"Don't be stupid."

"Where's the doctor? Why hasn't Tara interrupted him? She's useless."

At last, someone agrees with him about the woman.

"Here he is."

"Everyone sit down and give this man some air," Tara says.

"Jim! Jim, can you hear me?" Reckoning the voice belongs to the doctor, Jim opens his eyes and tries to sit up, but can't.

"We can't move him so just give him space please."

"Go back to your seats!" Tara growls.

Staring at the light on the ceiling, a cobweb hangs to the side and he wonders whether Tara knows.

He turns off from listening to the muffled voices as he wonders about the light. Is it one of those newfangled energy efficient lights? It's coldly bright and he's curious to ask if it saves as much money as they say. Perhaps he should buy one and find out.

The frowning doctor peers at him moving his lips.

Speak up, man. How can I hear if you whisper? he thinks. Jim's been going to him for years. Helen didn't approve of him because he'd once been a vet. "What's wrong with that?" he'd said to her. "He decided he preferred humans to animals. They don't bite him!" He'd laughed.

"He's a quack," she'd said. He'd laughed hard at her joke and wondered at the time why she didn't think it was funny.

The doc's whispering again.

"What?" he says. Why can't I hear him? Something about the hospital. "I'll be damned if I'll go to hospital," he says. "I've got things to do." But the doc doesn't seem to hear and disappears.

Another busybody in a uniform peers at him as he feels himself being lifted onto a trolley. He squints in the bright sunshine before he's slid into the back of the ambulance.

"What the hell is this thing?" Jim asks the smiling face who puts a mask over his nose and mouth. He tries to lift his hand to wrestle it off, only he can't seem to move it. Something jabs into his arm and he drifts off.

30

Into the Fog

Late into the night, the children are woken. Their crying and complaints go unheeded as they're hustled out of the warmth of the barns and into a grey shroud of fog. Olga and the other mothers urgently whisper instructions and coax the smaller children onto their backs. Chilled air bites them awake and they follow each other two by two in a line out of the tiny village.

Lazo and Dimitri fall into line with Dafina behind them. The thickening fog envelops them, and, with only dim light from a couple of lanterns, the children trudge slowly and in silence. Before long they hear the familiar boom of fighting somewhere far off. But for now they're safe.

"Stop, children," a mother calls out. Halting abruptly, Dafina and another child run into the back of Dimitri, and they huddle together to peer into the darkness.

"What are we waiting for?" Dafina says, jumping on the spot. "I'm freezing." Then she starts coughing.

"I can't feel my hands," says another child.

Nearby, Dimitri hears others crying. Then for no reason they start walking again.

"Watch out. There's a hole in the path," a mother in front of them calls out.

Their eyes search the ground, imagining a huge hole that might swallow them. But the fog is so thick, they cling to the jacket or shirt of the child in front of them, like an anchor.

They come to another halt.

"This is impossible," murmurs one of the women. "We should have waited."

"I know," grumbles another. "I don't know how we're going to get to the forest at this pace."

Dimitri blows warmth onto his hands and thinks of his mother. He wishes she'd made him wear something warmer. Not that he's ungrateful for the jumper but the cold biting his bare legs makes him shiver. He's sure the ground is frozen like his bare feet and wishes for the shoes made of soft hide that his grandfather made for him to wear each winter. His calloused feet sting and ache as he jumps up and down on the spot, hoping to get some feeling back into them before they begin walking again.

Dimitri thinks about his baby brother and wonders what he's like. He doesn't even know his name. He'll teach him how to plant the tomatoes, and how to gather the right wood to start a fire. He imagines playing with him, giving him a piece of bread just baked, telling him stories. But when he thinks about it, he can't think of one good story. He can't tell him about the soldiers, the bombs, the constant growl of hunger or the fear. His mind goes blank. Then he brightens. He can teach him how to skip stones across the river. Sadness tightens in his chest like a bolt and he bites down hard on his bottom lip until he feels the familiar taste of blood in his mouth. It's as if he knows that his brother will never be taught by their father.

The path is better, and the fog begins to lift in patches. The lantern lights ahead and behind are like welcome beacons and the path begins to slope upward out of the protective blanket of fog.

"How long's it been since we left home?" Lazo asks.

Dimitri shrugs. "Maybe four or five days?"

"Is that all? I feel like we've been marching to nowhere for years."

"It's been six days," Dafina says. "One of the mothers told me it's Saturday. Or maybe it's Sunday morning now. We left our village on Monday, remember?"

"It may as well have been years ago," Lazo retorts, rubbing his hands. "When are we going to get there? When are we going to eat? I'm starving. And thirsty."

"Shut up," someone says.

But Lazo's words remind Dimitri that his stomach aches too. That the skin on his lips is cracked and flaky, and that he's tired. So tired. All of his energy is used to put one aching foot in front of the other. If he thinks about his lost family, the hunger and pain, he might give up.

They stop again. Stiff and silent, they listen. The dull drone of an engine somewhere seems uncomfortably close.

"Keep going!" a mother hisses. "Don't stop."

A nudge in the back and he's urged forward. The lantern ahead of them goes out and the sky begins to lighten enough to make out patches of snow lying in the rocks at the edge of the dirt path. Out of the fog, the line of children snaking along the path look exposed on the mountainside and they're a long way from the forest of trees they need to reach to be safe.

"Snuff out the lanterns!" yells Olga. "Keep together. Hurry, before the sun rises."

The drone of an engine grows louder until they see the blackbird high above. Then they see another one. The children stop and cower in fear. Some whimper, others cry.

An explosion of a bomb is heard far below them.

"Hurry! Hurry!" Olga screams.

"Oh God. Please help us," another mother yelps. She's carrying two children on her hips and one clings to her back.

"Let me help," Dimitri says to her. He prises the clinging boy off. "It's okay. You can get on my back." The child's arms circle Dimitri's neck so tightly he has to pull at his tiny hands to loosen his grip.

"What's your name?" Dimitri asks.

"He can't talk. We call him Puppy. Thanks," she says, panting. "Let's get moving. Can you walk faster?"

"Okay, Puppy. Hang on but not too tight," Dimitri says. He jogs to catch up to Lazo and Dafina, his feet screaming with pain from jagged stones on the path.

They hear the roar of another blackbird before they see it. Puppy's arms and legs grip tight like a vice around Dimitri's body and he starts crying.

The pop of machine-gun fire echoes across the mountain. Is it close? He can't tell.

"Keep together now. Hurry!" Olga stands to one side of the path and urges the children past her. "Go as fast as you can. Get to the forest. Quick. Don't stop."

They know instinctively the forest will protect them from being seen and the first children desperately run to its safety. But too many are out in the open when a blackbird swoops past and the first ear-splitting explosion lights the side of the mountain.

31

Olga and the Soldier

Crouched behind a large boulder, with Puppy clinging to him, Dimitri trembles uncontrollably. The air is acrid and his eyes sting as tendrils of black smoke drift over them from the ridge below. The blackbird has disappeared; its roar replaced by screams of terror as children dart in all directions.

"Run into the forest. Go that way. Run!" Olga does her best to direct everyone but her voice cracks hoarsely as she yells.

The other women drag and push screaming children. Their terrified eyes search for escape and safety. "Hurry!"

"Where's my sister? I can't find my sister." A girl staggers around like a drunk, howling. "I have to find my sister!"

"Run! For God's sake, run! There's no time. They're coming back."

A young woman struggles to run with three children clinging to her.

The blackbird's roar echoes around the mountain. Frozen

with fear, Dimitri and Puppy watch the spectacle as if in slow motion, unable to move. He's resigned to it. The sound is unbearably loud. Perhaps this is the end.

In the scrap of grey light, a red and black ladybird lands on Dimitri's hand. Watching it, he imagines it's him, crawling into the boulder's crevice where no-one can see him. Fearless. Fly high above and away. It's good luck, his mother had said, when he showed her the one he'd trapped. Let it go. Back to its family, she'd said. But I'm one too and can fly, he thinks. And he's suddenly calm and the thunder of gunfire and explosions doesn't seem so bad.

The blackbirds roar above them. Another explosion. The ladybird abandons him. The rat-a-tat of gunfire close by. A hand tight around his arm tugging him upwards. He's propelled along and looks back for Puppy, but he's gone. Where is he? Run! Run as fast as you can! The hand is tight. His legs ache. Breathing hard, his chest hurts. He'll go back for Puppy and the ladybird later.

The path gone, they climb rocks. "This way. Keep going. We've got to get to the forest."

The blackbird's back again. *Rat-a-tat.* Keep climbing. Puffing hard, he stops and blinks.

"Come on! This way." It's Marika. Her fingers clench white around his wrist. Letting go, she leaves red marks on his arm. "We've got to catch up to Olga. If we lose her, we're lost." Marika touches his face gently. "Dimitri, come on, we're nearly there," she says softly.

He blinks again. He tries to swallow but can't, his mouth is too dry. He wants to say something but his voice has scuttled down his throat like a field mouse. He nods instead and looks in the direction where Marika points. Olga is climbing over boulders with a young child on her hip. It's Puppy. She pushes two other children in front of her. Even they've given up crying as they hurry away.

"Let's go," Marika says, taking Dimitri's hand. They keep Olga in their sights until she disappears into dense scrub.

The *pop* of rifle fire seems close, but it's hard to tell if the sound is just an echo off the mountain. The sun strains through the grey cloud. Their breath comes out like puffs of smoke as they scramble over boulders like mountain goats until they spy Olga at the top of the ridge. After placing a comforting hand on each child who grips onto part of her skirt, she swings Puppy onto her other hip.

They've almost caught up when Marika suddenly stops. She sees something that Olga has not. Pulling Dimitri behind a nearby bush, she holds her finger to her lips. He crouches with her, confused, until he smells cigarette smoke.

"We have to get to the others," they hear Olga say breathlessly to the children. "It's too dangerous here."

"It is far too dangerous," a deep voice says. A man in a tattered uniform, cigarette in his mouth, points his rifle at the small group. Puppy wails in fright and the two children whimper and cling helplessly behind Olga.

"Oh God!" Olga cries out as she turns around. Dimitri and Marika dare not move.

The soldier flicks the cigarette away with dirty fingers and moves closer. "It's you!" Olga says with a sneer.

"You're lucky it's me and not one of the others," he says.

Dimitri and Marika look at each other, puzzled.

"Move," he says, pointing with his rifle in the direction he wants Olga to go.

"Why don't you give up and come with us? Your brother would be proud."

He sneers and spits at her feet. "My brother is dead to me."

"You were always a coward and a traitor," Olga says, clenching the folds of her filthy dress.

"You're nothing but a Macedonian dog." His eyes narrow and he steps closer.

"These children are part of the evacuation order," she says.

"We know what you Partisans are doing. Do you think we're idiots? You're making them into foot soldiers to further your stupid cause. The sooner you give it up, the better it will be for all of us."

"That's not true. I'm holding a baby for God's sake. How can he be a soldier? And look at these two. They could hardly lift a rifle." He stares at the children and moves closer to peer at the wailing boy still in her arms.

Rocking him, Olga whispers something to Puppy, whose howls lull into a whimper.

"Is it yours?" he asks.

"No," she says, her voice cracking. A beam of sunlight settles on her and she looks like an angel. The soldier steps back to stare at her flushed face, her blue eyes gleaming.

"Put the child down," he commands.

She does what he asks. Puppy whimpers and clings to her skirt, sucking his thumb hard. The other two know not to move, and Olga briefly rests a reassuring hand on each child as if that will protect them all.

The soldier drops his helmet to the ground and moves menacingly toward her. She squares her shoulders and stares at him in defiance.

Marika touches Dimitri's arm and gestures to the approaching blackbird then to the bits of rock lying around them. There are two the size of their fists. He nods his understanding and they each pick one up. The roughness feels good in Dimitri's hand. Perhaps they have a chance.

The soldier is side on to them and he touches Olga's chin. She flinches. He says something to her that they can't hear. They watch him throw back his head and the roar of the plane overhead drowns out his laugh. Olga takes a step backward.

She bends to say something to the children and they run into the forest. "Follow the path and I'll catch up to you soon," they hear her call out.

The soldier begins to undo his belt.

Before Dimitri can understand what's happened, Marika has thrown her rock. It hits the soldier on the side of the head, and in the time he takes turning to see where the rock has come from, Dimitri has thrown his. His aim is good and it strikes the soldier in the middle of his forehead. Then another smaller one hits him. Dimitri knows it's Marika's special stone. Eyes glazed, the soldier crumples, hitting his head hard on the ground behind him.

Kneeling down next to the soldier, Olga looks wildly around as Marika and Dimitri run toward her. Dimitri stares at the blood on the man's face. Close up, he's young; his face peaceful and calm. Marika turns away to search for her stone, which has fallen next to his large mud-splattered boots. Pocketing it, she watches the sky for the plane coming toward them.

"Oh God," Olga says, crossing herself. She glances at the plane then back to them.

"We just wanted to stop him." Marika looks aghast. "Is … is he dead?"

The noise of the plane's engine draws closer and they all look skyward.

"He's knocked out." Olga is already on her feet. "Let's go. It'll be worse if they find us here," she says, pulling them both away. Something whizzes overhead and a shell falls nearby propelling them to run from the wall of heat and into the cover of the forest.

They blindly run following a worn path until they reach the other three children cowering behind a tree. Dimitri and Marika holding the hands of the others continue on as quickly as they can, leaving the deafening noise and the stench of smoke behind them.

32

The Hospital

"Dad! Dad," a voice softly calls. "Dad, it's me, Helen, can you hear me?"

"Of course I can hear you." He opens his eyes to stare at his daughter's tearful face.

"Thank God! You've given me such a fright," she says, holding his hand. "How are you feeling?"

"I'm all right. Where am I?"

"You're in hospital. You had some sort of turn and they're running a few tests."

He tries to sit up but a mask clings to his face, pinching his cheek. "How do I get this confounded thing off?"

"Dad, I think you have to stay still. I'll get the nurse and find out if we can get the mask off you. Okay?"

He wonders what the time is. He's hungry. He's in a cubicle cordoned off by curtains. Nothing to look at and nothing to do.

"Hello there, how are you feeling?" the nurse says, picking up his wrist and slipping on a cuff. "Just going to take your blood pressure now."

"Do you know what's wrong?" Helen's voice is urgent. Only he can't seem to see her. There she is, behind the nurse. Why doesn't the girl come closer? He can't hear what's going on.

"The results of your tests should be back shortly."

"Good," says Helen. "Dad, it won't be too long and we'll get you out of here."

"Oh, it might be a while yet," the nurse says, frowning. "Are you comfortable?"

"Uh," he mutters.

"He wants the mask off," Helen says. "Do you think it can come off now?" That's her sweet voice. He knows what she's like. She can get what she wants when she wants to. He almost feels sorry for the nurse. His daughter can be vicious like a dog with a bone. He smiles to himself. That's my girl. She'll sort this lot out, he thinks.

"It helps his breathing. Let's keep it on until the doctor comes in, shall we?" Damn, the nurse has won. Come on, Helen. Get stuck into her. Get this mask off.

But Helen is too busy smiling at the nurse and now she's on her phone. Doesn't she know she can't use her phone? He blinks. Why can't he speak? Is it that he can't be bothered? Yes, that's it, he can't be bothered and he closes his stinging eyes.

He jolts awake when he hears a voice, "Mr Philips, Mr Philips."

"Uh."

"I'm Doctor Petersen. The tests are back now and it looks like you've had a transient ischaemic attack. It's like a stroke and has similar signs."

"Oh God!" Helen exclaims. "Will he be all right? Will he speak? Is he paralysed?"

"It's very mild. There's no reason why he shouldn't make a full recovery," the doctor says.

"When can I get out of here?" Jim says, surprising himself.

"We'd like to keep you in here overnight for observation."

Is now the time to mention the fall in the bath? He thinks better of it. They might keep him even longer.

"We've organised a bed for you," the doctor says.

"I'm a bit hungry. Any chance of something to eat?"

"I'll arrange to get you some sandwiches," the nurse says.

Before long, he's in a ward with Helen at his side.

"I hate these places," he says, wolfing down the sandwiches.

"Me too," Helen says, squeezing his hand.

It reminds him of the hours spent there with Anna.

"Hopefully, you can go home tomorrow. That is, if you behave yourself." She smiles. "I'm going to get something to eat and then I'll come back."

"Why don't you have one of my sandwiches? They're quite nice, love." Jim holds out a withered corner.

"It's okay, Dad. You need to eat them. I won't be long."

"Look, why don't you go home? There's no need for you to hang around here all day."

"No, Dad! I'm staying."

He's actually thankful.

"Off you go then. Stubborn as usual. Just like your mother," he mutters, smiling.

"Or maybe stubborn like you," she says, grinning back.

He's alone in the ward with a nice big window where he can admire the city skyline above the trees. The sky darkens with heavy clouds. He turns on the television but merely stares at the pictures; no sound. A stroke. It's not that bad, they say. Still, it could have been worse. They'll up his medication now. Add it to the list.

"Mr Philips, would you like a cup of tea?" a voice asks. A young woman with a smiling face holds his tray.

"No thanks, love."

"You know it's not really PC to say that," she mutters as she sweeps out of the room.

"What the hell is she talking about?"

"Time to check you again," the nurse says, swinging the curtain around him, blocking out the view of the rain that's begun to fall.

She takes his blood pressure and writes down the results.

"Now, it says you have dentures. How would you like to remove them for me?"

He takes them out, hating the feeling of his collapsing mouth.

"What do you want with these?" he tries his best to ask.

"For a clean," she says. "Before you go to sleep."

"It's all right. My daughter will help me," he says, horrified. He's not going to let this woman handle his teeth. She won't clean them properly.

"No, no that's my job," the nurse insists, trying to wrestle them from his hands.

But he's got a tight grip. "No!" he says.

Helen comes in at that moment.

"Help," he implores her. "This woman is stealing my teeth."

The nurse turns red in the face and tries to explain. "His teeth need to be cleaned and he won't let me take them."

Helen looks at him, then at the nurse and sighs. "It's all right, I'll look after it."

The nurse frowns. "Suit yourself. Is he always this cantankerous?"

"Well, no, he isn't. How about you stick to helping people get better and keep your opinions to yourself?" Helen retorts.

"You tell her, love," Jim whispers, holding the dentures tightly in his hand.

The nurse opens the curtains in a huff and leaves.

"Dad. What are you doing? She's only trying to help. And you are cantankerous."

He slips his dentures back into his mouth. "You weren't very nice to her, Helen. She might smother me when you're gone."

"Don't be ridiculous. Now listen, behave yourself, otherwise they won't let you out."

191

"Do you think you could clean my dentures before you go?" He smiles his sweetest smile.

"Do they really need it?"

"What do you think? Don't you clean your teeth each day? The nurse will have a toothbrush and I'll tell you what to do."

"Ugh," she says, rolling her eyes. "If I have to."

33

Dafina and the Toddler

An icy wind whistles between the trees. Grey snowflakes begin to fall and swirl around them as they follow Olga. The sound of gunfire has died down and the blackbirds have gone. Thoughts jumble in Dimitri's head. He's sure he's killed a man. What will Lazo and the others say? The Greek boys won't mess with him after this. His chest swells with pride. He's a Partisan. He's fighting for the cause, even if he's not sure what the cause is.

"Say nothing about this to anyone," Marika's whisper interrupts his thoughts.

"Why?" he says, puffing to keep up with Olga, who is jogging ahead with Puppy on her hip.

"You really are an idiot. We've injured or even killed a soldier. There are spies everywhere and if anyone knows they could tell others. Then they'll be after us."

He hadn't thought about that possibility. He remembers

the stories of the Partisans who killed villagers who had betrayed them. The traitors had been strung up on poles in the village square as a message to everyone. The soldiers who'd marched his father away, executed collaborators. Surely as a Partisan and a killer, they'll be after him and Marika and he resolves never to tell a soul.

They trudge in silence through the forest to reach the shelter of caves set deep into the mountainside where they find the others.

The stench of human excrement hits him first. It's dim with the only light coming from the mouth of the cave, but Dimitri steps gingerly over the exhausted and sleeping mounds of the children who are crammed in everywhere.

"Dimitri!" a voice hisses. "Over here."

He recognises the voice, sees a hand waving and heads towards it.

"Where have you been?" Lazo whispers. Dafina lies slumped next to him and seemingly peaceful.

"I don't know what happened. I, I ... got lost." Dimitri wants to tell Lazo the truth but he can't tell him that he and Marika killed a soldier. He glances around for her, but she's slipped away into the dimness.

"Did you hear what happened?"

"What?" Dimitri asks. How could everyone know already? His heart thumps and he gnaws on his fingernail. Will he go to jail? He glances up and down the cave. Two women who're talking silhouette the cave's entrance. Except for their murmurs and a low sob somewhere near him, it's quiet.

"Some of them were on the mountain path when the bomb fell. We were lucky. We'd just passed through. We thought it was you. I'm glad it wasn't."

Dimitri drops his hand to his side. Absorbing the news, his head begins to hurt.

"Who was it?"

"I don't know."

Weariness spreads across his body. Dimitri sighs and looks for a space to lie down. All he can do is stand in one spot shivering with cold and fear, hands limp at his sides.

"Squeeze in next to Dafina. She's so hot she'll keep you warm," Lazo whispers. Dimitri shuffles then settles next to her and she moans in her sleep. He can't get comfortable and is wide awake.

"Did you get anything to eat or drink?" Dimitri whispers.

"Nah. There's nothing. They've got some water but that's for the sick ones. What I'd do for a sip."

"Yeah, me too." Dimitri leans on his elbow and peers beyond the cave entrance. "It's started snowing." Lazo groans. "It's heavier than before. I'll get some melted snow. We can drink that."

"Do you want me to come with you?"

"Nah. You stay with Dafina."

Dimitri heaves himself up and picks his way between the children. Some are in a fitful sleep while others lie on their backs and stare at the space above them. He stops short of the cave's entrance behind the two women.

"This is all we need," Dimitri hears one of them moan

softly. "Look at it. It's getting heavier. Do we stay until it stops or do we keep going?"

"We've no choice but to keep going. We can't stay here. The soldiers are too close. They could find us anytime." The other voice is Olga's.

He steps back, unsure of what to do.

"But look at them, they're exhausted. There's no food. Some are so weak they haven't the energy to cry anymore. To lose ten of them today is too much to bear. Melena is almost ready to give up and so are the others. Please, Olga, let's stay here for one more day, at least to rest. The soldiers have to give us safe passage. It's been agreed. They can't go against orders."

"Don't you get it. They don't care. If that soldier from my own village didn't, what makes you think any of the others will. He's dead and they'll come looking for us. My mind's made up. At dusk we leave. Now I want you and Effie to collect some water. Make sure each child gets some. It's the only thing we can do for them."

"But..."

Olga puts her hand on the other woman's shoulder. "Comrade, if we stay here another day, it'll be certain death for many of them, either from starvation or thirst or from the soldiers looking for us. We can only get to the border by daybreak if we leave tonight. Now, collect the water, then get some rest. You'll need every ounce of energy for what's to come."

The other woman nods and heads out, leaving Olga staring

after her. Her shoulders slumped, she rubs her neck before pinning back stray bits of her hair.

Dimitri's not sure what he should do. Her words about the soldier echo in his head. He feels sick. Should he tell her that he's sorry? That it wasn't his stone. Shifting the blame takes some of the weight off him but only until doubt comes crashing back. The sight of the soldier crumpling onto the ground swirls around and around in his head and he's forgotten what he'd set out to do.

His thoughts are interrupted by a whispered voice, and he blinks at the shadowy face above him.

"Dimitri, what are you doing standing there?" Olga says. "Go find somewhere to sleep."

"I will." He turns and threads his way back and lies down next to the now sleeping Lazo and Dafina. Using the crook of his arm as a pillow, he fights sleep.

He'd had a stomach ache once and his father had told him to think of something happy. The pain won't be so bad, he'd said. Then, he'd thought about his pet chicken who'd followed him everywhere until it met its end in a pot. He tries again for a happy thought. He pictures Kitty sitting on the step in the sun waiting for him to come home. He remembers her softness under his hand, the sound of her purr as she wound her way around his legs.

Soon his eyes droop as exhaustion sweeps him away to fitful dreams. He's back in the village playing with Kitty and throwing stones at the birds. The soldier is perched like a bird on the branch. He has wings as big as a door and he draws himself up on the branch, ready to swoop. Dimitri runs as fast as he can before the ground falls away from under him. The talons of the soldier bird pierce his skin taking a grip on his shoulders. With his arms and legs flailing around, he's dropped into the mouth of the first chick. He spirals headlong into the gullet of a dark world.

He wakes with a start. Dafina's damp hand reaches out to touch his. He peers toward the front of the cave. The snow has stopped and the dark-blue haze of dusk begins to settle.

Dafina moans, "Water."

"I'll get it," he whispers. He picks his way over the bodies of sleeping children to the mouth of the cave. Olga sleeps against the wall with a coat thrown over her.

Outside he sucks in the cold fresh air and warms his hands with his breath. Popping a lump of snow into his own mouth first, he scoops up a mound and carries it back to Dafina. What little is left in his cupped hands is held to her mouth and she sucks it noisily. Children are being woken. Some begin to cry. Others stretch and yawn, complaining of hunger and cold.

"How are you feeling?" The voice behind him makes him jump. It's Olga.

"I'm feeling better," Dafina says. "Are we going soon?" She sits up straight and her eyes glisten. Olga reaches down to touch her forehead.

"Yes. Get ready." Olga moves on to prod more children awake. "We're going." She checks on each child, barking orders for the women to carry the sickest and the youngest.

Lazo stretches and yawns. "Are you sure you're better?"

"Yes, of course I am." Dafina frowns then smiles when she notices Dimitri. "And where have you been? I was worried sick."

She hugs him tight and he hugs her back. It makes him feel better.

***

The mountain path is even steeper than before. At least the sky is clear and the moon helps light their way. It's not as cold as they expected. Some of the day's snow has already melted, leaving behind ridges of mud. Rivulets of water course between the rocks. The children slosh through the mud in the dark – one frozen bare foot in front of the other. The women are weary and frightened for their charges. But they push on. "The border is not far and the soldiers are gone," they tell the children. "We're nearly there."

A woman begins to hum. Then another. Soon they're singing quietly and some of the children join in. It's a song from home. A lullaby for babies. The children remember and for a short time they forget their tiredness, hunger and pain.

Dimitri sings too. But Dafina can't. She can barely walk. Her breathing is laboured and coughs wrack her small body. Lazo and Dimitri, on either side of her, drag her along with them. But the going is slow and others pass them.

"We're going to pick you up," Dimitri says after a while.

"No, I can walk," she protests.

"It'll be quicker. Anyway, you're only a bag of bones so you'll be light," Lazo says, grinning.

"Very funny. Are you sure?"

"Yeah, it's nothing for us," Dimitri says.

"Well, only for a little bit. Until I get my breath back." She puts an arm around each boy's shoulder. With their hands joined, the boys make a seat and slowly and awkwardly they walk sideways like crabs.

"I feel like a queen," she giggles, before she breaks out into a weak cough.

When the path widens, others pass them until it becomes even steeper and rockier. The boys puff hard as they navigate around large boulders. Some children ahead of them are on all fours scrambling along. Lazo stumbles and they nearly drop Dafina.

"Leave me," she wheezes. "It's too hard." They stop and she stands unsteadily. "You go ahead; I'll be all right."

Dimitri can hear her attempts to suck in the air. "We'll stop just for a minute. Okay?"

"Thanks." She sits on a large boulder to the side of the path. "I just need a bit more of a rest. You go on. I'll catch up."

"No. We're not leaving you." Lazo's voice cracks. "We can carry you."

"You can't. It's too steep. You nearly dropped me before."

More children pass them.

"I'll get someone to carry you," Dimitri says. "Someone bigger than us. It'll be all right, you'll see. It's not far now." He doesn't know why he says that. He hasn't a clue how far they have to go. It seems as if the mountain goes on forever.

He hates it. He looks up but can't see anything. The sky is dark; even the moon has abandoned them.

"Stay here. I'm going to get help," Dimitri says.

He pushes past children until he finds one of the women. He remembers her name is Menka; that she is nice and had played with the children back at the last village.

"Please," he puffs, "my friend can't go on. Can you or someone else carry her?"

Menka stops. She has two toddlers in her arms already.

"Where is your friend?" she says.

"Up there." He points.

He leads her to Dafina who is lying on the ground, curled up tight to keep warm.

Putting the sleeping toddlers down, Menka bends and whispers something to Dafina. The toddlers begin to wail their protest as they cling onto her legs. "If I carry your friend, do you boys think you can carry these two?"

"Yes," they say and reach out for a child each.

Menka murmurs something to Dafina, then hoists her over her shoulder. She's a powerfully built woman but even she is struggling to carry her. Children have been stepping around them and now they re-join the throng on the path. Lazo and Dimitri concentrate on carrying the toddlers, whose crying turns into whimpers. It becomes easier to walk and the path widens again. There's barely a tree the higher they go. "Just a little more to go," they're told. "It won't be long."

Dimitri knows it's a lie. It will be a long time. It already feels like a lifetime ago since he was with his mother and his grandfather, who told him the same thing. They all lie.

"Hey!" Lazo says. He's running after his toddler and picks him up.

Dimitri feels the deadweight of his charge slumped asleep on his shoulders. He tries to ignore his aching back and stinging feet; the gnawing pain in his empty stomach. His thoughts drift. He can barely remember what his father looks like. Does he have a moustache? What colour are his eyes? He's dismayed that he can't seem to remember his face. His mother's face is fading too. Olga was right – she is now his new mother.

After a while, the toddler on his back squirms to get down. He holds his hand to keep him from straying but the toddler has other ideas as he pulls away to get to Menka. Muttering something that Dimitri can't understand, he holds his hand tightly and forces him back in the right direction. They stop and the children bunch together to keep warm.

"We will rest here for a while," Olga calls out. The women drop their charges and bags onto the ground and rub their aching backs. Dafina, he sees, is sitting next to Menka with her arms wrapped around her legs, chin resting on her knees.

"The next part of our journey will be very difficult. Children, you must do exactly as the mothers tell you. There's hardly any light so you'll need to be very careful. There'll be mothers helping you but you must concentrate on where you walk and listen very carefully. May God go with us all," Olga says.

The rest over, they're soon up on their feet. They walk on, climbing higher and higher until the path narrows so much they have to stop. One woman gets them to line up in single file. Menka stands like a guard, directing the children to walk one by one across what seems to be a narrow ledge. Dafina has already gone ahead.

"Now it's your turn," Menka says. "You'll be all right. Hold onto the rope railing along the rock face there and follow the lantern's light. Take your time. There's no rush. Be careful," she says, holding the lantern up high. One by one, the children inch slowly along.

"It's best if you put him on your back," Menka tells Dimitri when it's his turn to go. "The path is very narrow. Be very careful and take your time." She pats him gently on the shoulder.

As Dimitri bends to pick him up, the toddler wriggles out of his grasp, slipping past Menka before she can grab him.

"Come back," she gasps as her light follows him disappearing into the darkness.

"Oh my God, oh my God!" she screams. "He's gone over!"

"Stop, children!" barks Olga as she rushes past Dimitri, who's standing frozen in shock. They peer down into the darkness. The light from the lantern arches across the narrow path, then nothing.

"Shh," another woman says, "I can hear something." All ears listen for the toddler. But the only thing they hear is the murmuring of children who have already crossed the ledge. Behind Dimitri are five children and three women.

"It's all my fault," Dimitri sniffs. "I'll climb down to get him."

"No, Dimitri, you can't, it's a sheer drop," Olga says quietly, putting her arm around his shoulder.

Menka is sobbing. "It's my fault. That poor, poor child. Oh God. I can't do this, Olga. I just can't." Then she wails and beats her head with her fists.

"Pull yourself together!" Olga commands, shaking her by the shoulders. "It's nobody's fault. It was an accident. There's nothing you could have done. You have to keep going. We all do. Let's go!"

Dimitri swallows and looks out into the darkness. The toddler was his responsibility. He feels numb. Olga's gentle hand on his back guides him to the beginning of the ledge.

"Come on, now. Walk carefully."

Clinging to the rope, he no longer cares what happens. He doesn't want to go on, but somehow he does. All he thinks about is the toddler whose name he never knew. He wishes for the warmth of his hand, his body on his back. But no amount of wishing ever gives him what he wants.

34

The Border

A darkness descends on Dimitri. He doesn't hear Lazo or
Dafina calling him. He doesn't notice Puppy tugging on his
sleeve. He doesn't notice the sun rising or feel the pain of his
feet anymore. He feels as if he's in a black hole. Olga takes his
hand and leads him to a mossy patch under a tree and there
he collapses into a dreamless sleep.

Stirring, he keeps his eyes clenched shut. Amongst the
usual waking moans and crying of the children, there are
urgent whispers from unfamiliar voices. He senses excitement
in the air, tempting him out of the darkness. But if his eyes
remain closed he'll be protected from what's going on around
him. If he can't see, bad things can't happen. His worries
are even worse than before. He stops himself from thinking
about what's occurred and what's next. Instead, he forces
himself to think only of now.

Stretching his blistered and scratched feet, he feels around.

He pulls at a plant with his bare toes and the pain wakes him. Under his head is his jacket, although he has no memory of putting it there. He realises too that he's no longer cold. He sees red through his eyelids and he guesses the sun is shining brightly. Then he hears a child's laugh and another's giggle amongst the crying. But what opens his eyes is the smell.

It's sweet and reminds him of something. Something from home. He can't pinpoint what. A blue sky greets him and he rubs his stinging eyes. They're in a field of white and yellow flowers and for a minute he wonders if he's in a dream. They're like the ones outside his village. Could he be home?

"You're awake." Lazo peers at him.

He blinks the grit away. Next to Lazo is Dafina. She's smiling. "Are you all right? Look where we are."

Children are everywhere, many more than before. The smaller ones are running around.

"Where are we?" Dimitri scratches his head.

Marika has two children jumping on her. She's smiling and he wonders why she looks so happy.

"We're at the top of the world. Well not at the real top but it feels like it." Dafina pushes a piece of bread into his hand. "We saved this for you."

"We're at the summit. Only a few kilometres from the border," Lazo explains. "We joined up with another group of children who were already here."

"But where did this come from?" Dimitri stares at the bread, hardly believing it's real. His fingers feel its freshness.

He brings it to his mouth, sinking his teeth into it. It's like a cloud.

"It's good isn't it? No stones or dirt in it." They watch him eat.

"Oh, there's this too." Lazo hands him a tin cup of milk.

"Is this a dream?" Dimitri asks.

Dafina laughs. "I hope not. I think things are going to be better now."

"Don't say that. The evil eye might turn on us," Lazo says.

Dimitri gulps the milk and runs his tongue around his lips. A small square of bread and half a cup of milk aren't much but they're enough to make him feel better.

"Where did it come from?"

"Some villagers snuck across the border and brought it early this morning," Lazo says.

"Isn't this a beautiful place?" Dafina hasn't coughed since Dimitri woke up and her eyes sparkle for the first time since he's met her.

"Yes it is."

He sits amongst the flowers and watches Olga. Her face is tired and drawn but she manages a smile when she bends to speak to two girls. She glides through the sea of children toward them.

"How are you feeling, Dafina?"

"I'm better. I feel much better." Olga touches Dafina's forehead. Then bends to look at Lazo.

"I see you've finished your bread and milk, Lazo." She smiles.

"How did you know?"

"There's a little on your top lip for later." Lazo quickly licks the remnant away.

"And you, Dimitri? How are you?" She touches the top of his head and at that moment he feels nothing. And he thinks that's a good thing.

***

"Stay here and rest," Olga commands her group.

It's still daylight and they've walked the few remaining kilometres towards the border. There's a hum of excitement and anticipation. Many of the children don't understand what a border is. Some think it's a wall in the middle of the forest, which is where they find themselves. The trees are tall and smell of pine. The milk and bread have made them hungry for more.

Dimitri, Dafina and Lazo are in a group of older children. Marika is there, too. All waiting, but for what they're not sure.

"My little comrades, you've done well. We're nearly there," Olga says to them. "I'll look for the border guards who'll escort us into our new country. Vangelia, can you come with me?"

Before they have a chance to leave, a group of five men in uniforms emerge from the woods nearby. A red star with five arms is emblazoned on the side of their jackets. Olga smiles in relief.

"Ah, you've found us. Can you escort us across the border?" she asks.

"Hands in the air!" one of the men shouts.

Vangelia and Menka shriek and some of the children begin to cry.

Dimitri feels dizzy with panic. They must know about the soldier and have come looking for him. He cowers behind Lazo. Can he run? He glances at Marika but she seems calm. Maybe he can blame her. It was her stone after all. The thought fills him with guilt. He's nothing more than a coward.

Dafina takes his trembling hand and gently holds it, rubbing her thumb against his. He concentrates on the movement and breathes until the panic subsides. If he stays hidden amongst so many children perhaps they won't find him.

"We're leading these children across the border into Macedonia," Olga says calmly, holding her hands high in the air.

"We have no orders to allow you to cross," the man says. All eyes are on him, waiting for the next move. Sobbing comes from somewhere behind Dimitri. Fear ripples through the group as the women try to keep the children calm but many are agitated.

Olga looks confused. "Please. We've come such a long way. Have some mercy. You can see we have sick and exhausted children."

The guards look at the squirming mass. All are thin and dirty and in rags. Some sniff, some cry. Others stare in fear through sunken eyes.

Another man steps forward and mutters to the leader, who shrugs.

"You'll have to take that path to the village of Dolno Dupeni."

The guards lower their guns and head back into the forest, and everyone breathes a sigh of relief.

"Let's go before they change their minds," Olga yells out.

Over a hill and through a grove they trudge, the dying afternoon sun warming their backs. Constantly glancing behind, Dimitri fully expects the guards to come after him. If only they can get across the border, perhaps he'll be safe, he thinks.

"We're nearly there," Olga calls out.

"She keeps saying that," Lazo grumbles.

But it's not long until they see the first house of a village and then another. The stone houses are clean and neat; the gardens green and lush. A goat bleats a greeting. Then women in aprons and colourful headscarves appear, smiling. It seems the whole village has turned out to greet them.

"We're finally rescued!" Olga cries out. The other women cheer, some kiss the ground, others kiss the grass and the trees.

"We're here!" Menka yells. "I can't believe it." The villagers rush toward them holding out their arms, crying, kissing and hugging any child they can.

"We've been expecting you," says one villager, holding and kissing a baby. "There's room for five hundred in the next village and you're the last group we've been waiting for. Follow us. We'll take you."

One by one, the villagers take the toddlers off the mothers and walk with them to the next village where there are more children.

"Have we crossed the border?" a child asks.

"Of course. You've been in Macedonia since the forest. Didn't you know little one?" a villager says. "Welcome to a place where there is no war."

"We're actually here," Dafina says, slumping against Dimitri, who looks around in awe. It's not a rich village but he's never seen anything like it. It's the closest thing, he thinks, to heaven.

They're given their first hot meal in ages. With so many children, Dimitri becomes separated. Lazo is on the far side of a large barn and he's lost Dafina, but settles himself next to an older boy to scoff the small bowl of hot bean soup as fast as he can.

"Slow down," Olga calls out. "Eat slowly. There's plenty for everyone."

Mountains of freshly baked bread, cheese, olives and cups of milk are handed out. With their stomachs full, they're put to bed on straw in a barn for the first time in a long time at night. Now warm and no longer hungry, his stomach aches and Dimitri can't sleep. He curls up hoping it will go. But it doesn't. He wonders where Lazo is. The boy facing him blows bubbles. He turns over to his other side, to the staring dark eyes of a boy he doesn't know. He rolls instead onto his back and thinks of the field of flowers and forgets the pain in his stomach and in his feet.

***

The next morning, Lazo shakes him awake. "Come on, they're giving us breakfast."

Dimitri leaps up. "More food?" He peers out of the barn. "It's daylight. We didn't march last night."

"You don't have to," Menka says from behind them. "From now on no more blackbirds. Come on."

Lazo and Dimitri run to jostle for a spot in the long line. More fresh bread, milk and cheese await them.

"I think I like this country," Lazo says, grinning.

"Me too."

After breakfast they're allowed outside to play.

"Let's find Dafina," Lazo says.

"Yeah, I haven't seen her since we got here."

They wander around until they see Menka. "Boys, Olga's looking for you. She's in that barn over there."

In the murky light their eyes find their way to Olga, kneeling over a sick child. When she notices them a shadow passes across her face as she hoists herself up and moves over to them. Dimitri feels queasy and his heart sinks. He's convinced it's about the soldier and she's made a decision to give him up to the authorities.

"You wanted to see us?" Lazo says.

She rests her hands on their shoulders. He can't escape, he thinks.

"I'm afraid Dafina's gone," she says, crossing herself.

"Gone?" Lazo frowns. "Gone where? How can she be gone?"

Dimitri breathes a sigh of relief until he thinks about what she's saying.

"Little comrade, she was very, very sick. She passed away into a happier place. I'm very sorry and I know you tried your best."

"But she was better yesterday. She said so. She looked better," Lazo cries out.

With his hands hanging limply by his side, Dimitri can't move.

Lazo sinks to the ground and bawls. He can't stop. Olga holds him close, trying to comfort him. She cries too. Swallowing the lump in this throat, Dimitri takes a deep breath and walks away from his friend. He can't stay here. He's too scared that once he begins to cry, he will never stop.

35

It's Not Cricket

Footsteps echo an urgency as buzzers go off and Jim opens his eyes, forgetting for a moment where he is. A gloomy dawn light spreads over the avenue of English elms outside his window and he admires the hues of green, gold and orange. A flame shoots up from two hot air balloons as they float across the gardens, their occupants oblivious to those trapped in hospital wards below. He no longer has the room to himself. A man with a grey beard now occupies the bed opposite. Pulling himself up to get more comfortable, the man notices Jim and smiles.

"Dobro utro," Jim says, nodding.

Frowning, the man looks uncertain and turns away. Annoyed, Jim grunts. A simple courteous good morning back would be sufficient. That's the trouble these days; simple manners no longer count. Jim liked greeting people with, "Good morning. How are you?" Col Johnson taught him that. "There's lots of things you have to pay for but good manners aren't one of them," Col would say.

Col was a salt-of-the-earth kind of man and had been like a father to Jim. In the early days, as young teenage newlyweds, he and Anna had lived in a boarding house owned by Col and his wife, Molly. The couple took them under their wing when they needed it most. Young and lost in a strange place, Col and Molly taught them just about everything. Where to get a job, what to plant in spring, the best places to buy meat, how to cook, what pub to drink at, and, most importantly, which footy team to barrack for – Richmond, where they first lived.

It was tough working in a textile factory during the day; Anna as a machinist and Jim as an errand boy. They studied at night. He'd been good at figures and studied accounting. They worked hard and there was little time for much else. Sometimes, Col and Molly took them to the beach, and once they spent a weekend at Mount Martha. There'd been no beach where they'd come from and they'd marvelled at the white sand, the red cliffs and the clear blue water.

One day, Molly asked Anna to join the local netball team. She was a natural goal shooter and loved it. When Col invited Jim to join the local cricket team, he was surprised how far he could throw the ball. Jim practised every chance he could get to be selected to the local team. Playing cricket was the one thing that made him feel like he fitted in. He enjoyed the camaraderie of the team. No-one cared where he'd come from. He developed his bowling skills and, after a few years, a scout saw him and invited him to play for the district division. Jimmy the Juggernaut, they'd called him back then; the district's best bowler. He missed playing cricket and Col and Molly. They'd been good friends but both had died within six months of each other nearly forty years ago.

"And how are we feeling this morning?" the nurse calls out. "Just going to do my checks before the doctor comes around. He'll tell you if you can go home today."

"Dobro utro." Jim puts on his best smile.

"Pardon?" the nurse says, frowning. She checks his chart.

"Dobro utro," Jim says again, wondering if the woman is deaf.

"We must have made a mistake. It says here English is your first language," she mutters, walking out of the ward with his chart.

What's got into her? Jim thinks, shaking his head.

Breakfast arrives before he has a chance to get any more worked up. He lifts the lid to find baked beans, soggy scrambled eggs, and bacon. He has a sudden yearning for feta cheese, bean soup and crusty bread. For a brief minute, he recalls the image of his mother at the stove stirring the soup and his hand quivers as he picks over the egg.

The nurse returns, frowning, and he tries to compose himself.

"Jim," she says, looking at him carefully. "How are you feeling this morning?"

"Si aren," Jim replies. Of course he feels fine. He doesn't like the disapproving look on this woman's face.

"Za sho ma pulish," he says. *Stop looking at me.* He squirms under her squinting eyes. It's his turn to frown. Why doesn't she understand what he's saying? He's being rude, he realises. Perhaps he is cantankerous after all. Who wouldn't be when they're stuck in here? He's got to get home. Feed the magpies. Put the buckets out. He's sure the forecast is for rain today.

The nurse busily writes something on his chart. He decides to keep quiet and eat the rest of his breakfast. Helen's right – if he doesn't behave they might not let him out.

The nurse draws the curtain around the man opposite him, giving Jim nothing more to see, and as he plays with the baked beans he can't help the rising feeling of melancholy when he thinks about his mother.

36

Where Is My Family?

It feels odd to be out in the sunshine. No noise of shell-fire; no blackbirds in sight. Every so often the sound of a backfiring vehicle makes Dimitri jump.

There's commotion in the village. Cheers, laughter and shouts of joy seem to come from the town square.

"What's going on?" Dimitri asks one of the mothers.

"Some of the families have managed to get out of their village and have come looking for their children. Go and see, Dimitri. Maybe someone from your family is here."

"Thanks." He runs as fast as he can to the square, hoping that his mother has come. He thinks about his baby brother and what he might look like. Or maybe it's his father. Then he worries. Will he recognise either of them?

"Petro!" a woman shouts. "My beautiful son!"

"Majka! Majka!" a boy yells.

Dimitri jostles to find a place in the crowd.

"I hope my mother's here," a girl says, elbowing him in the ribs.

"Elpida!" another woman yells.

"Here, Majka. I'm here!"

Wistful eyes briefly turn to watch the joy before turning back to search for their loved ones. It pains Dimitri to see Petro and Elpida reunited with their mothers. Then someone else calls out and on it goes. The tearful reunions lift everyone's hopes. Children strain to see if their family is there to greet them.

Surely someone is here, he thinks. The note about his brother and the jumper found him in the mountains, so they must know where he is.

"Vassili! Vassili!" The anguished cries of one mother is heard over and over again. "Vassili, my boy, where are you? Majka's here. Come to Majka," she calls out.

A boy in rags pushes past Dimitri, toward her, muttering that he's Vassili, then turns away disappointed. In desperation the woman climbs onto a chair someone has dragged from their house. Her red eyes scan the crowd, searching for her boy until they rest upon Dimitri. He recognises her. She's from his village and he elbows his way through the crowd, hoping his mother is somewhere near.

"Effie! It's me, Sophia's son!" Dimitri cries out.

"Dimitri! Oh my God!" Smiling with joy, she jumps down.

"Do you know where my parents are?" he asks.

"Is my Majka and Tato here? Have you seen my Majka and Tato?" a small girl asks, tugging at Effie's ragged dress.

Dimitri has never seen the girl, who moves onto another woman, asking the same question before being swallowed by the churn of the crowd.

Effie grabs Dimitri in a hug that squeezes the breath out of him. "Thank God you all made it," she says, letting him go. "You're okay?"

He nods.

"I can't tell you where your family is. I left two days after you. Your mother had a baby boy and she gave me a jumper to give to you if I ever saw you. I was trying to follow your truck when I ran into some partisans who thought children from our village were sent to Bitola. And I gave them the jumper and the message. Did you get it?"

His bottom lip quivers and he nods.

"Maybe your mother made it to Bitola."

His head drops to his chest.

"But it's good to see you. And here you are. Where is Vassili and the others? I've been calling out to every group who arrives. Dimitri, take me to where Vassili is. I can't wait to see him."

His eyes dart to her and then away. "It's only me and Lazo. We're the only ones," Dimitri says softly. He realises only then that he and Lazo are the lone surviving children from their village.

She clenches his arm tightly, her mouth set hard. "What do you mean, Dimitri? You were all on the truck. Where's Vassili?"

Dimitri swallows hard, trying to avoid her eyes. But she

won't let him. She takes his face into her sweaty, trembling hands. "Dimitri, answer me."

"They were ... they were all killed. Vassili too." He gulps in air as she lets him go before crumpling, almost as if in slow motion, in front of him. The noise of the crowd buzzes in his ears and he doesn't know what to do other than watch Vassili's mother pounding the ground with her fists. "Oh God. How could you do this?"

Watching the wailing woman, it occurs to him that it's not fair for either of them. And he drifts away from her and the crowd.

He bites hard on his lip and blinks back tears as he walks, wondering what he should do. He glances at the animals in a field and stops to stare at them. Squatting in the dirt, he busies himself by putting small stones into a pile. Then he looks up and notices Marika watching him. She smiles as she approaches. He doesn't want to speak to her. She reminds him of the soldier. But he can't avoid her and gets up, ready to walk away.

"None of your family here?"

He shakes his head and pulls at the wire fence. Two goats and a donkey raise their heads and stop chewing to stare at them.

"I'd head into those mountains if any of my family turned up here. This is a lot better than what I had at home."
He wants to escape but she keeps talking. He rests his head against the fence, its wire biting into his forehead.

"We could climb over, you know." She grabs the wire hard.

Alarmed, he yelps, "No!" They'd been instructed not to go beyond the fence.

She drops her hand and studies him. "At least the food's better here."

He doesn't argue with her and stares at the mound of stones he's built.

"Why have you been avoiding me?" she says, selecting a stone from the top.

He meets her steely gaze. "Well?" She aims for the donkey and throws the stone hard, hitting the animal on the rump. It scampers away.

"Well?"

Shrugging, he turns away. He's had enough. He decides he doesn't want her friendship. She's a reminder of his past, just as Lazo is. He's better off alone. But he's pulled back with a yank.

"Hey! What's wrong with you? One minute you're my friend and the next you act like you don't know me." She puts her hand self-consciously up to her shorn head. "Is it because I'm a better shot than you?"

He jerks his head up. "It's not that."

"What then?"

"We killed a man. Your stone and mine hit that soldier," he says flatly.

"No we didn't. That's not true. Olga said he was all right, just knocked out."

"I heard her say that he was dead. Any minute someone will come looking for us, to arrest us," he says, walking away.

"No-one's looking for us. We're in another country." He glances back and sees her standing with her arms crossed. He can tell she's angry. "You're still a baby," she calls out. "A big stupid baby."

He picks his way along the village road to the nearby lake. There, the crisp wind cools the stinging heat from his face. Marika's words hurt him. He hates her scorn. He doesn't know why her opinion matters so much to him, but it does.

He wishes he could stop his worries. Sitting down, his hands find a scab on his knee to pick at while he contemplates what to do. The mountains loom over the lake and he wonders where his family could be. He dismisses the notion of going back. He can't go through it again. Then there's the death of the soldier to consider.

Sitting on the grass, his gaze drifts to a group of children chasing each other. Prancing on her toes, a girl pretends to be a horse. Another bleats like a goat while one hee-haws like a mule. They trot, then run and make noises like the animals they pretend to be. They squeal with laughter in their make-believe world and he wishes he could be like them.

A plan forms in his head and he resolves to start again. He's heard they're going to Bitola the next day to be billeted until the end of the war. If no-one from his family is there, he'll start again, make new friends and forget what's happened, and after the war is over, he'll look for his family. But somehow the thought of tomorrow closes in on him like the claws of a wolf trap.

37

Bitola

Dimitri's dreams that night are filled with the image of the soldier. Crows peck at his eyes and his head. Risto lies across him, his boils have burst and pus has leaked and spread like a yellow river across the soldier's tunic. The soldier suddenly sits up with Risto and Dafina. They ask in unison, "Dimitri, come with us. Come with us now."

He wakes in a fright, covered in sweat, sure the dream is real. Rubbing his eyes, he's reassured by the steady breathing of the other boys around him. Lying awake he waits for dawn, hoping he'll feel calmer with the rise of the sun.

After breakfast they're allowed to play while they wait for the trucks to take them to Bitola. It's a habit to check the sky and listen for the drone of a blackbird. But there's nothing. They're a sad group, dressed still in the rags they arrived in; scratching at lice and fleas like dogs. Some stare back across the mountains in the direction from which they've come, wondering what's happening at home.

Dimitri and Lazo wander along the shores of the lake, which seems to go on for ever.

"It's freezing," Dimitri says as he wades into the water.

Lazo runs at Dimitri, splashing him.

"Hey, quit it."

They don't stay in the water for long and sit on the grass in the sun picking at the scabs on their legs. Some of the girls sing a Partisan song. Others run and chase each other.

Picking up a small stone, Dimitri examines it closely. It's almost perfectly round and smooth. He almost feels sorry to let it go. But he pulls himself up and throws it anyway. It skips across the lake, just like his father had taught him, and bounces, two, three, four, five, six times.

"Wow," Lazo says. "You've never done that."

"That's because we only had a river and our stones were never this round."

"I'm going to try."

Lazo's stone bounces four times and they spend the next hour trying to outdo each other.

After a while, they're called and they climb into open-air trucks. Dimitri finds himself seated on a bench next to Marika. Smaller children sit on the floor at their feet. Lazo is on another truck.

"I'm sorry for calling you a baby," Marika whispers.

Dimitri hides his surprise and looks at the waving villagers lined along the side of the road.

"It was really mean," she says.

He joins everyone else in waving back at the smiling line of faces, who can't guess that inside him is a slow crawl of anguish.

"Are we friends?"

He nods and makes a weary effort to smile. He doesn't know why he forgives her. Maybe their secret gives them a common bond. Not even Lazo knows about the soldier.

They jiggle and rumble over the dirt road alongside the lake.

"That's Lake Prespa, little comrades. It's one of the largest lakes in this region," Olga says.

"Can you go into the water, mother?" a small child asks.

"In summer you can go swim in the water and go sailing on a boat."

"I wish I could go on a boat," says another child, and they all imagine what it must be like.

"Did we come from over there?" another older child asks.

Olga points. "That's Albania. And over there is your homeland that you will see again one day soon."

Dimitri gazes at the mountains and wonders when he'll go back.

The convoy soon leaves the shoreline and heads inland. They pass farmers sowing crops. Donkeys loaded down with sacks trudge wearily along the road. People wave and they wave back. Dust billows hiding the trucks behind them.

"Are we going back into the mountains, Mother?" a child asks in panic.

"No, little comrade. We are going over a different mountain to Bitola. We'll be there very soon."

Dimitri hates that Olga says that. *We'll be there soon* and his stomach churns. Hungry and tired, he's been in the truck for too long.

The gears shift and crank as the truck climbs and the noise puts a stop to anymore discussion. They journey through dense forest where the trees are the tallest Dimitri has ever seen. Some of the children are sick and the air soon fills with the stench of that morning's milk and cheese. They stop for a stretch and to relieve themselves in a clearing covered in tiny purple flowers. It's not long until they must climb back into the truck. Some fall asleep to the rocking motion, while others complain of hunger and thirst.

The road hugs the mountain until they hear the squeal of the brakes taking them down the other side. In the distance is the twinkling lights of Bitola, which seems to spread for kilometres. The children stare in awe as they get closer. There are more houses than they've ever seen in their short lives. Trucks, horse-drawn carts and a few cars pass them by.

Finally, they stop and are greeted by smiling women in white uniforms. Children are everywhere as more trucks follow in behind them, unloading more. Olga tells them the women are from the Red Cross.

They've arrived at a large stone building used as an orphanage by the Germans during the war. Here they're given baths for the first time in weeks. Stepping into the murkiness of a large metal tub with two other boys, the hot water helps to soothe Dimitri's nerves. Closing his eyes, he takes himself off to the last time he'd had a bath. His mother splashing water she'd boiled on the stove; the soap in his hand making rainbow bubbles.

"Come on, it's time to get out," a burly woman says.

A once-white threadbare towel is thrust into his hands and he looks at the brown water as another boy is instructed to get in. Someone leads Dimitri to an adjacent room where an assembly line of boys wait to have their heads shorn, leaving locks of hair like small crawling animals on the wooden floor. The towel is taken and a bundle of clothes is thrust into his hands. His feet are measured. Socks and shoes are plonked onto the pile of clothing.

"Get dressed," a woman tells him. "In there." She points to another room filled with boys of all ages.

Dimitri pulls on stiff underwear then long cotton pants and a pale-blue cotton shirt. He's never had real shoes before and watches to see how others put on the socks and shoes, unsure of what to do next. He lifts his right foot and examines the callouses on the sole. There's a deep cut under his big toe and scratches across the top of his left foot and leg. He watches a woman shove a boy's foot into a shoe. The boy winces, trying hard not to cry. Dimitri looks at the black leather and squeezes his foot into it. When he gets the other one on, he stands and almost falls from the pain.

"You've got them on the wrong feet," a voice says to one of the boys next to him. Dimitri watches as she takes them off and holds them in front of the boy. He looks at his own shoes and realises he's done the same. Quickly removing them, he puts them on the right way and it feels a little better.

"These boys don't know how to tie their laces," a woman says to another. Bending down to help one boy, she shakes her head. "Poor things."

When it's his turn, he studies the starched white hat below him and it reminds him of the nurse he'd seen when the donkey kicked his head.

"Please," he asks, "can you tell me where my clothes are?"

She grunts as she hoists herself up.

"Oh, we're throwing those old rags out. Now off you go into that next room." She pats him on the shoulder before turning to the next boy. "Another one who doesn't know how to tie his shoelaces."

Dimitri walks tentatively as if he's on prickles. The shoes are tight and strange on his feet and he wants them off. But that's not as bad as the pain of losing his jumper, the one knitted by his mother. Its smell of home, of his past life, is gone and tears sting his eyes.

"I hate these shoes," grumbles Lazo, who's saved him a place at a long table in a cavernous room filled with the chatter of children. There's no sign of Marika.

"My feet hurt," Dimitri says and he wonders if he will ever be allowed to take the shoes off.

"And no itching. They put something on my hair to kill the lice."

"Yeah. It stinks," Dimitri says. "Can you smell that?" He licks his lips as he watches women bring trays to each table.

There's beans, rice and potatoes swimming in sauce on each plate placed in front of them.

"Whoa. Look at this," Lazo says, tucking in. "This is a feast."

"Is this meat?" Dimitri asks, filling his mouth.

"Yep."

And the hall falls strangely silent while they eat. After dinner, they're told they're getting dessert.

"What's dessert," says one boy on the other side of Dimitri, who shrugs.

"I don't know."

"Maybe it's the name of the fruit they have here."

"Nah. You have it after dinner. It's like a drink."

They're given something in a wrapper. The boys look at the block and then at each other.

"What are we supposed to do with this?"

One boy rips the paper off and they all watch as he holds something brown in his hand. He sniffs it then licks. "Mmm," he says before taking a bite. "It's good. It's really good."

"This is the best thing I have ever eaten in my whole life," Lazo says.

Dimitri murmurs. He loves it. He bites down on it and licks what's melted on his hand.

"How are my boys? Do you like the chocolate?" Olga has come to see them. She, too, has bathed and looks beautiful in fresh clothes. They look up and nod vigorously. She beams.

"I thought it was called dessert," Lazo says. Olga laughs as she wanders across to another table.

"If only Dafina were here. She would have loved this better than roasted goat," Dimitri says sadly. "It's so good."

After dinner they're shown to a large room filled with beds. Lazo and Dimitri are side by side and tentatively give the beds a bounce.

"Hello everyone, I'm Sister Danisha. This is where you'll sleep while you're here. There's a nightshirt at the end of your bed. Put that on and take your shoes off. Put your clothes in a bundle under your bed."

"We have to change again?" asks a boy.

"Of course you do. When you get up in the morning you must make your beds and fold your nightshirt and place it under your pillow."

"Sister, I don't know how to make a bed. Back home I slept on straw," a small boy whimpers.

"We'll show you how," she says, smiling. "Don't worry."

The boys scramble to change.

Dimitri slips under the cool crisp sheets. He rubs his hand up and down the pillow. It feels like he's floating on a cloud and soon he's asleep dreaming of chocolate.

38

Who are You?

The doctor's soft voice rouses him. "Jim. Sorry to wake you."

Jim grunts.

"How are you feeling?"

Why do they keep asking that? "I'm feeling good. When can I get out of here?" Only he doesn't say it in English.

The nurse cocks her head, raises her eyebrows and gives the doctor a knowing look. "See what I mean?"

"When can I go home?" Jim asks again, wondering if the doctor is deaf.

"Interesting," the doctor says, frowning. "I think we need to run some more tests."

"Do you know what he's saying?" the nurse asks.

"He asked when he can go home." They turn to stare at the

middle-aged woman who's come in with his cup of tea. As she places it on the table she smiles.

"You understand him?"

The woman nods.

"What language is he speaking?" the doctor asks.

"He must be Macedonian. He's speaking Macedonian."

The nurse looks uncertain and all eyes drill into Jim, who stares back. He feels the need to say something but his mind is jumbled.

"No, I'm not," he says. "I'm Australian."

"We all say we're Australian. It's okay, you can tell people about being Macedonian. Discrimination is not like it was in the old days," the woman replies gently.

He clenches his sweaty hands and is surprised when he recognises the woman is not speaking to him in English.

"Get lost, you interfering busybody," Jim hisses. Her kindly smile quickly disappears and he knows he's gone too far when she turns abruptly away from him.

But an unsettling feeling creeps over him. Has his accent come back? In his younger days, he mimicked Col's accent, practising hard until he sounded just like him. Everyone laughed at first when he said, 'boody make', instead of 'beauty mate'. It was hard twisting his tongue around words, getting the nasal twang just right and understanding the sayings. He loved to call Anna his cheese 'n' kisses. She liked it better than being called the trouble and strife.

He breathes heavily and his chest thumps. The nurse and doctor have disappeared. He swings his legs over the side of the bed and makes for the door barefoot, in his pyjamas. He ignores the shouts as he makes the split decision to turn left, hoping he's heading for the exit.

"Got to get out of this madhouse," he mutters.

He makes it to the nurse's station and barely glances at the shocked look on the young nurse's face. He thinks he hears his name and suddenly chuckles, he's too fast for them. He's taking a run up. They'll never catch up to Jimmy the Juggernaut. But they do.

***

"I'm glad I caught you, doctor. Is he ready to go home?" Helen strides in, pecks Jim on the cheek, then peers into his eyes. "You look pretty good, Dad. How're you feeling?"

Avoiding her gaze, Jim wonders where his breakfast tray has disappeared to. He hopes the doctor doesn't tell Helen about his attempt to escape. He'll never hear the end of it.

"All indications are that he's fine. However, there is a slight complication. I think your father has selective aphasia. This happens sometimes in stroke victims. The blood flow to the brain may have been disturbed, either because of a haemorrhage or if a blood vessel is blocked. I think it may have affected his language function. Bilingual patients can revert to their native language."

"What? I'm afraid I haven't a clue what you're talking about." Helen frowns. "My father isn't bilingual. I don't know where you got that idea."

"He's been speaking to us in Macedonian," the doctor says. "We'll have to perform a scan to see what's going on."

"Macedonian? Are you joking? He had a scan yesterday and everything was fine. He doesn't know any language other than English. He was communicating perfectly well last night. What the hell has gone on here? Dad?"

Jim sits quietly absorbing the doctor's explanation and tugs at a thread that's come away from the faded blue cotton blanket.

"Say something." Helen glares at him.

But he's too scared to utter a word.

She turns to the doctor. "How do you know it's this Macedonian language? Maybe he's jumbling the words. Look, he's been through a lot. My mother just died and he's not coping at all well. He's confused, that's all. Even I get my sentences and words mixed up. It happens to all of us."

Helen looks close to tears. Could the doctor be right?

"I'm really sorry about your mother. It might explain his blood pressure levels. They're quite high at the moment. But this is not an issue of confusion. He is speaking an actual language. I know because the Macedonian orderly interpreted for us. He asked to go home."

Jim tunes out as the doctor tells Helen about his near escape. He's too busy staring at the gathering clouds outside. There'll be rain for sure and he's stuck here, instead of being at home organising the buckets at each downpipe to collect the runoff.

"We have to take him now for a second scan. He could have had another mini stroke in the middle of the night," the doctor says.

Helen nods as she sits down hard in the chair. "Yes, of course."

She stares at her father in shock. "Dad, did you learn Macedonian when you were younger from someone in the factory. Or maybe from a neighbour?"

He glances at her sunken, bloodshot eyes and doesn't trust himself to speak.

"Dad? Talk to me. I'm your daughter. You can trust me. You must have learnt this language somehow."

The nurse returns with the orderly.

"This is Effie. She'll explain to you what he said."

Jim's not ready for Helen to know and it's all he can do to restrain himself. He can't protect her anymore. He tugs the thread so hard it comes away in his hand as the orderly finishes relaying her story to Helen, who shakes her head.

"I can't believe it. Who are you? What have you been keeping from me?" she whispers.

Bewildered, he's wheeled away from Helen before he can tell her. Noticing the nurses' station opposite his door, he can't help feeling disappointed when he realises he hadn't got as far as he'd thought. The old feelings of being totally alone engulf him as he lies amidst the loud thumping noises of the scanner.

39

It's a Train

For the next few days, the children settle into a comforting routine. Woken early, they wash, dress and make their beds, watched by a stern-faced woman who keeps them all in line. Then it's outside into the cool air for exercises on pockmarked asphalt before breakfast. Afterwards they're steered into classrooms to learn songs they've not heard before. The one Dimitri likes best is the Macedonian national anthem and it stirs him enough for the melody to stay with him. He thinks he's heard it before, when he was very small. It reminds him of happy times.

Gorite Makedonski shumno peat
novi pesni, novi vesnici
Makedonija slobodna
slobodna zhivee!

Makedonija slobodna
slobodna zhivee!
(The Macedonian forests sing
new songs and news
Macedonia is liberated
It lives in liberty!
Macedonia is liberated
It lives in liberty!)

They're taught for the first time in Macedonian; a jolting language for many used to their village's own dialect. The Greek children struggle the most, relying on their bilingual friends to interpret. They don't understand what's being said and they don't like it much and scuffles break out between some of the boys during playtime. But the food is better and the women in charge are nice, and, for the most part, it's a relief to feel safe.

Families arrive looking for their children and each day two or three beds in their dormitory are vacated by lucky boys reunited with their loved ones. Dimitri prays, willing his name to be called, but it never is.

Lazo pleads to everyone for news of his sister. "Please," he asks, "she's with the Partisans." But here, no-one has heard of her.

On the seventh day, without warning, they're told they're leaving. With just the clothes on their backs, they're loaded onto trucks and taken to the railway station. Dimitri is wide-eyed as he's herded with everyone else onto the platform. His stomach flutters in anticipation and fear. Olga divides them into their villages but as they're the only survivors, Dimitri and Lazo are put into a group from nearby settlements.

"I'll be going with you. We should be there in a couple of hours," Olga says. "Listen very carefully to my instructions."

Marika is in his group too, rolling her stone in the palm of her hand like a set of worry beads. He'd hardly seen her during their stay. She nods her greeting but Dimitri is wary of her.

"We're going on a train," Lazo says, nudging Dimitri, and hardly containing his excitement.

"Stay together in your groups. We're going to Skopje on this train," Olga yells, but her voice is lost amongst the excited shrieks from the children.

"It's coming, it's coming!" yells an excited boy. A train chugs into the station like a giant metallic worm.

Dimitri's jaw drops. Like most of the children, he's never seen a train before. A whistle pierces the air, making everyone jump. Some of the girls cover their ears. Then another train pulls in on the other side of the platform, marooning the children in the middle. Steam billows like great clouds and the whistle blows again. Mesmerised, Dimitri steps away from his group to get a closer look. The metal gleams a shiny blue and silver. He studies the driver and envies his cap. The driver stares back, then nods and smiles. Dimitri itches to climb up to get a better look but someone pulls his arm and he's caught up in a tide of children being swept along the platform.

In the ensuing confusion, Dimitri loses sight of Lazo and

finds himself with a group he doesn't know. He tries to go back but there are too many children pushing him along.

"Lazo!" he yells, but his voice is drowned out by the noise. Pushed in, he's rammed against the far side of a box car. He thinks he sees Lazo in the crowd near the train opposite. He tries to get the attention of one of the women. "Please, I'm not meant to be here. I'm in another group."

Before she can answer, the door slams, shutting them in dimness. Dimitri hammers on the door loudly. "Lazo! Let me out. I have to get out." He tries to prise the door open but it doesn't budge.

Children jostle into each other and some tumble onto the hard floor as the train jolts and begins to move. It seems as if the crying and screaming will never end.

"Sit down everyone," the woman calls out, trying to get order. "Don't be scared. Remember I'm here. You're not alone."

"Ljubica, I've got a sore leg."

"She pushed me."

"I did not!"

"Now stop arguing," Ljubica says. "We've got a long way to go so settle down onto the floor. Kosta, for goodness' sake, will you sit down before you fall on someone again?"

"Please! Where are we going?" Dimitri asks, tugging at the woman's worn brown dress. He wipes his eyes and his panic begins to subside.

Ljubica squints. "Who are you?"

"I'm Dimitri."

Her face crinkles, her glasses drop to the end of her nose. "You're not in my group. Whose group are you meant to be in?"

"Olga's group."

"What's her last name? I know three Olgas."

"I don't know. Please, can you tell me where we're going?"

"Why Mikulov, of course," she says frowning. "Didn't Olga tell you?

"Where is that?"

"Czechoslovakia. Your group is probably in another car. We'll find them when we stop. Now sit down over there!" Ljubica leans down to pick up a crying child. "There, there, little one. It'll be all right."

Dimitri sniffs and wipes his nose on his sleeve as he tries to remember. Where did Olga say they were going? But he can't remember. All he knows is that it's a town in Macedonia; that they should take a few hours to get there. But what town? Why didn't he listen? The train picks up speed and the whistle blows again.

He tries to wrap his mind around the word Czechoslovakia. Where is it? Is it far? Will his parents be able to find him there? What will happen to him? Where's Lazo? But the woman is too busy trying to comfort other crying children. Maybe she's right. Maybe his group is somewhere on this train.

Dimitri uneasily resigns himself to watching the countryside blur through the slats. Some of the girls are singing and playing games by clapping their hands. Some sleep, others complain about being hungry or thirsty and some cry quietly. The box car smells of animals long gone, despite the clean straw on the floor. He's lost and alone and surrounded by faces he doesn't know. He buries his head into his knees to avoid their curious stares. There's nothing he can do but squint through the cracks and listen to the rhythm while hoping his group is in another car. *Clickety-clack, clickety-clack, clickety-clack.*

After a while, the train slows and stops.

"All right, everyone, we're here," Ljubica says. "Get ready to hop out."

Dimitri yawns and stretches. Finally, he'll re-join his group. As they file out, they blink in the harsh sun and growing heat. Unlike some, he's held on and can finally relieve himself behind the bushes they're shown to. Dimitri has little time to scan the length of the train that's disgorging its noisy passengers onto the platform before they're quickly led to a picnic area nearby, which is scattered with wooden seats and tables. A stream furiously gurgles a greeting as they trudge across the bridge and colossal fir trees surround them in a protective circle.

He watches hefty women in bright scarves ladle steaming soup into cracked bowls from makeshift fires. The smell reaches him and his stomach rumbles. The women smile and speak in a language no-one understands. The soup, with its smattering of vegetables and meat, tastes good. They're given water and the clearing is filled with tired children.

"Stay here, Dimitri, and I'll see if I can find your group," Ljubica says.

Dimitri does as he's told and settles himself cross-legged on the damp grass. He anxiously searches the faces around him for someone he might recognise. He watches Ljubica talking to two other women, whose frowning eyes bore into him. She shrugs and walks over to another woman, who's breaking up a fight between two boys. She waits and speaks to her then walks on until he loses her in the crowd.

Two boys pick up stones and toss them into the stream. Then more boys join in, collecting stones and sticks and throwing them across to the other side. Others try to hit the giant fir trees and he wishes that he could do it too, but keeps a fretful watch for Ljubica instead.

He jumps when he hears his name.

"Dimitri. I should have asked you what village you're from." Ljubica holds a child on her hip.

He panics. His mind is blank. "I ... I've forgotten," he says finally.

"Well I can't find Olga."

"I remember Olga said that we'd be on the train for a couple of hours, so she must be here somewhere."

"Oh dear, in that case you should have been going to Skopje. Mmm ... you're on the wrong train then." Her frown deepens. "Look, I can't leave you here. You'll have to go on with us and we'll see what we can do at the other end."

Dimitri feels the warmth drain from his skin.

"Don't worry, Dimitri. I'll look after you. It'll be all right, you'll see."

His worst fear is realised. Lazo and Marika are somewhere else and he should have been with them. If only he'd stayed with his group and listened.

"Come on," she says gently. "It's time to return to the train."

"Aren't we at Mikulov?"

"No, dear, we're not. We've still a very long way to go."

Dimitri's stomach lurches. Trapped in the crowded box car, his mind fights the idea of being on the train for longer than he wants. He gulps in fresh air through the cracks of the carriage where he's edged his way to a paltry space along the wall. What he wants to do is cry. But he can't. He'll be called a baby by the other boys. Or worse, a girl. Friendless, he can't afford to draw attention to himself. He prays for sleep and when darkness falls he drifts off to the rattle of the train, which is taunting him with its chant over and over again: *you'll be there soon.*

***

Late the next morning they arrive in Budapest, where they're sprayed with a mist of disinfectant. Afterwards, they're taken to a large hall to eat before returning to another train.

Dimitri is sure the other children whisper about him and he takes great care not to meet anyone's eye. He listens carefully to Ljubica though, and does what is asked of him.

The second leg of the trip is boring. With nothing to do the children sleep, cry or argue.

"Get away from me," an older boy says. The pain from the punch reverberates down his skinny arm as Dimitri crashes into another child who's fighting for the same space. It occurs to him that the children allowed him to have the space against the wall earlier, but now they know he's just like them.

"Don't fall on me!"

"Watch it. There's not enough room."

"Settle down," Ljubica growls.

Sliding to the floor, Dimitri no longer cares and sinks into his own sad thoughts. The train is taking them further and further away from his friends, his village and his family. It's for his own good, they tell him. He's clean, has new clothes but nothing else. He's worried that he won't remember his parents or his grandfather; that when it's time to find them he won't recognise them. He knows he will never recognise his baby brother.

An elbow digs into his back. His leg is wedged under someone else and feels numb. Light flickers through the cracks and when he lifts his head he meets the dull eyes of a girl opposite. He shifts his weight to hug his legs closer and rests his head on his knees, making his body as inconspicuous as he can.

He thinks about the train taking him further away from the soldier. The realisation that he can't be tracked by the authorities gives him some relief, but not enough to take away the sickening feeling of being lost and alone.

He's woken in the night when the train stops. They line up for toilets. His stomach grumbles and he shivers in the unseasonal cold snap. Snow is falling. His jacket long gone, he's dressed for summer that's still a month away. Back in the box car, he cups his hand around his nose to stop the foul smell created by the children who've soiled themselves. The thought of escape lingers for a moment as he weighs up his options. The idea, like his footsteps in the snow, is left marooned on the platform. Dimitri leans his weight into a space between two older boys' backs and allows tears to slip down his cheeks.

Someone asks how long, but the response is always the same, "Soon."

40

Mikulov, Czechoslovakia

Dawn streaks rays of light through the cracks of the carriage. Dimitri jolts his head from the steel pole he's used as a pillow. His stomach aches and he licks his dry lips, wishing for water. When he squints through the slats, he can make out a blur of buildings outside. The other children begin to wake and yawn, their sunken eyes are weary. Two small girls lie asleep on Ljubica's lap, their arms entwined around her and each other, while Ljubica snores.

When the train eventually comes to a stop, everyone is awake and alert with expectation. The door is heaved back by a small man in a cap, who moves quickly on without a glance.

"Everyone out but stay together," Ljubica says. They eagerly push their way onto the platform and blink in the bright light. "Wait here and don't move!" she commands as she goes to talk to another woman.

"Mikulov!" another man says. "Mikulov."

The air hangs with the warm smell of summer after the stench of the night. Children mill about impatiently on the platform, itching to jump and run.

"Are we here?" a girl says.

"Yes, almost," Ljubica answers. "We're in Breclav and we're waiting to get a bus to Mikulov."

"I'm hungry."

"And I'm thirsty. When will we get to our new home?"

"Soon," Ljubica says, craning her neck for a signal. "But we have to first wait here for a little while longer."

She glances at the piece of paper in her hand. "When I call your name, put your hand up and leave it up."

They wait. Wait to be told what to do, where to go. Waiting for their new lives to begin. What they know for certain is that they don't know when or if they'll ever see their families again.

One by one the hands spring up.

"All right," Ljubica says after she calls out the last name.

Dimitri's shoulders sag in disappointment as his arms hang down by his sides. He bites his bottom lip while he waits for Ljubica to look his way. She's busy counting the numbers on the ragged piece of paper.

"Can we put our arm down now?" a child calls out.

Then Ljubica's gaze skims the children until she rests on one.

"Dimitri!" And he quickly thrusts his hand into the air. "Arms down," she says, smiling. "You're all here."

"This is it," a boy says to no-one in particular.

There's not much to see beyond the platform of fidgeting children.

This is where I start a new life, Dimitri thinks. His earlier thoughts of escape are completely abandoned. Having nowhere else to go, he resigns himself to whatever is to happen next.

"I'm Pando," the boy says. He blinks constantly as if he has something in his eye.

"Dimitri," he replies.

"How old are you?"

The boy looks to be his age. His black hair reminds him painfully of Lazo. It's a strange question to ask of someone.

"About twelve," Dimitri lies. If he's to make a new life, then he wants to be older. "You?"

"I think ten," Pando says. He cocks his head. "Want to stay together?"

Dimitri shrugs and nods. He has nothing to lose. "All right."

Pando walks alongside him as Ljubica directs them along the platform to an area where a dozen old buses are lined up.

"I lost my friends when a bomb hit our truck."

Dimitri nods and glances at Pando, realising he is just as alone. Everyone else chatters excitedly as they're loaded onto buses. Dimitri boards first, finds an empty seat and slides across to the window, willing Pando to follow.

"My little sister was killed so my father joined the Partisans. I think my mother is still in the village with my aunts," Pando says, settling next to him. "But they'll come and get me soon."

Dimitri admires his hope and peers at his companion. "How do you know? How do you really know?"

Chewing hard on his thumbnail, Pando shrugs. "They told me."

"Who?"

"My mother and my aunts. Even Ljubica told us that eventually we'll be going home."

Dimitri's not so sure. He's had enough disappointment not to hold out hope. But he says nothing. And he's glad Pando doesn't ask him any questions. He doesn't trust himself not to cry if he has to explain. "Where are we going?" he asks instead.

Pando shrugs. "Some place safe."

Dimitri nods. Then, out of the dirty window, he watches a line of children bustling over the gravel, kicking up the dust as they get on the bus next to them. The engine roars to life and Ljubica walks along the aisle counting heads. She clings onto the unpainted iron rod hanging from the roof. The bus is filled with noise like birds gathered in a tree. Dimitri stares out the grubby window at the old buildings that have been standing for centuries and an old woman in a scarf hobbles along a worn path. The bus winds left, then right through rough cobbled streets before accelerating into green countryside. Before long they reach another village where the bus slows. The children are suddenly silent and press their heads to the glass, staring at a massive building surrounded by a high stone wall. The bus swings through a carved wooden gate and stops.

"This is Mikulov," Ljubica announces. "Your new home."

Children spill out from other buses following behind. They're bustled across a cobblestone courtyard into a large stone building with a terracotta roof, and into a hall with dozens of wooden benches and long tables. Jugs of milk are brought out by two round women in colourful aprons. They smile and welcome each child as they pour milk into glasses in front of them.

A woman with a giant mole on her face sets down large slices of fresh white bread smeared with something pink. "It's strawberry jam," she tells them with a smile. "You'll like it." And they do, wolfing down as much as they can.

Ljubica calls Dimitri aside. "I've found out you should have gone to Skopje. But there's no way to get you back. So you'll have to stay here for now, I'm afraid."

"Okay," he says, hiding his disappointment. He goes back to his place at the table to finish his piece of bread but finds no appetite for it and pushes it away.

"If you're not going to eat that, can I have it?" Pando asks.

Dimitri shrugs and nods. He looks at his surroundings. This is to be his new home.

The woman with the mole stands back to watch them. "Those poor Greek children," she says to another woman. "Look how starved they are."

For some reason it disturbs Dimitri. After they finish eating, they're sent out to play. As he passes the woman he says, "We're not all Greek, some of us are Macedonian."

"Oh," she says, showing her surprise.

Dimitri runs to catch up with the others outside. It feels good to run because he wants to, not because he has to. It feels good knowing he doesn't have to go anywhere else.

"The buses have gone," Pando says.

"Yes." Dimitri, with his hands in his pockets, kicks an acorn toward Pando. They kick it to each other for a while until Dimitri tires and finds a bench. Pando sits next to him.

"How old do you think this place is?" Pando asks.

"It looks old."

"It's probably a castle where a rich king once lived."

Dimitri doesn't want to show his ignorance that he doesn't know what a castle is, but he does know about rich kings and queens. They're the ones in his homeland fighting the Partisans. He remembers his grandfather cursing them.

"I wonder if our King and Queen live in something like this."

They speculate what might have happened in the castle until there's nothing else to talk about. They watch a group of girls running after each other; another group sing and laugh. Some of the other boys are collected around something they've found on the ground.

It piques their interest. "Let's see what's going on," Pando says.

Dimitri nods. But Ljubica walks out and scans the courtyard to interrupt them. "Pando, Dimitri. My group. Come over here!" she calls. Half a dozen faces turn in her direction and a group of twenty-one gathers in front of her.

"Now, I want you to file in through that big wooden

door." She points. "You're going to get new clothes and be shown where you'll be living. I'll see you tomorrow. Off you go now. Don't run."

The room is dim after the sunshine. Lining up in front of a desk, a thin blonde woman with smiling eyes writes something in her notebook.

It's Dimitri's turn to stand in front of her.

"What's your name?" she says in Macedonian, smiling at him.

"Dimitri Filipidis," he replies.

"What village are you from?" Her eyes bore into him. He can't remember and he doesn't know why. He remembers what the village looks like; the rough stone houses, his own house with three stone steps, the church with its majestic carved door. He shifts from one foot to the other, staring at his newly scuffed shoes, but all he hears is her pencil tapping on the table in front of him.

"I don't know," he says finally, in defeat.

"That's all right. We'll put down Ptolemaida. There are lots from there. That'll be close enough. You're all from the same region."

"Now for the last question. Do you know when you were born?"

He thinks. He doesn't quite know what she means. His mother said he was born on a stormy night in the house where he grew up. He never knew when. "Ah, no."

"Well then, do you know how old you are?"

This he can answer. Before he opens his mouth he

remembers Pando is behind him. He can't afford to jeopardise his tenuous friendship. "I think I'm twelve," he lies.

Her pencil poised, she sizes him up and squints. "You're all small," she mutters while writing something.

"All right then, Dimitri. Remember this date. February 6th 1936 is your birthday from now on. That's the opening day of the Winter Olympic games when I represented my country in ice skating. Never forget that date. Now you have a birthday and you can celebrate on that day every year from now on." She smiles and shows off the whitest teeth he's ever seen. And for some reason it feels good to know he has something. "Off you go now to find your dormitory."

The boys' dormitory is airy with ten steel bunkbeds lined on either side like a row of vegetables in a garden. Each child is given two sets of underwear, shorts, shirts, socks and another pair of black shoes. Beside each bed is a double cupboard to store their possessions in, which for most of them is more than they've ever had in their lives.

The bed above him is occupied by a pale, freckled boy called Kosta, who's as thin as a reed. He tells Dimitri that he's come from Ptolemaida too. Pando ambles in and smiles when he's allocated a bed next to Dimitri.

That night, after a meal of bread, beans and meat, they go to bed. Dimitri lies awake for most of the night listening to the sounds of quiet crying, sniffles and coughs. He wants to cry, too, but bites his lip and tries to listen to his own breathing instead. He looks across at his new friend, Pando, and thinks about Kosta above him, and hopes they don't disappear like everyone else.

41

When Your Time is Up.

When they wheel him into the room after the scan, Helen is there, waiting. Her sunken eyes are red and she's holding a bunched-up tissue in one hand and her phone in the other.

Jim's already decided it's better not to speak, at least until he can figure out what to do. He's tired. Anna, where are you? But she's not coming back.

After he's been made comfortable, and the nurse leaves, Helen leans over and he feels her warm lips brush his cheek. "How are you feeling?"

Her breath smells of spearmint. He shrugs and grimaces.

"Won't you talk to me?"

Her gentle gaze almost breaks his heart. He wants to tell her not to worry – that he'll be all right.

"Dad, I know what the orderly said but I think it's all just a mistake. I'm sure they've got this all wrong. It happens sometimes. You've had a stroke – we know that. And sometimes it affects speech. You probably said something that sounded like another language." She leans over and strokes his hand. "Or maybe you learned this other language when you were working in the textile factory. There were lots of migrants there. I wouldn't put it past you to pick it up. You've always been clever. I'm sure it's as simple as that. Anyway, I've asked them to run more tests. I know it's tough for you but we've got to get to the bottom of it. What do you think?"

He knows they haven't got it wrong. He shakes his head and closes his eyes, hoping she'll get the hint and leave.

"That's okay. There'll be a perfectly logical explanation. You rest for a bit, Dad."

He must have dozed because when he wakes she's still sitting next to him, fiddling on her phone. For goodness' sake, hasn't she seen the sign about mobile phones? She lifts her face toward him and he snaps his eyes closed. It's better if she thinks he's asleep.

Footsteps thump across the lino past his bed.

"I came to see," the voice lowers to a whisper, "how you're going." It's the no-hoper his daughter now lives with. Jim imagines him kissing her. He's probably wearing a crisp white shirt with teddy bear cufflinks, a pink tie and blue suit. Jim thought he'd looked like a sissy when he saw him last time and thinks he may have hold told him so. Perhaps that's why Jim doesn't see him much.

"I'm okay. But Dad…" She sighs. Even with his deafness, he can tell how upset she is. "They don't know what's going on. They say he's had a transient ischaemic attack, which is like a stroke, and he may have had another mini stroke last night. He's had a scan so we'll know the results hopefully soon."

"He looks all right," the no-hoper says.

What would you know? Jim thinks.

"If it's a mild stroke he should be fine. My uncle had one a few years ago and it took him no time to get back to normal."

So you think you can waltz in here and give a diagnosis?

"They think there's something wrong with his speech." She blows her nose loudly.

"It'll be all right. He's tough. You said it yourself. Nothing gets the better of him. He'll pull out of this, you'll see."

Jim likes what the no-hoper says. He is tough. She's just too protective. Suddenly, he's glad the no-hoper is there. Maybe he's not so bad after all. Helen seems to like him. Perhaps he should give him more of a chance.

"He'll be back to his obnoxious cranky self in no time."

Hey! Watch who you're calling obnoxious.

"In no time, you'll be calling him every name under the sun and wondering what all the fuss was about."

What was I thinking? The no-hoper's had his chance and now he's blown it.

"I suppose," she says.

"Come on. He's still asleep and you need to get something to eat. I bet you haven't eaten, have you? I can't have you fading away on me now."

He's got a point. She's far too skinny. Their footsteps and

murmuring voices fade into the corridor. Peace, at last, to think about what to do. He needs the bathroom. He opens his eyes and meets the eyes of the man in the bed opposite. Jim makes a big show of lifting the sheet to his chin and adjusting his pillows.

The man continues to stare. What *is* his problem? Jim wonders as he gazes out of the window. It's a clear day; no sign of rain. Then he remembers the garden. It needs a water. He'll tell Helen to drop by and water it tonight. Then he remembers. Blast! How is he going to tell her?

The nurse comes in and heads to the rude man opposite. He'll try to attract her attention first and see if she understands him.

"Moshish da ma pomoshish?" *Can you help me?*

The nurse glances at him and raises the palm of her hand. "I'll be with you shortly," she says tersely.

Did she understand him? He watches her fling the curtain around the bed opposite. A buzzer sounds and a doctor and three other nurses rush in and disappear behind the curtain. There's some sort of commotion but he can't make out what's going on.

Jim begins to feel irritated. The nurse has probably forgotten him. He's hungry now and glances at his watch. But it's no longer on his wrist. He stares at the tan mark around where the watch should be and tries to remember when he'd last worn it. But he can't. Deciding the man opposite has it, he yells to the nurse asking her if his watch is there. But he gets no response.

He flings off the sheet and swings his feet over the side of the bed. Looking around, he grabs his walking stick as he slides off the bed. Funny how he forgot it during his failed escape attempt.

He walks gingerly toward the bathroom. Relief at last. When he emerges, he sees that the man has gone, leaving a dent on the pillow where his head was. He stops to pull his pyjama pants up high and suddenly wonders where they've come from. He doesn't remember putting them on. Helen must have brought them. As he shuffles back to bed a strong hand grips his arm from behind.

"Jim! You should have called me before getting out of bed. You might have fallen. From now on press the buzzer and someone will come with you."

"I did call you. But you ignored me like everyone else," he growls, forgetting he's not speaking English.

But she acts like he's said nothing at all. "What was that?"

He rolls his eyes. "I did call you."

"I'm sorry, Jim, I can't understand what you're saying," the nurse says slowly and loudly.

"I'm not an idiot. And while I may be hard of hearing, I'm not deaf!" But his outburst seems to have no affect on her.

"Let's get you back into bed then, shall we?"

Gripping his arm, she helps him onto the bed before tucking the sheet around him.

He points to the bed opposite and raises his eyebrows.

"Oh, Mr Vincent? I'm afraid he's gone."

He nods.

"Now use … this button … next time, Jim," she says slowly. She peers into his face. "Okay?"

He nods, if only to get rid of her. But she whips a cuff around his arm and sticks a thermometer in his mouth. His stomach rumbles. He points to his wrist where his watch used to be.

She writes something in his chart, then opens the drawer of his bedside table.

"Is this …what you …were after?"

He nods and puts on his best smile as he slips his watch over his hand. It's only eleven thirty.

"I'm afraid we can't give you anything to eat until the doctor comes by … just in case you need more tests. It shouldn't be too long now." She must have read his mind. She heads toward the bed opposite. Another nurse comes in and they strip the bed. He hears a snippet of the conversation.

"The family are on their way. Such a pity it was so sudden."

"I know. I only checked on him half an hour before. But then, these things happen. He was old anyway and when your time's up, it's up."

42

Fractured

Alone on his bed, Dimitri runs his fingers over the handwritten letters of his name on the front of the grey envelope. Someone has written to him, remembers him, knows him. He hardly allows himself to think what's inside. The stamps are postmarked Skopje.

"Aren't you going to open it?" Mary asks. She's come to the library specially to give him the letter. As a Senior, he studies at this time every day in preparation for exams in the week to come.

"I will later." He slips the letter into his textbook.

Mary smiles. "Take your time. I'll be in my office if you need me." After the sound of her heels have faded into the corridor, he picks up his books and scurries to the dormitory to be on his own.

He turns the envelope over and over in his hands. He's

waited so long for this day. For more than five years, he's watched everyone around him receive letters from family.

When he first arrived in Mikulov in June 1948, life was tolerable. He'd made new friends with Pando and Kosta. The arduous journey over, they'd settled into a routine of classes, sport, play and chores. After a few months, Pando's parents arrived to claim him. A month later, Kosta left too. Alone again, Dimitri withdrew into himself. His silent days were followed by nights haunted by the fear of nightmares about the dead soldier or Risto or the child who fell off the path.

Children and teachers coaxed him, yelled at him, cajoled him to speak, to play – but he never would.

One teacher, in exasperation, yelled at him, "Dimitri, spell pencil!"

When he didn't respond, she smacked a pencil across his knuckles, spelling out the word to him and the class. "You'll remember for next time," she said smugly.

Still, he had nothing to say.

"What's wrong with you?" a boy asked.

"You're a dummy, you're a dummy," another sang, until Dimitri was surrounded by children chanting until they grew bored and moved on when he failed to respond.

All he wanted to do was read and be alone, and spent hours in a happier world of his making in the library. He was sent to the psychologist, who told everyone to leave him be; that he'd speak when he was ready.

The teachers had bigger problems. Some of the children misbehaved. The Greek boys fought with the Macedonians, blaming each other for their predicaments, until they were finally put into separate dormitories. A girl decided she was a donkey and pranced everywhere she went, eating only carrots. Another never stopped screaming and she eventually disappeared.

His silence lasted months in that first year until Mary, an aid worker from England, arrived to teach English to any child who wanted to learn. With her gentle ways, she was loved by everyone, and Dimitri was sent to her class where he sat on his own. When Mary asked him a question, he stared blankly, even though he knew the answer.

"Don't ask him, Miss. He can't speak," a boy explained. "He got a knock on the head or something." The others agreed, but he noticed how unconvinced she looked.

At night, when he couldn't sleep, he'd mouth the English words he'd learnt. One day, Mary found him in the library at lunchtime alone and asleep. The English version of *Twenty Thousand Leagues Under the Sea* by Jules Verne lay open in his lap. She was sitting cross-legged on the floor next to him when he woke, and she smiled.

From then on, Mary came to the library each day and sat with him, encouraging him to ask questions until one day, six months later, he finally did. "How do you say this?" he asked in English, pointing to a word on the page. "Miscellaneous," she said, smiling. Then she told him what it meant and they discussed the meaning in the sentence. It was the first time he'd smiled. A short while later he gradually began mixing again with the other children. Besides English, Greek and

Macedonian, he learnt Czech and Russian and fell in love with language. He, like all the children, eventually settled into their new lives.

But on bad days he clung to the idea of his parents coming for him. They'd smile and he'd run toward them. Their arms around him, he'd feel safe. They'd be proud, exclaiming how athletic and smart he was when they found out he was always top of his class. They'd be shocked by how much he'd grown and how his once-blond hair had darkened to a mousy brown. Undersized no longer, he was now one of the tallest at one hundred and seventy-nine centimetres.

In 1949, when the Civil War ended, Dimitri and the rest of the Macedonian children were told that the Greek Government had decreed them to be Greek, and the teaching of their language stopped. The Red Cross interviewed them and tried to reunite children with families. One by one they left until the only remaining children were orphans who became wards of the state. Alone and abandoned, Dimitri was fractured like the rest of them.

Hoisting his legs on the bed, he scratches the growing stubble on his chin with one hand and clutches the precious envelope in the other, trying to gather his courage. Children squeal, playing outside the window. Some are singing. A teacher's dull words lumber monotonously somewhere nearby. Chewing his bottom lip, he carefully prises the envelope open and brings out two pieces of paper and reads the Macedonian words.

Skopje, 25 May 1953

Dear Dimitri,

I am your Aunt Vera, your mother's elder and only sister. The last
time I saw you was when you were two years old, so you
probably won't remember me. I lost contact with your mother
when the Germans arrived and travel was difficult, but I always
held out hope I'd see her again. Then the Civil War began and I
had to wait until it ended to search for her. I heard she had a baby
boy in 1948. I was so happy – she had two boys after losing five
other children in between you and your brother. But it is with
heaviness in my heart that I have to tell you that your mother and
your little brother died with your grandfather when bombs fell on
your home in May 1948. I searched for your father and found
that he too had died on the island prison of Gyaros in January
1949. Since then, I have searched for you, my only nephew. I
always held out hope that I would find you. Everyone I talked to
told me you'd gone south but there was no trace of you.

By pure chance I met a boy a couple of months ago. He was a
friend of yours, I believe. His name is Lazo and he lives here in
Skopje. He told me that you had travelled together before you
became separated. He thought you went to Mikulov. I asked the
Red Cross to check and they gave me the address of where you are
living. I can't tell you how happy I am to discover that you're alive
and well.

I live in Skopje on my own, since my husband and your two
cousins passed away ten years ago, and I would very much like it
if you would come and live with me.

My address and map is on the attached piece of paper. Please write back and indulge an old lady by coming.

Much love always and God's blessings,

Tetka Vera.

He's secretly known all along, yet the finality of the words blisters him like a burning piece of coal. A breathless heaviness starts in the pit of his stomach and works its way up until the sob, kept at bay for so many years, escapes like a howl.

"Majka, Tato, Dedo," he whispers, as if the words themselves will make a difference. He slumps into his pillow, the letter limp in his hand. Wiping his nose on his sleeve, he closes his eyes. The scene of his mother and father in their small stone house with Dedo, talking, eating and laughing, has played over and over in his head for years. Now just a memory, the fracture will never be made whole.

After a while he re-reads the letter. His old friend is in Skopje, and an aunt wants him. Sitting up suddenly, he forms a plan and resolves to leave. But he's behind the Iron Curtain.

Taking his letter to Mary, he stands in the doorway of her office.

"Are you all right?" she says, studying his face.

Nodding, he gives her the letter.

"I'm so very sorry about your family."

"Thank you. I think I knew deep down years ago. They would have come if they could have." He swallows hard, shifting from one foot to the other. "I think I'd like to go to my aunt."

"You're seventeen with a bright future here. You could finish school at the end of the year and be sponsored for university. Are you sure you want to give that up?"

He nods. "I have to go. Will you help me get the papers to leave?"

"Of course."

43

The Diagnosis

Jim hears her voice in the hallway.

"Do you know how long the doctor will be? My father hasn't eaten yet, has he?"

The answer is muffled but he hears Helen clearly.

"Well, that's really not good enough is it? Is there a phone number? I'm happy to call him."

He cocks his ear, hoping she's not going to make a scene otherwise he'll never get out of here. Smoothing the sheet around him, he sits as straight as the pillows allow and waits for Helen. For some reason he's nervous.

She enters the room and he puts on his brightest smile. She smiles back but he can tell she's anxious.

"How are you feeling, Dad?" She puts her hand on his arm and bends to kiss him. His palms clammy, his fingers find the hem of the bedsheet and pulls it up to his chin.

"The doctor will be coming by very soon to let us know

about the tests. We'll get it sorted out so you can go home. Oh, and Tony came in to see you but you were asleep. I guess this whole thing is exhausting for you."

She looks at him intently and feels his forehead. He waves her away.

"Okay, I'm just checking. You look a bit flushed. They told me you were at the doctors when you collapsed. What were you doing there? Without me too."

Already she's asking questions he can't answer. He doesn't remember being at the doctor's surgery. Why would he have gone without her?

She shakes her head as she checks her phone. A nurse comes in and addresses Helen as if he's not there.

"The doctor will be coming to see you in the next half an hour. The test results are now back."

"Thank you so much," Helen says, smiling her best smile at the nurse, who's already halfway out of the room.

"Well at least you have this nice room to yourself," she says. "I brought you something." She pulls the newspaper out of her large handbag and hands it to him. He smiles his thanks and begins reading. At least he can still read English. And he understands as well. Surely that's a good sign?

He's engrossed in an article about the drought when the doctor comes in and Helen jumps up to greet him.

"Hello there, Jim. I'd like to introduce Vera, who will interpret if we need her."

Jim jerks his head. He knows that name from somewhere, but for the life of him he can't remember from where.

"How are you feeling?" the doctor asks.

"He seems good," Helen answers.

Jim gives a thumbs up to the doctor and looks warily at the younger woman. The doctor moves his lips. He must concentrate.

"The tests have come back and everything looks fairly normal. However, from the scan we can see a tiny blockage in a blood vessel."

"Oh God, what does that mean?" Helen looks as though she's going to burst into tears.

"It means that my original diagnosis was correct. I believe he has a type of aphasia. In all likelihood it came from the stroke but it can occur from a trauma to the head. He did present with a bump and there were signs of bleeding. Jim, did you fall at some stage?"

They turn to stare at him and he shrugs. He says nothing and Vera repeats the doctor's words in Macedonian. But he can't remember falling.

"I've no idea. They told me he was at the GP when he collapsed. Dad, did you hit your head? Is that why you went to the doctor without me?"

"He's lucky. He seems to be able to understand and he can read. In severe cases, communication can be adversely affected, but, for your father, I think it's relatively mild. Normally, work with a speech pathologist should get him back on track. The next thing I'd like to do is book him in to see a neuropsychologist. He may want to conduct some further tests. I'll arrange a referral for you to see someone after you're released from hospital."

Helen slumps into the chair, rubbing her head.

"Doctor, I follow everything you're saying, but there's one problem. I don't want to sound like a broken record but he's Australian. He's only ever spoken English, which is his native language. The fact he speaks this other language now makes no sense. How can he speak it if he's never learnt it?"

"I'm afraid I can't answer that. This could possibly be a temporary condition, but to be on the safe side we should start him with the speech pathologist as soon as possible. He can go home tomorrow. Does he live at home on his own?"

Vera is talking to him, translating, and he waves her away. He can't concentrate.

"Yes he does, but I'll stay with him for a couple of days to make sure he's okay."

"That's probably a good idea."

"Look, just one other question. Why does he need to go to a neuropsychologist?"

"The scans show that there may be some abnormality in the frontal lobe. The specialist will take him through some additional tests. Look, I don't think it's anything to be worried about. It may be that his frontal lobe, which seems a bit smaller than normal, may be normal for him. We don't know. It's just a precaution."

"I know it's difficult for you to comment, but from my understanding of the frontal lobe, are we talking about memory loss or dementia?"

"Possibly. We'll know more after he's tested."

"So I can take him home tomorrow?"

"I don't see why not," the doctor says, smiling at Jim, before writing something on his chart. "I'll look in on you before you go." Then he leaves with Vera trailing behind him.

"What are we going to do, Dad?" Helen says mournfully.

He shrugs and holds out his arms and while they hug each other, Jim can't help feeling saddened for his daughter. As for him, it's all too much to absorb as he racks his brain, thinking about the name Vera.

44

Skopje

Two months later, getting off the train, Dimitri walks along the platform looking for the station exit. Carrying one bag containing everything he owns, he hails a taxi and hands the driver the address. The streets are fresh and bright with the bustle of shoppers. A couple stroll arm-in-arm licking ice-cream. The shop windows gleam with hanging sausages and goods. Excited and anxious, Dimitri knows he's embarking on the next stage of his life.

When the taxi pulls away, he stares at the double-storey stone house. On either side of the large black door are two windows adorned with red and white flowers. Hesitating, he again checks the address. The number on the door is the same and, as he raises the brass knocker, the door swings open.

"My darling boy." A stocky woman beams before clutching him in a tight embrace. "How I've longed to see you."

Her smile reminds him of his mother and he brushes aside the nagging pain of her loss. He's taken aback by their similarities. Her short thick hair is grey, but her eyes and the shape of her nose are the same. He walks into the cool of the house, which is adorned everywhere with homemade doilies atop dark wooden furniture. She shows him to his room upstairs.

"Make yourself comfortable. You can put your clothes in this cupboard where I've made you some space."

The room is simply decorated with a single bed and white bedspread. A small wooden table sits in the corner, and when she opens the cupboard he notices someone else's clothes hanging inside.

"They belonged to your cousin." Vera's eyes fill with tears and she sniffs in between the awkward silence.

"Thank you, Tetka. I'm sure I'll be very comfortable here."

She shows him the bathroom on the landing, and he follows her downstairs to a small room where a table is covered with food; soup, homemade bread, a spinach pastry he remembers from his childhood called zelnick, and roasted meats. And he realises how hungry he is as she piles his plate high. She begins to pour some red wine and he shakes his head.

"No thank you, Tetka. I don't drink red wine. It doesn't agree with me." He has never been able to stomach it.

His aunt watches him eat, her hands clasped in front of her on the table. He looks up and smiles and her face is full of joy.

"It's been so long since I've had zelnick. It's just like…" he's about to say Majka but checks himself with a cough instead. The taste is as he remembers and he suddenly feels a lump in his throat. He loved the smell of the baking pastry and begged his mother for a piece straight from the oven.

"I can't tell you how good it is to see you. Your mother would have been proud." She wipes the tears away with her apron, just like his mother used to do. "You're a big, handsome boy." Then she begins to cry. "How I miss her."

Not knowing what to say, Dimitri finishes eating. He's not ready to talk about his mother.

"Would you like more?" she says.

"Thank you but no more for me," he says. "You're not eating?"

She shakes her head. "I had a little before."

He sits back in the chair and glances around the room as his aunt clears away the dishes. There are photos on the mantelpiece and he gets up to inspect them. There is one of his aunt with a man and two boys.

"That's me with your uncle and cousins. They were killed by a German bomb." She picks it up and her eyes fill with tears. "You would have liked them. Good boys. They would have been a bit older than you now."

Putting the photo down, she clears more dishes.

"Would you like some help?" Dimitri asks.

"Oh no. No, Dimitri," his aunt says, shaking her head. "Sit. Read the newspaper."

He glances at the folded newspaper on the side table next to a big floral-patterned chair. He notices on the other side of the room another photo. He recognises her in an instant. His mother is much younger with her head tilted back in laughter. He runs his hand across the glass of the frame.

"It's so unfair. Why take her? A good woman. Hardworking. All she wanted was to be with her family," his aunt says behind him.

"Yes. She was a good mother," he says, putting the photo back.

"If she hadn't married …"

He's not sure why she stops and wonders if the marriage to his father was frowned upon. But he's in no mood to hear it. The rich food begins to sit like a log in his gut. He doesn't want to be reminded that he no longer has parents.

"Thank you, Tetka Vera, for the meal. If you don't mind, I think I'd like to stretch my legs and go for a walk."
"Of course. We'll talk later," she sniffs.

He hears her sobs as he gently closes the front door. He wanders around the city, losing himself in the gardens along the Varda river, in the laneways and in the bustle of the day.

Eventually he tires and, with the setting sun, he finds his way back to his aunt's home – his new home, she'd declared.

Vera watches him carefully as they make small talk over dinner. He tells her what he's seen and where he's been, but he can't talk to her about his family.

After dinner, he excuses himself and goes to his bedroom, where he lies awake for hours working out what he should do. There's no reason for him to go back to his homeland and even if he wants to, the new law that all returning refugees must declare themselves to be Greek as a condition of entry doesn't sit well with him. He has no reason to return to Mikulov and decides to stay with his aunt, who's alone. He'll look for work and find Lazo. Having formulated a plan, he falls into a deep sleep.

The next morning, before leaving the house, Dimitri tells his aunt about his decision and she smiles with happiness.

He first returns to the university library, which he'd visited the day before. He'd noticed a sign asking for someone to shelve books and hopes the job has not gone. He's in luck. The job is his after they discover his linguistic skills and love of books. For the first time in a long while, he feels his life is changing for the better.

At home, his aunt announces that Lazo is coming for dinner.

Dimitri is nervous and excited waiting for Lazo to arrive. What will he look like? Will he be taller than him? Will they still like each other after all this time?

Dimitri almost runs to the door when he hears the knock. His friend stands there, grinning and looking like a bigger version of his childhood self.

"Where the hell did you get to?" Lazo beams, grabbing Dimitri and hugging him tight.

"I guess I took the wrong train."

"They must have had better food – you're taller than me."

"I always was," Dimitri laughs, slapping Lazo on the back.

Dimitri doesn't know why he'd been worried. They take up from where they left off all those years ago. When Lazo lost Dimitri he was distraught. He found out where the train was going and tried to get on the next one. But there wasn't another one. He had no choice but to go to Skopje where he went to an orphanage on the outskirts of the city. His sister found him twelve months later. She settled in the city, married and had two sons.

"I live with them still," Lazo says, grinning. "You'll come over to dinner and meet the family?"

"I'd like that. And your parents?" Dimitri asks tentatively.

A shadow crosses Lazo's face and he shakes his head. "Gone. The same as yours. The whole village went. Firebombs were dropped from the blackbirds and no-one got out in time."

They sit in silence for a while eating.

Dimitri brightens. "Do you still throw stones at the crows?"

Lazo laughs. "Not any more. Do you remember when you tried to throw a stone at the blackbirds? You were convinced that your stone could knock those bombers right out of the sky."

Dimitri frowns before he smiles and remembers. "Yeah. That's right. I was so sure that I could hit them."

"You were determined all right."

They chat and reminisce some more, careful not to talk too much about the march across the mountains. Before long the evening draws to a close and they say their goodbyes with plans for Dimitri to go to Lazo's house the following night.

Dimitri has a job, a place to live and his best friend. Finally, he feels he's in a place where he truly belongs. He lies in bed that night happier and more optimistic about the future than he's ever been.

45

Home at Last

Helen helps him up the concrete steps. The garden has grown without him, even though it's only been a few days. Rosebuds are now open and the grass seems longer. Treading heavily through the front door, Jim breathes in a comforting smell – lavender. Touching Helen's arm lightly, he smiles to tell her he's noticed. Out of season red tulips sit in a vase on the coffee table, and the whole house is airy and clean. The piles of newspapers next to his armchair are gone, as are the rolls of toilet paper he used to blow his nose, now replaced with floral tissues. The windows sparkle clean and the place almost doesn't feel like his own, but he's glad to be back.

He follows his daughter inside and heads to his bedroom, where she plonks a plastic bag of his things on the immaculately made bed.

"I'll sort out your stuff later."

Even here, the aroma is clean, almost as if the odour of him and Anna has been wiped away.

"I'll make us a cup of tea," she says as she leaves him.

He nods. His head feels heavy as he sits on the bed he shared with Anna. A place where they were bound together in a conspiracy of private conversations, intimacies and, most of all, their love. Now, all he feels is his immense age.

Finding his tattered slippers in a neat line in the cupboard with his dress shoes and runners, he removes his old brown leather walking shoes, tossing them carelessly aside. A quick check of the rest of the cupboard where her dresses still hang satisfies him – all still in order. He wanders into his study. Everything is as he left it; the boxes piled up, the stone still in the desk drawer, and Anna and her lovely smile in the photo on his desk. "It'll be fine," she'd always say. "You worry too much."

She was right. He did worry too much. He never remembered a time when he was free of it. He'd been afraid on the ship and what he'd find in a country he'd barely heard of. He feared not being good enough no matter how hard he worked. He was whole when he was with her and could do anything. Her constant belief helped him tolerate his worries. Now, he's not sure of anything except the slow creep of a headache.

"It's all very well for you. I have to deal with her questions. You know what she's like. She'll overreact," he whispers.

He's surprised at Helen's patience and consideration. He'd always indulged her. Mother and daughter clashed. She's our only child, he'd say in defence when Anna complained about how much he spoiled her. But he wanted her to have everything he'd never had. "I do too, but we've got to set boundaries," Anna had said. "She has to learn toughness too."

"Dad, it's ready," Helen yells from the kitchen.

"How could you have left me with this?" he whispers to the photo.

On the spotless kitchen table is a cup of tea, a plate of scones and a notepad and pen.

"I thought this might help. You can write down what you want to say. Is that okay?"

He raises his eyebrows and nods approvingly as he blows on the tea to cool it enough to sip. Then picks up the pen and writes: *Thank you for cleaning the house. It looks as good as new.*

"I can't say I did it all. I got a cleaner in. See how good it looks when it's clean? No more mouse droppings." Helen nervously chuckles.

He forces away the alarming thought of having a stranger in his house.

Did you make the scones?

"No. I bought them. Do you like them?"

Very nice. Better than the swill in hospital.

He's happy she's eating a scone too.

"It can't have been much fun in there."

They lapse into an awkward silence. Outside, a car drives past. Beyond his walls are the neighbours, their dogs, cats and children. He wonders for a minute if they have had to live with secrets like him, or is he the only one?

"Dad," she takes a deep breath. "Dad, I don't know if you noticed but I made up my old room and, well, I'm going to stay for a few days. Just to make sure you're all right."

If he could he would protest and tell her that he'll be perfectly fine. That he really doesn't need her and he likes being on his own – he can look after himself. But he can't say that. In truth, he's scared about everything. The stroke, the speech and all the tests he's yet to do. They'll find more things that he's not ready for.

"Dad? Dad?"

He's still poised with the pen in his hand.

"Are you all right with me staying?"

Thanks love. That would be good. What about

He's forgotten the no-hoper's name.

"Tony's fine with it," she says, reading his note upside down.

And work?

"I'll work from here. I brought my laptop."

And the kids?

She frowns. "They don't live at home anymore. Remember? Jasmine lives in Brisbane and Alex moved to New York."

He smiles, more in relief than anything, and nods.

"Dad, there's something else." She sweeps the crumbs on the table into a neat pile with her forefinger.

The muscle in his neck tightens and his head begins to thump.

"Dad, I have to know. They said you're speaking your first language. Is that true?"

Her question is not unexpected. He feels her bright-blue eyes boring into him while he doodles on the pad. He's drawn a box inside another box and wishes he had a different coloured pen.

"Dad?"

Concentrating on the drawing, he nods without looking up.

A small groan escapes from her. She shifts on the chair, causing it to creak.

The dog next door takes up its mournful bark of loneliness and Jim gives up the box and draws a continuous circle instead.

Leaning forward, Helen sweeps the crumbs off the table into her hand, sliding the tiny pile into her empty cup.

"So does that mean you're Macedonian and were born in Macedonia?"

He stops doodling and considers. What's on the piece of paper can't change the subject – won't distract her even though it's filling with pictures. She wants to know. The pen and paper will tell her. It won't be him. And he turns the paper over where it's blank and writes slowly. He has to get it right.

I was born in Northern Greece and before I came to Australia I considered myself to be Macedonian.

He can't bear to look at her.

"Oh my God!" The chair scrapes back as she gets up and goes to the sink. "This is unbelievable."

She sinks into the chair again, pulling it close to the table to rest her elbows and cradle her head in her hands. Jerking her head up, she exclaims, "But I'm sure my birth certificate says you're Australian."

Lied. No-one checked.

"Jesus. So this means, then, that I'm half Macedonian?"

He writes: *Actually your background is 100% Macedonian.*

"Fuck! Dad. I mean, sorry for the language. You mean Mum was Macedonian too?"

She gets up, starts pacing, and he stares at the new box he's drawn. It hadn't occurred to him that his daughter is anything other than Australian. He'd not given her heritage, or what it might mean to her, a single thought until now.

"I can't believe this. I can't believe that you didn't think this was important enough for me to know. That you've been living a lie. Be honest in life, you always said. Ha! What a joke. You can't even look me in the eye."

She's right. He can't bear to see the pain on her face. *I'm sorry. But it's a long story.*

She looks over his shoulder. "I'll bet it is. So Jim Philips is not your real name, is it?" She resumes her pacing. "Of course not. What is it?"

Dimitri Filipidis. Your mother was Marika Anna Ginova.

"Sweet Jesus. When I think … I can't think. I just can't fuckin' think. How could you do this? Everything I've ever known about you is a lie. And Mum. She's just as bad. I can't deal with this. I'm sorry but ..." She walks out of the kitchen shaking her head. "I have to go out for a bit. Clear my head," she says, then slams the front door.

He stops doodling and stares at the page of lines and realises he's drawn rows of flowers. A tear escapes and drops into the middle of one, blurring it. He hauls himself up and walks forlornly around the house until he stops in front of a photo of the three of them. He hears Anna's voice in his head. "She'll come back. She's in shock that's all. It's a lot to take in."

"I don't know," he says out loud. "It's not the same as when I told her about your accident."

He walks to the bedroom and lies on the bed. "Why can't you still be here?" he whispers. "Why?"

46

A Chance Meeting

Dimitri settles into life with his aunt and his new job. Each morning, when he walks into the library, a whiff of ancient mustiness, old leather and dust prickles his nose. His first task of the day is to sort returned books into their correct places on the shelves. When he's sure no-one is looking, he can't resist reading snippets. He saves books of interest and takes them home where he reads every chance he gets. It takes his mind off the loss of his family.

Luckily, the main librarian, Katerina, a kindly middle-aged woman, is understanding. Once, when he tried to take home five books because he couldn't decide which ones to read, she suggested he write reviews so they could be featured on a display.

Today, as he greets her, he's proud to see the typed blurb about the five books he read last week displayed on the table inside the entrance.

"Good morning, Dimitri. One of the books you recommended was borrowed by the Mayor after he read your review," Katerina says, smiling.

Dimitri beams. Returning books to the shelves, he daydreams about a novel he's been reading, *The Good Soldier Švejk* by Jaroslav Hašek, a book by a Czech author published in 1923. Contemplating how to write his review, he spies a girl through the other side of the shelf. The space from the book he's pulled out frames her in a shaft of dust-filled light. Dark glossy hair falls between square shoulders. Dust motes drift around him and it's as if he and the girl are cocooned in an aura of shimmer in the turbid light. He wills her to turn around but she's engrossed in reading.

"Excuse me, do you have books written about the Ottoman Empire?" a stooped man asks.

Dimitri jumps. "Ah, yes, in the opposite aisle." He points.

When he turns back to peek through the shelf, she's gone. Rushing to replace the book, he pushes the trolley toward the counter and collides with the girl coming out of the aisle.

"Sorry," he says.

Her deep-blue eyes burn into him like the flame of a gas burner. He's sure he's seen them before.

"You should watch where you're going," she says, rubbing her leg.

"I'm really sorry. I didn't see you. Are you all right?"

Gaping, he's almost certain he knows her. Eyes hooded by a frown appraise him.

A shaft of sunlight falls between them and he takes her in.

Dressed in a floral blue dress and low-heeled shoes, she flicks her hair impatiently. He's confused. The long black wavy hair is no longer bowl shaped. Her boyish figure has filled out. "Marika?" Dimitri says softly.

She frowns, looking confused. "Do I know you?"

"You should know me." He nervously laughs. "But I suppose you might not remember me."

She cocks her head. "I don't know you."

The tilt of her chin reminds him of when she apologised for calling him a baby. Right before they left Bitola. "It's me, Dimitri Filipidis. We walked through the mountains together."

"I don't know what you're talking about."

It's his turn to be confused.

"Do you work here?"

"Ah, yes, I do. So you didn't walk over the mountains during the Civil War?"

"I most certainly did not! I've lived here all my life. Can you help me find a book or not?"

He's sure the heat he feels is spreading a hue of red across his face. Trying to hide his embarrassment, he gropes for the last book in the trolley, hoping that Katerina will call him and release him from his awkwardness.

"I'm sorry, I thought you were someone else. What book are you after?"

Locating the recently released novel she wants, she stands close enough for a faint waft of lavender to drift toward him as he hands the book to her. He has an urge to touch her hair and hold her soft hands.

Her smile of thanks feels as if a difficult chasm has been crossed, until she turns abruptly to walk purposefully to the front counter, leaving him bewildered. It's as if she knows he is watching her. Then she disappears.

He can't get her out of his thoughts for the rest of the day. That night, the old nightmare comes back to him. The dead soldier knocks on his door with a warrant for his arrest. He's dragged down the street and, as the gun is turned on him, he wakes suddenly in a cold sweat. He hasn't had the dream for years and it unnerves him. He thought he was free of it, until now.

Lying in the dark, he thinks of the girl, and the more he thinks of her, the more he convinces himself she is Marika. He has to find her and for the rest of the night plots how.

When he arrives at work he puts the books away as always. He remembers the title she borrowed and he finds another book written by the same author.

"Excuse me, Katerina. Do you know how I can find out who borrowed a book by this author yesterday? I think it was a young girl."

Katerina, with a pencil behind her ear, is busy reading a letter. "Why?" she says without looking up.

"She mentioned that she wanted another book by the same author, but I couldn't find it yesterday."

"So?"

"Well, I told her if she came back today, she might find it's been returned."

Barely glancing at him, Katerina holds out her hand. "Give it to me and I'll check when I get a spare minute."

Dimitri swallows hard, clinging the book to his chest. "You're busy. If you show me where to look I'll check." He isn't allowed behind the counter and doesn't have access to the cards where the members' details are kept.

"What?" Katerina squints and considers him for a moment. "Oh, all right. I suppose you could learn about the library cards. Look in that pile on the other desk. They're from yesterday. After you've checked, you can file them for me in the cabinet over there."

He nods, happy that his plan has worked, until he finds the card. The title of the book the girl borrowed is listed on the card, but the name listed is Irina Pandev. He stares at it for a moment, wondering if he's mad. She was telling the truth. Quickly, writing down the name and address on a piece of paper, he slides it into his trouser pocket.

Casually, at a soccer match with Lazo the next day, he broaches the subject of Marika.

"There's not much to tell. We went with the others to Skopje, then they split us up. She went to one orphanage and I went to another. After a few months, I heard she was adopted."

"And you never saw her again?"

"Nope. Hey, do you remember that kid Petro? You know,"

the one with the scars all over his arms and the enormous ears?"

"No!"

"You know the one they called Puppy."

Dimitri pretends interest but isn't listening to Lazo as he rattles off information about Petro and other children they knew. The names mean nothing to him. He's only interested in finding out about Marika, and Lazo can't help him.

After work, he doesn't know why he goes out of his way to casually walk past the building where Irina Pandev lives. It's a three-storey stone building with a faded blue picket fence. He strolls up and down the street twice, pretending to be looking for an address, and scarcely considers what to do if he actually sees her again.

Every day he walks an extra half an hour home past her building, hoping for the chance to see her again. Once, he thought he saw her walking ahead. He ducked and weaved around people to catch up, but lost her.

The thought of her gnaws at him until she becomes an obsession. What he remembers of her becomes amplified – her eyes, full lips, the curve of her waist, the dimple on her left cheek – and reduces him to a desperate bleakness.

His aunt notices his appetite has waned. He makes excuses not to go out with Lazo and his demeanour is explained away as melancholy for the loss of his family. The lie only deepens his guilt.

47

Future in a Coffee Cup

The chill of winter settles with the weeks and Dimitri still walks the extra two kilometres out of his way past the girl's building. Realising the futility of his efforts, he finally gives up.

A week later at work he deals with a queue of people who wait patiently to return books. Piling them neatly onto a trolley ready to be returned to the shelves, a precariously balanced book falls.

As he bends to pick it up, he hears a voice ask, "Do you have a book by this writer?"

His gaze coasts along the floor and climbs to the height of a girl pointing to a ragged piece of paper in her gloved hand. Hoisting himself to his full height, he stares. She's dressed modestly in a navy dress and wears a small hat.

Lifting her chin, she searches his face as if she's trying to get a measure of him. It's all he can do to compose himself. It's the girl who's occupied his thoughts these last weeks.

Wrenching his gaze from her enquiring face, he reads the words on the paper and jerks his head back as if he's been slapped. One eyebrow arches quizzically and a glimmer of a smile dances on her lips. He knows the book – it's about the famous Macedonian dissident, Mirka Ginova, who died during the Civil War. He remembers Mirka is Marika's aunt.

He closes his gaping mouth abruptly and gulps. "Ah, er, I can look for you. It should be this way?"

With quivering legs and clammy hands, he strides toward the far corner of the library, her footsteps keeping pace behind him. He selects the book from the shelf and when he's sure they're out of earshot, turns to her. "Is this the book, Marika?" He almost stumbles on her name and looks for her reaction.

"Thank you, Dimitri," she says, running her fingers over the hard cover and down the spine.

"It is you."

"What time do you finish?"

"At four."

She nods. "Meet me tomorrow at 4.30 at this café," she whispers before thrusting the book and another piece of paper into his hand and walking briskly away. His heart thunders so loudly he's sure everyone can hear it.

***

Arriving early, he finds a seat in the café where he can watch for her. Ordering a Turkish coffee while he waits, his mind is in a whorl. What should he say? The coffee arrives and he sips the thick liquid slowly and watches as the café fills. After what feels like an hour, he asks a man on the next table for the time. It's only been fifteen minutes. Nervously tapping his fingers on the table, he watches each person who enters. The bulk of a man blocks the doorway and he doesn't see the red polka-dotted dress until it nears his table. A strange feeling of elation comes over him when he sees it's Marika, and his nerves calm when she smiles.

"Hello," she says. Sweeping the expanse of her dress underneath her as she sits opposite, she opens her handbag and brings out a packet of cigarettes. Handing Dimitri the matches, she leans in expectantly. He lights it and, as he does, it occurs to him how different their lives are – she with her smoke ring and he tongue-tied. She seems so much older and worldlier.

"You're persistent aren't you?"

"Wha, what do you mean?"

She cocks a dark thin eyebrow.

"Following me."

His face burns with an inelegant glow. "You knew?"

Leaning forward she hisses, "Of course I knew. I saw you every day."

"I thought the name and address were wrong. Your library card lists you as Irina."

"It belongs to my mother."

"Why did you pretend not to know me?"

"I wasn't pretending. I don't want to be reminded of my

ugly past. I have a new life here." Strands of dark hair, escaped from her ponytail, hang limp along the side of her face.

"What happened to you?"

She hesitates. The waiter places coffee in front of her. She scoops two generous teaspoons of sugar into the thick glug. Stubbing her half-smoked cigarette, she sips. Her full lips hide white teeth; one slightly crooked. A small mole on the side of her cheek edges a dimple when she smiles.

"It's simple. I took the train meant for us and you didn't."

"I was stupid. But what happened after that?" He scratches the prickle of new whiskers on his chin and wishes he'd gone home first to shave. "I've seen Lazo and he never mentioned you, not once."

"That's because he ended up in another orphanage. They split us up."

"Where did you go?"

"I went to an orphanage just outside of Skopje. Luckily for me, a young childless couple adopted me. They gave me everything I wanted." Her eyes glisten fiercely. "Beautiful clothes, an education, a magnificent house to live in. I wanted for nothing. For the first time in my life, I was loved."

Finishing her coffee, she flips her cup upside down on the saucer. "You at least knew what it was like to be loved. You knew your parents. I never knew the love of mine. Can you imagine what that was like for me? As far as anyone knew, I had no-one. I hated my great-aunt and great-uncle and most of all my horrible cousin. And they never cared for me. My new parents took in a poor refugee orphan. End of sad story."

Turning the coffee cup right side up, she peers in and frowns at the thick goo of brown coating the sides. "Have you finished? Turn yours over and I'll tell you your fortune."

He does as she asks. "You're a fortune teller? What does yours say?"

She screws up her face. "It always says the same thing." She picks up his overturned cup and peers into it. Time seems to stand still. "Mmm, yours is the same as mine. We're destined to travel to a faraway land. We're already in a faraway land, don't you think?"

Dimitri can't think. All he wants to do is touch the hand clasping his cup.

"I was in Czechoslovakia so I guess I've been and come back."

She smiles.

"I'm really glad to have found you, Marika." He means it. He's always been drawn to her even when they were children. Being with her now gives him an unaccountable happiness he's never felt before.

"Actually, I've changed my name to Anna. A new identity … a new life."

"Do you … do you ever think about the soldier?" he blurts.

Stiffening, she puts her cigarettes into her bag and stands abruptly. "Thanks for the coffee. I have to go."

Dimitri wants to kick himself. She made it clear she didn't want to be reminded. However, he still needs to talk about it and she's the only one who understands. He should have waited, he tells himself. And he wonders how he can see her again.

He doesn't wonder for long. Coming out of the café, he sees her standing across the street smoking. Her stare pulls him across the road.

"Marika, I'm sorry," he says.

"If you want to see me again, you must promise me two things. You're to call me Anna and never ever talk about what happened. Ever!"

Staring into her blue eyes, all he can say is yes.

***

He sees her three more times before he has the courage to kiss her. At a movie, putting her hand on his arm, her touch burns into his skin. The screen is blank to him as he feels for her fingers in the dark. Walking home, they chat about the movie.

He's about to say goodbye when she lifts her head. "You can kiss me if you like." He's never known lips could feel so soft. He's falling. The feel of her tongue. He's falling into abandonment. Whatever it is, he understands he wants only more and for it to never end. But end it does as she pulls away, breathless.

"Okay," she says, laughing. "I think that's enough." She looks back through the front door and winks. "See you tomorrow?"

"You sure will," he says.

After that, they see each other every day. He meets her adoptive parents and she meets his aunt. She doesn't want to see Lazo – he's a reminder, she says. Yet she doesn't seem to mind that Dimitri is a reminder too.

He feels like a bumbling fool when he's around her but she doesn't seem to notice. They talk about books. She loves to read too. They discuss her work. She's apprenticed to a highly regarded dressmaker. Each time they go out she turns up in a different dress she's made. He likes her best in blue, which suits her eyes, he tells her.

Then, one chilly day a few months later, when they're strolling through the gardens nearby, he puts his arms around her and tells her he loves her.

She pulls him close and kisses him.

"Will you marry me?" he blurts.

A ragged breath escapes her. "I'm only fifteen and so are you."

"Actually, I'm pretty sure I'm already sixteen. Besides, everyone thinks I'm seventeen."

"What do you mean?"

"You're the only one who knows my real age. I was given a new birthdate so my papers state I'll be eighteen next month."

"What about your aunt? She'll know."

"My aunt has no idea. She thinks I'm almost eighteen and, besides, she likes you. She says you're a good Macedonian girl." He laughs.

"What's so funny about that? I am a good Macedonian girl." She smirks.

"Of course you are." He grabs her around her waist and bends to kiss her again.

Drawing away, she shakes her head. "And what about Lazo? What's he going to say?"

"Don't worry about Lazo. He's going to Germany to work and leaves tomorrow. He asked me to go with him but I told him I couldn't leave my aunt." He lifts her chin and kisses her deeply.

"And you didn't tell him about me?"

"No. You told me not to, remember?"

He pulls away and searches her face. "So was that a yes?"

"This is madness," she says frowning, and he sees she's thinking. "It could work."

"What do you mean could work. You haven't said if you love me and want to marry me yet. We can work everything out after that."

She laughs, puts her arms around his neck and kisses him deeply. He knows her answer.

Three months later, in April 1954, Dimitri and Anna are married.

48

The Knock at the Door

Jim washes the dishes and wanders around the garden feeding the magpies. It's hasn't been long but it feels like a lifetime since he was at home. He checks the water meter, then the gas meter and takes a photo of the numbers on each. He picks a sprig of parsley, sniffs Anna's blood-red roses and sighs.

"You've pruned them too hard," she'd growled. "They're ruined!" He'd been itching to use the new pruning shears and the six-foot rose bushes were reduced to six inches. Now the roses are bigger and better than they've ever been. He wishes she could see them.

He wants to dig up some weeds but is worried about bending down. Then he remembers, his pendant alarm is on his bedside table. Limping inside, he puts parsley he's harvested in a jar of water and makes another cup of tea. Sitting alone at the kitchen table, the house is silent except for the tic toc of the old clock on the mantelpiece. He writes down the figures from the photos in his book and compares the water usage to the last recording five days earlier. More water has been used while he's been away than for the whole month. He should be angry. But he isn't and can't muster up indignation to figure out why. He has bigger concerns.

Without finishing his tea, he wanders the house and notices the light flashing on the phone, which must have rung while he was outside. He plays the message. "Hi, Dad, I'm sorry but I got caught up. I have to do a few things but I'll be back later, probably after you've gone to bed. I've called Flo and asked her to check on you. There's a chicken casserole in the fridge for dinner. Don't wait up."

She doesn't sound too upset, he thinks. He replays the message and is annoyed that she's asked Flo to come. He's a full grown man who is perfectly capable of looking after himself.

The clock on the mantelpiece chimes two times. He'd given it to Anna for their third wedding anniversary and just after her first miscarriage. It took nearly ten years before their baby girl came along. The doctors told them they couldn't have any more, which made Helen all the more precious to them.

It's not as if they ever lied to her. She didn't ask the right questions, that's all. And now she has and the whole thing is a mess. He's lost Anna and now Helen – the two most important people in the world. What if he has dementia? Will that mean he loses his recent memories? What if all he remembers is the childhood he's spent a lifetime trying to forget?

Rubbing his head, he slumps into his armchair, hoping to be distracted by the television, until he hears a knock at the door. Composing his face, he swings the door open to his smiling next-door neighbour, Flo, who's holding a casserole dish in her hands as if it's an offering to the gods. She's the last person he wants to see.

"Hello, Jim. I thought I'd come and see how you are."

He watches her eyes dart around the hallway as if looking to find fault and make a comment. He waves her in and heads toward the kitchen. Her fake jewellery jingles as her large frame bounces behind him and he waits for her inevitable opinion.

"Oh, the place looks amazing!" she exclaims in a high-pitched voice before sniffing. "And everything is so fresh."

He nods, knowing Flo will pass on her observations about him and the house to the rest of the street. He glances at the grey line zig-zagging down the middle of her head and the fluff on her faded grey oversized jumper. She's let herself go quite a lot, he thinks.

Flo and Ian had moved in next door a few months after them. They'd been friends and helped each other over the years. Their daughter Emma had gone to school with Helen.

He leaves her standing awkwardly while he seats himself at the kitchen table. He leafs through the notepad to find a blank page and writes, *Would you like a cup of tea?*

"Oh no thank you, Jim. I brought you a casserole." She lifts the dish toward him. "It's chicken with vegetables. I hope you like it. I cooked it this morning. It'll keep for a few days or you can freeze it. I'll just put it into the fridge, shall I?"

He nods, then remembers the other chicken casserole. *Thank you. It's very kind of you*, he writes.

"Ian and I were so upset when we found out what happened from Helen. It's so good that she's staying with you for a while."

She waits for him to write.

He wants to tell her to nick off.

Thanks. It's nice to have her here.

Flo sits down at the table. Frowning, she leans toward him and touches his arm gently. "You know, your speech can come back. My sister-in-law's brother lost his speech and it came back in just a few months. Mind you, it's worse if you don't get medical help quickly. Isn't it lucky that you had the stroke at the doctor's and not at home?" She sits back triumphantly in her chair waiting for him to respond. He has a mind to write down what he really wants to tell her but he knows Anna would've been cross. Forgive, forget and move on was her motto.

Yes, very lucky. Are you sure you wouldn't like a drink of something?

"Oh no, thank you. Look, Jim, if you need anything, anything at all just sing out. I mean..." She stops in her tracks and he sees her thinking. It makes him feel better seeing her squirm; that she has really put her foot in it this time. "Well... you know what I mean. Best be off."

He has an urge to snigger but instead walks with her to the front door until she stops at the photo of Anna in the hallway.

"I really miss her smiling face. It's been very hard ... you know, after the accident."

He nods and hopes he has a sympathetic enough look on his face. He remembers Flo had broken her arm and leg.

"It's not been the same since. I don't think I'll ever get over it." She sniffs. "Anyway, I'd better go. You take care of yourself, Jim. We're only next door if you need anything at all."

He waves and closes the front door, relieved she's gone. It's actually nice not to speak. It cuts the conversation off. Flo has tried many times to discuss what happened but he can't talk about it.

It really wasn't her fault that the truck came through a stop sign and hit them on Anna's side. The truck driver on his mobile phone didn't see them. Yet he can't help feel animosity toward his neighbour, who'd come over and also admonished him over his harsh pruning of the roses.

"Really, Anna, you should get a gardener in," Flo had said. "Now the real reason I came over was to tell you that the Zumba class is on in half an hour."

"Half an hour? Oh, I don't know. I've got to clean up all this mess," Anna said, picking through the piles of rose cuttings on the lawn that he'd left.

"Come on. You said you'd come with me," Flo pleaded. "You promised."

"I'll pick this up if you want to go," Jim had grumbled.

"I don't know, Flo. I've never done Zumba. Aren't I a bit old?" Anna said.

"Nonsense," Flo said. "It's Zumba Gold for oldies. Now get changed and come. You've got fifteen minutes."

"Oh, all right. Jim, don't touch any other bush while I'm gone," Anna said, pecking him on the cheek.

And that was one of the last things his beautiful wife had said to him. He hadn't touched another bush since. In her hospital bed, she made him promise to tell Helen everything and he's botched it all.

He wanders into his study and turns on the computer. Anna, as usual, stares at him.

He lived his whole life thinking he was never good enough for her. She'd been smarter and never worried. He'd loved her more than she loved him. He knew that. She'd never known love as a child. Her mother had died on the floor of an old abandoned cottage after giving birth to her. Her great-aunt and great-uncle had never wanted her. The aunt had turned crazy after losing two sons in a house fire, and the only son who survived gave Anna hell. Jim had hated to hear of her suffering as a child. Not that she talked about it much. Like him, she tucked it away forever when they got off the boat.

He glances at his watch. It's 5.30. Helen's been gone for over two hours. Where is she? Maybe she's been called into work. What are the things she has to do? Or maybe she's crying somewhere in a park. As she grew up he was always fearful for her. What if she got lost?

He can't eat and goes to bed early, tossing and turning,

keeping an ear out to listen for any sign of her. Fatherhood was tough and he worried constantly. A light sleeper, he was up first whenever Helen made a sound in her cot. He'd hated her going to school. The fence was too low. She could wander out, he'd said. The monkey bars were too high – what if she fell? In her teens, she fought for her independence. She caught the train on her own because Anna had intervened in their arguments.

"She's old enough. I trust her," Anna had said.

"What if she gets lost?" he'd huffed back.

"She won't get lost." Anna knew of his own terror. She had always soothed his worries. Telling him how life here was different, reassuring him she'd be back. And she always was. It took him a long time to adjust when Helen left home and made her own life.

Now, he wants her to be small again, to take her in his arms and cuddle the hurt away. Laughing when he threw her into the air. Watching her ride her bike, throwing the ball, taking her for swimming lessons; soothing her with an ice-cream after her first belly flop. Now he can't soothe her. He can't remove the pain for her or for him. Has he lost her? Will she ever come back?

Drifting off to sleep, he's alone with his emptiness.

49

The Job

After Dimitri and Anna are married they live with her parents, much to his aunt's distress. They're the lucky ones in the city. The house they live in belonged to Anna's adopted grandmother and was passed down to her father until a few months ago when the government expropriated their building, like everyone else's, to become social property. Anna's parents were devastated when they were advised the house was to be split up to allow more families to move in. Dimitri's aunt was forced to give up her house and was confined to a room and kitchenette. Most young people were expected to live and work communally on plots owned by the government, barely making ends meet.

Anna goes off each day to her job as an apprentice dressmaker. Dimitri continues to work in the library where he's given more responsibilities. They let him search for books to buy and he spends many a day in bookstores. He can tell if a book is good within a few minutes of reading it and has the gift of speed reading.

Although they bring in just enough money to live, life is hard and food shortages are rife. Still, Dimitri is happy with his new life with Anna, although discontent is never far away as things worsen.

"I didn't escape that hell hole in Greece for another here," Anna complains after she and her mother have spent hours in queues for a few vegetables and a cup of flour. "It's getting worse."

"If your father hadn't gotten sick, there'd be more money," Dimitri says. "Maybe we should go out to one of the farms. I've heard there's plenty to eat if we grow it ourselves."

"My parents and your aunt need our money more than ever. On the farms, there's no money for us to send back."

"But we could send back food. Isn't that better?"

Anna shakes her head. "It's hopeless. Sophia's friend lives in one of the villages and they have to give more than three-quarters of what they grow to the government. They've barely enough to feed themselves." Anna paces. "The only way is out. Like Lazo's done. He's making a heap of money in Germany."

Dimitri is thoughtful. Lazo left just before they married and his letters, although irregular, are full of excitement. Working in a steel factory, he made it sound as though his wallet was overflowing with cash.

"Maybe I should go to Germany. Lazo said there were jobs there. There's not much of a future at the library and it wouldn't be for long. The government will let me go if they know I'll send money back."

Anna's face falls. "Do you really want to go? I couldn't bear to be apart."

Dimitri puts his arms around her and whispers into her ear. "It was just an idea. I don't want to leave you either."

"Maybe we could go to Canada."

Dimitri looks at his wife. "Why there?"

"They're taking in child refugees from the Civil War. That's what we are. Aren't we?" She stares at him and he sits heavily on the bed.

"But that means declaring ourselves as refugees. I thought you wanted to put that behind you."

"I do." She paces the floor then stops. "No. I don't want to go down that path. They'll ask lots of questions. I just can't deal with it."

Dimitri holds her. "Don't worry. We'll work it out."

***

The food shortages worsen with the approach of winter and the chill wind whistles about Anna's legs as she waits, hungry, in yet another line.

A few weeks later, she arrives home breathless with excitement.

"You'll never guess what happened today."

"What?" Dimitri says, smothering her with kisses in the privacy of their bedroom. His hands slide up under her sweater.

"Dimitri, stop and listen!"

Letting her go, he sits on the bed. "All right. Tell me what happened. Then can I ravish you?"

She smiles indulgently. "I've been offered another job. A better job with a lot more money."

"How much more?"

When she tells him, he picks her up, and swings her around the room.

"I'm so proud of you." He finally puts her down to kiss her properly.

"It's a wonderful opportunity. Any of the other girls could have been asked but I was chosen. It's a huge honour."

"So what's the job?"

He should have known from her hands. She'd always find something to twirl whenever she had something difficult to tell him. Sometimes it was her hair, a serviette or even her necklace, as she was doing today.

"Sophia is leaving and she wants me to go with her to work as a dressmaker."

He whoops again. "That's incredible! That means you've finished your apprenticeship?"

"Yes. But there's something else."

"What?"

"There's a tiny detail that I have to tell you."

"What?" The tone in her voice alarms him.

"She's going to work in Malbun or something like that. I'll find out more in a few days."

He lets out the breath he'd been holding. Relieved. "So we have to move. We wanted to move anyway. It's perfect."

She flings her arms around him and kisses him. It wasn't until after they'd made love that he begins to wonder where they're going.

Leaning on his elbow while she dresses and fixes her hair, he asks her.

Staring into the mirror, she doesn't miss a beat. "Oh, it's somewhere in Austria, I think."

He nods and his mind races. They have no ties. He knows how to speak German. He'll find a job there.

They're excited when they break the news, but her parents aren't quite so happy, and nor is Dimitri's aunt. But their excitement is infectious and soon both families are happy for the young couple. The money they'll send back will be worth it.

A week later, Anna arrives home crestfallen.

"What's the matter?"

"It's the new job." Her eyes are downcast.

He lifts her chin to kiss her but she twists away. "Don't."

Walking to the other side of the room, she begins to cry. "What? Tell me what's wrong. It can't be that bad."

Sniffling, she wipes her eyes. "Tell me that you'll be with me, that you'll come to the end of the Earth with me."

Puzzled, he nods. "Of course. Nothing is that bad. And if it is, we can fix it. Together we can do anything. You know that." He's referring to the trek and the soldier. What could be worse than that? he thinks.

She's thoughtful. It's enough to hold her head high and dry her eyes. "You're right. We can do anything. It doesn't matter that we are going to another country. It's still a foreign country. We'll still write to Majka and Tato and to your aunt and our friends."

"Of course. You're just getting cold feet, that's all. It'll be an adventure." He's full of confidence.

"It's just that when I told you that Malbun is in Austria, I was mistaken. It's not in Austria."

"So what? That doesn't matter. Where is it then?"

"Australia, and the town is called *Melbourne*."

"Great. That's fine." He nods. He's never heard of the country. "Is it far?"

"I ... I think it's very far." She ducks into her father's study and brings out a globe. "It's here." She points to a huge continent on the other side of the world and Dimitri's heart sinks.

"Shit!" He sits down heavily. "How the hell do we get there? What do they speak? Why there?"

"I know, darling. So many questions. Sophia doesn't want to go without me. She needs a good dressmaker and she says there's so much opportunity there. We can make money, send some back and have plenty left over. Not like here. There's barely enough to feed us now and if we have children, then it'll be even harder."

Drying her eyes, she searches his face as he thinks about this new country, Australia.

"I'm sorry, but I thought it was Austria. Apparently they speak English. I can speak a little bit of English that Tato taught me, but I'll have to learn it." It all pours out of her in a rush. "They gave me two tickets for a boat that leaves in two weeks. Her sister is already there and..."

"Hold on. I can barely keep up with you. English. That's all right. I learnt English back in the orphanage. I can teach you. We have to leave in two weeks? That's sudden. What's the urgency?"

"Sophia is leaving tomorrow and she bought our tickets when she bought hers."

"We have to get our papers sorted first."

"It's fine. She's got it all done for us. We just have to sign these documents and lodge them."

"How much were the tickets? We'll have to pay her back."

"We can pay her back when we get there."

Dimitri scratches his head and begins reading the paperwork she hands to him. Then he looks up. "Where will we live?"

Anna is lighting a cigarette. "Her sister found a place for us to live. She's the one who got us the jobs. Stop worrying, Dimitri. It'll be fun."

"I have to think about these things even if you aren't. You said us. Is there a job for me too?"

Anna drags on the cigarette and blows a smoke ring over him. "Didn't I just say that? She has a job for you on the factory floor."

"What do I have to do?" Dimitri is worried and the old feelings of anxiety flood back. He's not sure he wants to uproot. He's been happy and felt like he belonged for the first time since he left his village.

"Stop frowning and looking so grumpy. We talked about this. Remember?" Anna settles on the bed next to him and gently puts her hands on either side of his face and settles her lips on his. He puts his arms around her until, finally, she pulls herself away. "I know you're worried about leaving. But this time it will be different. You'll see. It's going to be much better."

He smiles. "It looks like we're off to Australia. I better study about this place tomorrow at work when I tell them I'm leaving."

Her face breaks into a smile and she jumps into his lap, smothering him in kisses.

"This is our chance," she says, "to put everything behind us. No-one will know us there."

"Except for Sophia, her husband and soon her sister," Dimitri says, counting on his fingers. "And all the others they've asked to come who we don't know yet."

"But they don't know about what happened."

"You mean the soldier and the fact that we're from Greece."

She nods.

"I thought you never wanted to discuss that."

"I don't. But I know that this move means we can turn our back on everything. Make new memories and push away that horrible time. You'll see. We won't ever have to be reminded of it. Living here still brings it back. Our life before Skopje is gone. And a new one begins."

"A new beginning." He smiles, trying to ignore the nervous flutter in his stomach.

"We are never to speak of that time again. Promise?"

"Promise."

***

On Monday, 3rd January 1955, after a month of travel, they join the throng of excited passengers on the deck of the ship moored to Port Melbourne dock. The blistering hot wind engulfs them as they search for Sophia. She's jumping up and down in a bright-yellow dress, waving her arms in excitement. Next to her stands an older woman in a suit, shading her eyes with a white-gloved hand and holding her hat with the other.

"Hel-lo," Anna yells out excitedly. "We'll see you soon." But her words whip away in the fierce wind.

Dimitri is tired and hot carrying their two large suitcases down the crowded gangplank. He's barely brought a change of clothes to make way for his books and Anna's belongings. Despite his protest, she packed her mother's mauve floral dinner set, thrust upon them at the last minute.

"You'll need something to eat on," her mother had said, wiping her eyes.

Saying goodbye was more difficult than he'd thought. Tetka Vera's tearful face dredged painful memories of leaving his mother. The nightmares came back to toss him around on that first night away. His parents, the toddler and the dead soldier.

They shuffle silently in line like all the others, waiting their turn to tell their story to immigration. The pit of his stomach in a knot, Dimitri worries about being stopped. The train trip across Yugoslavia, checkpoints, questions and examination of their papers had made him feel like a fugitive and brought back his old anxiety. Crossing into France was an ordeal. The French officials had kept them for hours while their papers were checked, for what reason they never knew. The dead soldier's face had taunted his mind along the way.

He'd been ready to give up and turn back but Anna talked him out of it. She urged him on. They'd been excited when they saw the sea for the first time. Excitement turned into a nightmare. Holed up in an overcrowded cabin with seasickness, he'd been filled with doubt about the wisdom of leaving. It will get better, Anna had said, but he shuddered with dread.

As if she can read his worried mind, Anna puts her hand gently on his arm and whispers, "It's all right. Our papers are in order. Don't worry."

The line is unmoving and he feels lighter when he drops the suitcases and wipes his face with his handkerchief, appraising the other worried and worn faces around him. He sways as if he's still on the boat.

When it's their turn, a red-faced nugget of a man barely glances at them, then holds out his hand. "Next!"

The papers are pushed across the counter and Dimitri notices the sweat beading on the man's balding head as he studies their documents. Finally, the man lifts his head and eyes them to assess what type of people they could be.

"You're a commie then?"

"We're Macedonian, sir," Dimitri says immediately in his own tongue. Anna looks from the man to Dimitri in panic.

"What's he saying? What's happening?" Anna asks.

"I'll tell you later. Just keep quiet," Dimitri says.

"Listen, mate, you're going to have to learn to speak English." The man rolls his eyes and turns to his colleague next to him. "I got another coupla commies here."

"I'm sorry. We come from Macedonia." His stomach churning, Dimitri speaks slowly in a perfect English accent. "And we have jobs here."

The man stares in surprise then nods in approval. "So, mate, is your name Dimitri Filipidis? And your wife, Anna?" But he stumbles on the name, unable to get his tongue around the syllables.

"Yes, sir."

"And you've got jobs?"

"Yes, sir."

The man asks a few more questions about the jobs and where they'll be living, then signs the form. "I reckon we'll call you Jim and Anna Philips. You'll fit right in with that English accent of yours. A word of advice," the man lowers his voice and beckons him closer, "don't tell anyone you're a commie."

"What is a commie, sir?" Dimitri whispers.

"It's a communist. Some don't take too kindly to them."

"We're escaping from the commies, sir."

The man sits upright in his seat and grins. "Welcome to Australia, then."

"Thank you. Thank you very much," Dimitri says, grasping the papers in his sweating hands.

When they're out of the building, he tells Anna what was said.

"Oh God. I have to learn English fast."

After hugging Sophia and making their introductions to her sister, they get onto a crowded tram, where they find seats while Dimitri stands. The women are talking so fast they hardly take a breath.

Dimitri watches the other passengers. Most are well-dressed. Some stare at them. He feels self-conscious in his old grey pants and patched tweed jacket, which he takes off and folds over his arm. The heat is almost intolerable. They've come from a cold winter and hadn't realised the seasons were the wrong way round. As the tram lurches through the city, he closes his stinging eyes and tiredness envelops him.

When he hears a couple speak in Greek, his eyes spring open and he looks about wildly. Panic rises but he listens. They discuss people they've visited. The tram stops and people get off. Dimitri shuffles to a new spot as far away from the couple as he can get. He's convinced the man looks like the officer who took his father away. Sweat pools under his arms and down his neck, and he wants to get off. Instead, he clings onto the railing and tries to concentrate on the buildings he sees through the dusty window. When the tram stops he looks hopefully to Sophia and is disappointed at her shaking head.

A seat becomes vacant and he finds himself on the opposite side to the Greek couple. What are the chances that the man is the officer? If he is, he will surely not recognise him. But his tension doesn't ease. The couple stop talking to stare at Anna, Sophia and her sister, whose excited voices shrill loudly in Macedonian. Dimitri follows their glance to the suitcases on the floor, then back to the women, and the Greek man whispers something to his partner, who stares ahead grim-faced. Dimitri is reminded of the fear of being Macedonian in a Greek village.

The tram ride isn't helping his rattled nerves. His hands are clammy and he wipes his hands up and down his worn trousers. He tries to breathe but an acrid smell, like burning compost, assaults him. It's the smell of drying hops at a brewery nearby but he doesn't know that until much later. Today, he wants to retch. When he's almost at breaking point, the tram stops and he's ushered off by Sophia and her sister. They've arrived.

Later, in the privacy of their own bedroom in the boarding house in Richmond, Dimitri tells Anna about the Greek couple on the tram.

"That's even more reason to become Australian. We'll eat what they eat. Learn their ways and act as if we've always lived here. We don't need to mix with anyone other than Australians."

"That's a bit unrealistic. I don't know how we're going to do that."

"With a lot of hard work. You'll see. We'll do it."

And he knows Anna is right.

That night in bed, with a mosquito buzzing around his head, Dimitri wonders again if they've done the right thing. Suddenly, he misses the rocking of the boat and the smell of the coal smoke of Skopje.

***

It only takes a few weeks to settle into their jobs; Anna a machinist, and Dimitri, or Jim as he's now known, sweeping the floors and doing odd jobs in the textile factory. Months later they marvel at their new life and their freedom. They love everything about their new country and, in letters to their families and friends, describe the strange animals they've seen and the beaches with sand, which in the fierce sunlight is the colour of snow.

They leave out the flies, snakes and spiders, the insulting names they're called, and the bushfires. They don't care. They've seen and experienced much worse. They make enough money to send some back to Anna's parents and Dimitri's aunt. What is left over is used to save so they can build their own house in the paddocks of Glen Waverley.

Then, in 1963, they hear about the earthquake that wipes out most of Skopje. The letters from Lazo, who has returned from Germany, his aunt, and Anna's parents, stop. The only good thing to come out of that year is the birth of their baby girl, Helen; named after his grandmother, Elena – their one concession to their background.

50

The Apology

Jim wakes and sniffs. Light creeps in around the curtains. The time on the clock is 6.25 a.m and he hits the alarm before it goes off at 6.30. Sniffing again, he smells bacon and he's relieved. She must be back. Searching for his slippers, he pulls on his dressing gown and pads into the bathroom. The smell makes his stomach grumble, and he remembers that he'd forgotten to eat the night before. After he washes and dries his face, he wanders into the kitchen.

Helen hums softly as she stands with her back to him at the stove while pushing the bacon around the pan. A carton of eggs sits next to her on the laminate bench and bread is perched in the toaster, waiting. The jug whistles and he watches as Helen leans across to turn it off. There are two settings on the table and, as she turns around with the jug in her hand, she sees him leaning against the door and smiles.

"Good morning," she says, pouring the hot water into the teapot.

He smiles and sits at the table.

I'm glad you're back. I was worried, he writes on the pad while she concentrates on cooking. She breaks three eggs into the pan while he pours the tea and milk into the mauve floral china cups.

Putting crisp bacon on each plate, she reads his note and looks at him sadly. "I know. I'm sorry. I got back at around eight but you were already asleep."

Four slices pop and he collects the toast, butters them and puts two on each plate.

The eggs ready, Helen slides them onto the buttered toast and sits down.

This looks nice, he writes.

"Thanks," she says, watching him taking a bite. She eats half the toast, leaving the bacon, and sips her tea. He's enjoying the breakfast and gives her a thumbs up. He hasn't noticed a glob of egg on his chin and she leans forward with a napkin and gestures for him to wipe it. "There's a bit there."

The circles under her bloodshot eyes are worse and she looks as though she's been crying for hours. It hurts him to see her so pained. But what is there to say? He can only wait for her to ask, but silence falls between them. Finally, he finishes and after she clears the table, she sits down and chews on her thumbnail.

"Dad, I'm really sorry for the way I reacted. Running out yesterday like that was unforgiveable. But I needed to think."

It's all right. I understand, he writes. *Where did you go?*

"I went into work for a bit."

He nods and waits for her questions. He doesn't know how he'll answer them or if he can, but all he wants to do is help his daughter. He hates that he's the cause of her anguish. Isn't it a parent's job to make their child happy? But in this he can't.

"Dad, I did a lot of thinking and as you can imagine there are hundreds of questions. When I got back last night after you went to bed, I had a look at what you've been writing."

Picking up his pen, he doesn't know what to write and puts it down, settling for his teacup instead.

"I sat up all night. I read it all. And, and I want to tell you is that I ..." Tears roll down her cheek. "That I ..." she takes a deep breath. "I was so very moved. What you and Mum went through was unbelievable." Her voice cracking, she wipes her eyes. "I'm so sorry about the way I behaved. It must have been hell to keep it a secret. I just wish Mum was here too."

Me too. We wanted to tell you but didn't know how. It was difficult but putting it behind us was the only thing we knew to do.

"I understand. I'd like to know about my heritage and I'd like to learn the language."

He nods and writes.

I hadn't thought about what happened until your mother died. Did you see the stone and her diary?

"Yes, and I read her diary too. She always loved you. Right from when you met in the mountains."

I was a wimp as a kid.

327

"Not from what I read, Dad."

I killed a man. But it was war.

"You saved Olga, Dad. He might have killed you all."

Maybe

The tea has grown cold, and the sun streaming through the window warms them. Helen gets up and puts the kettle on. "Another?"

He nods and writes something else. *You know that I'm really only 78 not 80.*

She raises her eyebrows. "Looks like you're angling for another big birthday party in two years time," she says smiling.

Then she moves to her father's side and kneels down to kiss him and they hug each other tight, tears flowing from them both, interrupted only by the kettle's whistle.

"Why don't you turn on the news?"

He nods and takes his pad and pencil with him.

In the lounge with a fresh cup of tea, they sit quietly, each with their own thoughts, staring at the early morning news on the television.

There's more fighting in Syria and refugee children trudge in the rain across the borders to Macedonia. Jim shudders and flicks the vision off.

***

A week later, they walk arm-in-arm, approaching the crossing to go to the shops. The sky is a brilliant blue and the sun warms him.

Helen thought his story should be made into a book. Jim

was reluctant. The soldier was haunting his dreams and he wanted nothing more than to forget it all. He'd done his job. Helen knew everything, even his true age and that was all that mattered. Anna's wishes were fulfilled. But Helen wouldn't let it be.

"You know, I was thinking about that soldier."

Jim stops and raises his eyebrows. He doesn't want to think about him.

Helen frowns as she stares at him. "I can't see how you could have killed him."

He fumbles for his notepad. *We did*, he writes. *Let's leave it.* They continue walking.

"But, Dad, you were starving weak kids. I doubt you would have had the strength needed to hit him hard enough and in the right spot to kill him. Think about it."

Helen's words begin to make sense. Flashes of memory burst into his head.

He'd picked up a rock. She had her perfect stone. They each threw them. He remembers the surprised look on the man's face as he turned toward them before he fell. They ran to Olga. Marika looked for her stone.

"Dad, where was Olga after the soldier fell?"

He limps along deep in thought.

She was kneeling next to the soldier, he remembers. His heart beats madly in his chest.

"Where were the other children? Were they next to her, too?"

He shakes his head and shrugs. Why can't he remember them being with Olga?

"When you ran to her, what did you see?"

He shrugs again.

A flash of his face. Blood trickling from a cut on the soldier's forehead.

"Wasn't she a soldier too? Surely she would have been armed. I just wonder what she was doing?"

She stood up when we ran to her, he writes when they stop at the crossing, waiting for the lights to change. *It was war then and a long time ago.* His head begins to pound. Why doesn't she stop? If only he could shout at her.

"Was she checking if he was alive?"

He shrugs again and shakes his head. Why can't Helen let it go?

"It's not your fault."

The lights change. He's slow to cross and shrugs off his daughter's help. He wants to get away from his daughter's persistence. The soldier's blood. Where was the blood? He's sweating. He needs a glass of water. It's too hot.

The engine of the blackbird looking for its prey behind the gloom of smoke. Run, run, run. His legs won't move fast enough. It hurts to run. Blood. Screams. His walking stick flies. Screams.

There's a siren. *Hurry!* Marika's voice calls out like a singing nightingale.

51

The Magpie

"We're not sure if Jim knows what's happened or if he knows where he is," the nurse whispers.

His mouth is dry. Water? he wants to ask.

"He can probably hear you so feel free to talk to him."

"His name is Dimitri. He's Macedonian and so am I."

He hasn't heard his old name for years. It sounds odd. It's not him anymore.

"Dad, I'm here. Can you hear me? There's been an accident. You tried to run but were hit by a car."

I hear you, love, he wants to say.

"I'm here. You're going to be all right," she whispers. "You've got to be."

He moves his head and tries to smile but his lips won't do what he wants them to. He squints at his surroundings and feels lucky to be given such a fancy room. There's a view over the garden and a gigantic water tank. He wonders how much water it holds. When he's up to it he'll go outside and check. A magpie sits on the top and stares. Its feathers are black with streaks of grey; a sign it's not quite full grown. He's fed his magpies for years in the backyard. Every morning they come, a whole family waiting at the back door expecting to be fed. He lifts his hand and hopes they see he has nothing for them today.

"Feed my maggies," he whispers. "And Kitty."

"What did he say?" a nurse asks. "He's groaning."

"Is he in pain?"

The doctor puts the stethoscope to his chest. It's cold. Cold like the snow on his bleeding feet. He remembers the blood. The soldier's blood. He's sorry, he wants to tell him. But it was war.

"I'm sorry," he murmurs to the white uniform.

"What's wrong? Why is he moaning?"

"We're making him as comfortable as we can. The tests are in. I'm sorry."

They're talking about someone else, he thinks. Why is Helen still crying? She needs to pull herself together. She always was a crier, not at all like her mother. More like him when he was a kid.

Why is the uniform white? It was khaki with blood all over it. He'd looked back when they were running from the blackbird. There was only a little blood on his head where they'd struck him. She was kneeling on the man's left side away from them.

He remembers now. They were on his right side. He

remembers. Something glinted in Olga's hand. She wiped it on her skirt. But the blackbird is back. Bombs are falling. Run. Run hard.

He remembers. The blood. It's everywhere. The soldier's eyes are blank.

It's not our fault, Marika. It was never our fault. It was war and we got through it.

The light is dim. It must be dark. The kiss brushing his cheek accompanies a quiet sob. "Come on. He's resting. Let's get you a coffee and something to eat," says a hushed voice.

He's too tired to tell Helen she was right. If only they'd told her before.

Later, when she comes back.

He feels light as if a great weight has lifted from him.

He gasps.

His throat tightens, his fingers quiver and he's set free, soaring, like the magpie.

Author's Note

In times of war, people who have the least power, suffer the most.

Removal of children during war is not new. Before the Greek Civil War, in which this novel is set, children were separated from their parents during the Spanish Civil War ten years earlier, civil wars of Russia (1918–20), Finland (1917–18,) and Britain during World War Two.

Displacement of children from their homes continues to evoke widespread condemnation in the years since – Vietnam, Cambodia, Uganda, and, more recently, Syria. Australia's own indigenous children continue to suffer the consequences of removal. A United Nations report in 2014 listed fifty million refugees in the world, which is higher than the total number after WW2. Half of this number, according to UNICEF, are children.

During the Greek Civil War, it is estimated that there were up to 38,000 Aegean Macedonian and Greek children removed from their homes.

There is little information from the perspective of the

refugee children as many chose not to talk about or document their experiences. Some died from malnutrition and disease as a result of the war or the journey, and there is an absence of any official numbers. Of those who survived, many ended up staying in their respective countries, losing links to their heritage. Some never saw or heard from their parents again.

The Greek Communist Party formed the Democratic Army of Greece, backed by Yugoslavia, Bulgaria and Albania, and fought against the Greek Government, which was backed by the United States and the United Kingdom from 1946 to 1949. This war was the first conflict of what became known as the Cold War, and represented a struggle between left and right ideologies that germinated during World War Two.

After almost two years, the fighting intensified, and, in January 1948, the Greek Communist Party made a plea to Yugoslavia to help the children. The Yugoslav Government agreed to a limited evacuation. In March 1948 it was announced that children from the fighting zone of Northern Greece between the ages of two and fourteen would be sent to Bulgaria, Yugoslavia, Albania, Romania, Hungary, Poland and Czechoslovakia. The Greek Government, informed of this plan, announced three days later the relocation of some 14,000 children from what they called the 'bandit-controlled areas'. There started the propaganda war from both sides justifying the two removal programs; one side claiming it was a form of ethnic cleansing as most evacuations were from predominantly Macedonian areas, and the other claiming the abduction was intended to produce more communist soldiers. Either way, children at the centre of the tussle suffered tremendously.

It is said that more than 158,000 people were killed during the conflict, leaving a million homeless, but like many conflicts the true figure may never be known.

My research took in documented stories from surviving child refugees in Melbourne, Macedonia and Canada, and those of my own family. My mother-in-law, Anastasia, with her own father in jail and her mother dead, told me stories of hiding with her younger siblings so they would not be taken. Her older fourteen-year-old sister was handed a neighbour's newborn baby to deter the authorities, who allowed her sister to stay.

One aunt was not so fortunate. Effie was only five when she, her twin brother and two older sisters were taken while their parents were in the fields nearby. She barely remembers the journey but has happy memories of her time in a Czechoslovakian orphanage, where she recounts being educated and well treated. She wasn't separated from her siblings but many children were. With help from the International Red Cross, she was reunited with her parents when she was fifteen years old. She later married and now lives in Melbourne, Australia. I am very thankful for her willingness to share what painful memories she could remember. I am indebted to my extended family for sharing their experiences of the Greek Civil War and what it was like being a Macedonian living in Northern Greece.

Mirka Ginova is a real person who died in 1946. It is true that she was tortured and executed. It is not known if she had any family and the connection of the character, Marika Anna, is purely fictional, as are all the characters of this story. Any resemblance to anyone living or dead is purely coincidental.

Following the 1913 Treaty of Bucharest, existing Macedonian place names were gradually changed to Greek names. This included people's family and given names. The assimilation process was called Hellenisation. It became official in 1927 as the Greek Government Legislative Edict declared that, "there were only Greek people in Greece". From 1934 to 1941, the Military Dictatorship of General Ioannis Metaxas in Greece prohibited the speaking of the distinctive Macedonian language, with fines and jail for those who did not comply.

My own surname, Karakaltsas – taken when I was married – is a Greek name changed from Macedonian in the early 1900s.

The village of Baeti is purely fictional and bears no relationship to any known village in Greece.

Any inconsistencies or fallibility found in my depiction of life during the Civil War in this novel are my own.

My thanks and appreciation for their feedback and wise counsel goes to the writers at Phoenix Park and, in particular, Nicole Hayes, Nikki Bielinski and Peter Lingard. A huge thank you to Katharina Fares who helped me understand what the textile and fashion industry was like for new migrants in Melbourne. Special thanks to Colin Denovan,

Claire McGregor, Ron Mitrovski, Jack Lyons and my entire family for their counsel, love and support.

A Perfect Stone is a work of fiction inspired by my Macedonian family. It's for every child who was, and is, a refugee seeking the right to a better life.

About the Author

After many years in corporate life, S.C. Karakaltsas began writing her first historical novel in 2014. *Climbing the Coconut Tree* was released in March 2016. Since then she released *Out of Nowhere: a collection of short stories* in 2017 and has short stories published in the Lane Cove Literary Award Anthology and the Monash Writers Anthology.

S.C. Karakaltsas lives in Melbourne, Australia with her husband, daughter and elderly cat.

Would you like to know more?

Drop by and say hello at sckarakaltsas.com.

Other Books

Out of Nowhere: a collection of short stories by S.C. Karakaltsas

I hear a woman's screams, deep in my head. Mine.
I'm out of control.

Hot on the heels of her debut novel, Climbing the Coconut Tree, S.C. Karakaltsas showcases a collection of relatable yet at times unnerving and riveting stories where the unexpected takes us by surprise.

In the story, 'On The Side of a Hill,'- first included in the Monash Writers Group Anthology 2016 – a couple make a shocking discovery during their summer evening stroll. 'The Surprise,'- shortlisted in the Lane Cove Literary Awards 2016, – follows a mother and son's life changing journey. Transported to a café in 'The River,' a woman wonders, "Am I the only one who sees?" before the screams begin. And in the unforgettable title story, a man grasps why his wife is unhappy – too late.

***

Climbing the Coconut Tree by S.C. Karakaltsas

Inspired by true events, this is a story about eighteen-year-old Bluey Guthrie who, in 1948 leaves his family to take the job of a lifetime on a remote island in the Central Pacific. Bill and Isobel, seasoned ex-pats help Bluey fit in to a privileged world of parties, dances and sport.

However, the underbelly of island life soon draws him in. Bluey struggles to understand the horrors left behind after the Japanese occupation, the rising fear of communism, and the appalling conditions of the Native and Chinese workers. All this is overseen by the white Colonial power brutalising the land for Phosphate: the new gold.

Isobel has her own demons and watches as Bill battles to keep growing unrest at bay. Drinking and gambling are rife. As racial tensions spill over causing a trail of violence, bloodshed and murder, Bluey is forced to face the most difficult choices of his life.

All publications are available online and in print on Amazon, Booktopia, Fishpond, Kobo and Apple bookstores around the world.

Lightning Source UK Ltd.
Milton Keynes UK
UKHW010816210223
417383UK00001B/86

9 780994 503268